The One Behind the Psychologist

By Courtland O.K. Smith

Contents

— <u>The One Behind the Psychologist</u> —
The Two Behind the Psychologist
The Three Behind the Psychologist

Chapter 1

MacGuffin

Discontented, I frowned.

Still looking away, I responded with stony silence to Bill's inane suggestion that I write it all down like some kind of third-grade report. The potential benefit escaped me and—despite the fact that we had been friends for more than twenty years, through college, graduate school, and beyond—I was unsure of his allegiance, unsure with whom he stood.

As my left wrist was handcuffed to the metal table between us, I was forced to lean left and slouch to cross my arms and this definitely detracted from the disdain I was trying to convey; also not helping was the fact that my metal chair was bolted to the floor. Bill watched me in silence as he sat across the table in an identical chair, also bolted to the floor. I looked sternly at him and hoped his chair was even more uncomfortable than mine, but the handcuffs shackling me to the table ensured that my suffering was greater. It was an almost skin-piercing reminder that, when his visit was over, I would continue to be caged in this prison while he would return to work.

"Do you know who Judas is?" I asked after some thought.

Bill furrowed his brow. "Why do you ask?"

"You know who he is, don't you?" I persisted.

"Of course. He was the apostle who betrayed Jesus and gave him up to the Romans."

"And you don't see the connection, Bill?" I queried, again looking away.

"Nick, all I'm asking is that you take some time and write down exactly what happened in the week prior to your arrival here." He gestured around the small windowless visitation room. "Maybe if you write it all down, you'll remember something new."

"I remember everything!" I shouted, glaring at him, his head framed in the door's safety glass behind his back. I attempted to shift my position for dramatic emphasis, but was abruptly pulled back toward the table by my shackle.

Bill said, "Perhaps having it all down on paper will help you see the bigger picture. It could only help."

"What bigger picture?" I questioned. "How is any of this supposed to help me get out of here?"

Bill continued to respond calmly despite my angry tone. "Maybe we can get a better idea of everything that happened. We'll figure out a more productive way to approach things."

"You mean for the trial?" I asked, finally feeling as though he had been listening.

Bill nodded. "Writing down the events of that week will give me and the people I have helping us a better understanding of everything that was going on. I only have so long to sit here and ask you questions and at this rate it will take months to get the whole story. However, if you write it down over the next week or so... you get the idea. And, at very least, it'll help you pass the time."

I thought for a moment, considering his unquestionable logic as I unfavorably judged his appearance. His long white lab coat spoke volumes about his hollow confidence. He could have taken it off before coming here, but instead he chose to keep it on so he could convince himself that everyone was looking up to him. I scoffed quietly at his terribly obvious low self-esteem. Sad, what some people will do for a little attention.

"But what does Judas have to do with any of this?" Bill continued, interrupting my sartorial critique.

"At first I didn't know what your intentions were when you asked me to write about the week leading up to my incarceration. I called and requested you come here because it was my lawyer's incompetence during the hearing that led to my imprisonment. And now I have to deal with this brilliantly flawed legal system; my fate in the hands of a bunch of degenerate morons who couldn't even figure out how to get out of jury duty.

"I solicited your help for the trial and now you're sitting there asking me to write my memoirs? I'm not sure whose best interest you have in mind, maybe you made a deal with my wife's family and their lawyers, the very people persecuting me. It just sounds to me like tomorrow is going to be the worst day of my life, if you get my drift." I spread my arms apart the best that I could given the shackle and leaned my head back with what I hoped was an expression of despair.

3

Despite the fact that I had nothing left and my wife was lost to me forever, her parents would stop at nothing until they felt vindicated—and who knew when that moment would come. They were not the type to let go of the past and they had always thought the worst of me; but they were warranted in their conviction. They would never get back the beautiful, confident Julie who had twined her life with mine. To them too, she was lost forever.

"Equating yourself to Jesus?" Bill asked insightfully.

"Well, I'm glad you finally managed to decipher my complex metaphor with absolutely no help whatsoever," I said.

"You always were the smarter one, weren't you?" he asked with years of emotional scarring beneath his voice.

"I think you mean 'more obnoxious,' " I said with a self-deprecating bow, belatedly remembering that *he* was there generously attempting to help *me*.

Bill smiled at his small victory. "And isn't this the principle upon which you based your *thriving* practice?"

"My practice is not and has never been *thriving*," I replied.

"Sorry, but I'm right, aren't I? This is what you do, you have your patients reflect on their week in writing then you discuss it with them. Correct?"

I frowned. "I'm not one of your patients, Bill, and are you implying some kind of psychological basis as a reason for me being in here?"

"Nick, all I'm suggesting is that the process is a helpful one, a therapeutic one even. And it's not like I'm asking you to keep a *diary,* right?" He smirked at his question, attempting to lighten the tense mood.

"Then what are you asking me to do?" I demanded.

Bill sat back, tented his fingers, and pondered for a moment. "I'm asking you to keep a *retroactive diary.*" The ends of his mouth flickered up for a second, but settled horizontal when he saw that I was not amused.

"You're making this sound less and less appealing," I told him.

"If for no other reason, do it because it will save us time. It will speed things up immensely," he said.

I sat back which forced my arms to uncross as my left wrist pulled against the tension of the shackle. I felt the horizontal sections of the immobile chair sliding up and down against the vertebrae in the lower section of my spine. The room was quiet. No windows, just thick cinder block walls separating the cell from the rest of the world. None of the city's taxis and sirens and horns infiltrated, not even a stray bird chirping; just silence. I could have been anywhere, for all I knew.

As I thought, my eyes wandered around the room's monochromatic palette, seemingly inspired by the unremarkable color of fresh vomit.

I smirked a bit. "Can you imagine the interior decorator who worked on this place? Probably an inmate after this job."

Bill laughed. "What self-respecting interior decorator would take a job like that?" he asked, smiling out of the left side of his mouth.

I smiled as well. "How badly does business have to be going to take a job decorating a prison?"

"Can you imagine getting that call?" he asked, smiling fully, both sides of his mouth curled up.

"I know I'd be insulted," I said before mimicking the hypothetical phone call with a nasal high-pitched voice. *"We saw some of your work and thought you'd be perfect for the job!"*

"It's like commissioning an artist for a bathroom painting," Bill said before laughing excessively.

"In all seriousness, Nick," Bill said after he had finished laughing at his own comment. "This will be helpful, saving a lot of time and maybe even uncovering some details that weren't focused on previously."

"I'm going to trust your judgment here, old friend," I said, speaking with confidence despite the fact that I had none left. "This is my chance to get out of here so let's not mess it up."

Bill smiled wide. "Great!"

Limitations then began to trickle into my mind. "But, I won't be able to write everything. I saw all my clients that week before it happened. You know I can't write about what happens during sessions; doctor-patient confidentiality."

"Do you call them your clients or your patients?" Bill asked, distracted by semantics. "It suggests a completely different kind of relationship."

"Bill, I call them *friend.*" Sarcasm overpowered my tone. "But my word choice isn't relevant. I can't write about my patients' sessions. I think of it like Omertà."

"Omertà?" he asked.

"You know, like a code of honor, a code of silence. The mafia used to use the word. It actually dates back to the sixteenth century though, adopted by the Sicilians when they opposed Spanish rule."

Bill furrowed his brow. "Doctor-patient confidentiality is like Omertà? Who do you think you are? Where do you think you are? When do you think you are?"

Bill's questions were all valid.

I looked at him with a blank face before I responded. "My word choice doesn't change the fact that I will not write about my sessions with patients."

"Use different names then?" he suggested. "Change your own name if you're worried about people being identified indirectly should this report somehow get into the wrong hands."

"The names have been changed to protect the innocent?" I questioned archly.

"Put whatever disclaimer on it that will help you write," he replied with an encouraging nod.

"Did you know, Bill, that in 360 BC, Plato criticized writing by saying it would indulge forgetfulness?" I remarked, fully aware that he did not know that fact.

"Can't say I knew that," he admitted.

Thus encouraged, I continued on the topic. "People used to recite whole stories, entire epic poems by heart. Writing made that a useless skill. You know, if I were a layperson, I would assume a man dressed the way you're dressed, in that professional looking long white lab coat, would know a piece of information like that."

Bill's quick response to my assertion was equally condescending. "If I were a layperson, I would assume a man dressed the way you're dressed wouldn't know a piece of information like that." My dark blue one-piece prison clothes allowed Bill the aesthetic upper hand.

I ignored his comment. "I have to say that I disagree with the master. I believe writing is a remarkable way to aide one's memory."

"Yes!" Bill agreed excitedly, finally knowing I was on board with writing about the events leading to my incarceration. Then, with a drollness to his voice, he added, "But, *Plato* was the *student. Socrates* was the *master.*"

"True," I conceded.

"You were always the raconteur of the group back in college. This will give you a good outlet for those skills. You'll be like a prison Shakespeare!" He laughed as though his comment was in some way humorous.

"You know what Shakespeare said about the past?" I asked.

"No," he admitted after several seconds of thought. "What?"

"Shakespeare said, 'What's past is prologue,' " I informed him. "I recall you using that quote recently."

"So he agrees with us both!" Bill said with a tone of finality; our conjugal visit was clearly over in his mind.

"Indeed," I said as we arose from our uncomfortably stiff metal chairs. I was, of course, violently wrenched back down by the handcuff on my left wrist while he turned to knock on the thick safety glass so the guard would allow him passage.

But questions arose as quickly as Bill had when I realized that I would not see him twenty-three hours later at the bar, as I normally did. "When should this thing start?" I asked. "And how will this work exactly? The Monday or Sunday before ...it happened? Just go chronological, I'm assuming."

"Starting on Monday makes the most sense. Sunday is still part of the weekend," he said.

"Alright. So then…" I began.

"Actually," he said, interrupting. "Start now. Start when I asked you to write down the week approaching this situation. Then go to Monday."

"Why should I write about you asking me to write?" I asked.

"Just to keep a comprehensive record," he replied.

"Okay," I said, still not seeing the value. "Won't that be confusing? Maybe this record can go somewhere else? Another report maybe?"

"Place it wherever you want to," Bill agreed amiably.

Sarcasm then returned to my voice as I asked, "How about between Monday and Tuesday?"

"Sure, do that," Bill replied.

"What? That makes no sense," I said, protesting my own idea. "It would seem like an afterthought."

"Do whatever you want, Nick."

I thought for a moment and decided not to argue. "Okay," I replied. "I'll put it first, but what should I call this section?"

"What do you mean?" Bill asked.

"Well, it's easy to title the other sections because they're the days of the week, but what about this one; 'Prison Meeting with Bill'?"

Bill exhaled with a bit of disgust in response to my seemingly meaningless questions. "Call it whatever you want; it doesn't matter at all."

"How about 'MacGuffin'?" I asked, sarcasm coloring my responses.

"What's that? Someone's name?" he asked, giving me the perceived upper hand; allowing me to explain to the less knowledgeable of us.

"It's a term they used to use in the film industry," I said, allowing a slight smile at the small impending victory. "It refers to a plot element that serves to set the scene and drive the plot despite having no intrinsic importance to the story. In other words; it doesn't matter at all."

Making the connection between my words and his own, Bill pursed his lips as silent commentary for several seconds, indulging his lingering hurt pride, before responding. "Just make sure to indicate what all the sections are called and what order they are in. Write it down somewhere."

"Like a Table of Contents?" I asked.

He nodded with the same purse-lipped facial expression as before; he was clearly getting a bit frustrated.

A thought then broke the mounting tension. "How am I supposed to write? By hand?" I asked.

"No," Bill responded. "They'll give you access to a computer. Internet too."

"Our tax dollars at work…" I rolled my eyes at my piercingly true words.

Bill nodded then turned to again inform the guard of his desire to exit, but was stopped by another question.

"Oh, and how should I narrate this?" I asked.

"All these questions…" he said, clearly not enjoying being held back from work.

"I just want to make sure I do this in the right format," I said.

Bill's tone had started to sink toward that of a hassled doctor. "I appreciate your concern, but it doesn't really matter. What's important is the information."

I said, "You seemed to have a pretty particular idea of how and when I should start this. I thought maybe you had a preference for the narration style as well."

"Narrate it however you want," he said before asking, "do you even really need narration? Can't you just write down what happened?"

"That would be a little dry," I told him. "How about I do it like one of those old TV shows that has the main character do the voice-over of both what he was thinking while it was happening and what he is thinking retrospectively?"

Bill blinked several times while staring at me. "Please try to keep your flair for gimmick out of this one," he instructed. "Just a straightforward recounting of the week narrated by you will do just fine."

"I thought you said I could do it however I wanted to," I argued.

"Just keep it authentic, simple, and straightforward. Like you're writing a book. But it's just for my eyes and the people I'm working with, no one else. Okay?"

"Okay," I agreed.

Bill began to exit through the door that the guard had rudely opened during my line of questioning.

"Wait," I shouted, struggling for control.

"What?" Bill asked as he rotated his right wrist to look at his old-fashioned watch that did nothing but tell the time; two rotating hands.

"So I should start with this section about you asking me to write down the week leading up to my arrest?" I asked.

He rolled his eyes and said simply, "Yes."

"And I should start that section right in the middle of our conversation?"

"Sure, why not? Lots of books start like that," he responded.

"Who's writing a book?" I asked.

Bill shook his head. "You're the one asking about narration style and format and structure and chapter placement and character development…"

"I never asked about character development, but that's a good topic to discuss. How should I approach that?" I asked.

"Nick," Bill said slowly, "don't get caught up in the logistics. Just do it." With that he took a step through the door, then paused, turned, and walked back toward me. "I'm headed back to my office to see Kristin soon, your patient."

"Oh yes…" I responded. "When I perish, the meek shall inherit my patients?"

"Nick, we discussed this and you and I both felt that it was appropriate for me to take over your patient load until you… are available again."

"I'm just kidding with you," I said, attempting to pat him on the back with my unshackled hand, but only having the reach to skim the front of his shoulder with my right fingertips.

"Best of luck, Nick," Bill said as he exited.

"Wait," I said, verbally holding him back. "Are we fading to black then?"

"What do you mean?" he asked.

"Well, this is the end of a section, right? You said to write about this; the 'you asking me to write about the week leading up to my incarceration' section; then to write about the week starting with Monday. So should I fade to black at this point? You know how these things work; fade to black, wait a moment, then fade back in to the next scene?"

"Nick, you don't fade in and out when writing unless you're writing a theatrical play or a screenplay." Bill was clearly frustrated by his forced tardy status; the control squarely out of his hands.

"Well, *friend*," I began, "I don't know what I'm doing. You tell me."

"It's up to you, Nick," Bill said as he began walking away, his back shrinking in my visual field. "As long as you explore in depth the week leading up to this situation and as long as you keep a record of our meetings, you can do whatever you want."

"Fade to black it is," I said quietly to myself. "Fade to black it is."

Chapter 2

Monday Morning

The absence of restful slumber... the prevalence of aches, pains, fatigue, dissatisfaction, and middle age... It was dark in the bedroom. Not a hum of light but that of the blinking green dot on my cell phone balancing on the edge of the nightstand.

Julie must have set it to charge, I thought. I had been exhausted the previous night; too tired and sick to do it myself. Too tired and sick to do much of anything other than collapse onto the bed.

In my groggy state of unrest, I struggled to deduce that she had shut the blinds, but only after opening the bedroom window looking out onto the busy street below. Those thick wooden blinds did nothing to muffle the sounds of early summer in the city, but the city's acoustic expressions were not the immediate problem. It was the absence of the sun that eliminated any chance my already disrupted circadian rhythm would reassert itself.

Two weeks earlier she had—without consulting me—painted the room a deep dark rouge. When the wooden blinds were up, the reflection off the walls stirred something in me that helped with my slumber in no way at all. She told me I would get used to it. Why she painted our bedroom the color of rage was beyond me.

I lay there in bed in a perpetual state of sickness-induced jet lag, wondering if or why I should put both feet on the floor.

Can't think of anything, I thought, knowing well that *can't* meant *don't want to.* Regardless, to the best of my ability, I attempted to rub the sleep out of my eyes, but to no avail.

Luckily, or unluckily, the chirping of the birds living in a tree growing out of the concrete in front of our Brownstone made it impossible to sleep. I knew I needed to get up and start the day, but I also knew I had time. I only scheduled clients for the afternoon and evening hours if I could manage it and Mondays required managing it.

When I was a child, I had loved the sounds of nature. They made me feel like I was part of something bigger than myself. Lacking siblings, cousins, or any real family, I needed that feeling from time to time, that sense of a greater being, that purposeful organization in a chaotic world. That connection to something, anything, always made me feel safe, allowed me to sleep soundly.

Years later, in the middle of my estimated life span, I wanted nothing more than to hang out the window and kill every one of those cheerful baby birds. I thought long and hard about yanking the pole out of the closet and knocking those shrill hatchlings down to the pavement. Luckily, or unluckily, fatigue overpowered my great desire to silence them and so there I lay helpless, irritated.

For millions of years, species have learned to relax when they heard birdsongs. It was a natural indication of safety in the wild. So, despite my aggravation about the haphazard and arrhythmic chirping patterns, I credited this innate, universally mammalian trait for my ability to drift off, back to sleep.

I was whipped from my quick shallow slumber by the sound of water against the bottom of the tub in the bathroom just across the narrow hall from the bedroom. I turned over, trying to orient myself in the dark. I was in the middle of our king bed, a bed far too large for the tiny room.

With great effort, I lethargically crawled my way toward the blinking green light of my phone, turning it over to reveal the time. 10:18 a.m. Despite my inability to locate a good reason for doing so, I put both bare feet on the rug covering the wooden floor and then shuffled my way toward the door.

It opened slowly, squeaking slightly and allowing the dim reflection of the sun off the tan hallway to trickle into the bedroom.

"Let there be light," I whispered to myself as my eyes slowly and painfully adjusted.

I knocked on the bathroom door and called to Julie over the sound of the water. "Are you in the bathroom?"

"Of course I am," she shouted through the door.

I stumbled back over to the bed then slid away from reality to return only when Julie exited the bathroom. It was still dark until she pulled the string on the blinds, shifting the wooden slats horizontal, allowing light to pour in and set fire to the red walls.

"Feeling okay?" she asked, presumably mockingly.

"Not really, no," I grumbled, still in a bit of shock after being wrenched back into the world by the harsh sun.

"Soon enough you'll be as healthy as a horse," she assured me.

"What?" I asked, not quite comprehending her assertion as I attempted to bring my mind up to operating level.

"You're going to be all better soon. You just need a hot shower."

By that time I had processed her vocal noises as words directed toward me, so I responded with the appropriate level of sarcasm as I assumed I was being equated to a horse. "Thanks, Doctor. You know what they do with horses that get hurt?" I asked rhetorically. "They shoot them. I would prefer to not suffer the same fate."

Julie walked away, seemingly disgusted with my morning greeting. Then she stomped back into the room seconds later.

"I know you're sick, but I don't feel well either."

"What's wrong?" I muttered as if, at that point in the morning, I cared in some invisibly meaningful way.

"You don't give me much attention or respect..." She trailed off as far as I was concerned.

"Whatever you say, Julie," I said after the sounds stopped.

"That's exactly what I'm talking about," she responded.

It appeared that she was still angry despite my agreeing with her, but I was not interested in another fight, especially before noon.

"Let's talk about it later," I said, tone muffled by the pillow over my head, articulation masked by the covers over my body.

"Whatever, Nick," she said before stomping out of the room.

"I hope you feel better," I pushed out with early morning fatigue in my voice, but she likely heard only a muffling of my words.

I turned over again, this time frustratingly more alert and less likely to drift away. I knew it was I who was enticing Julie's verbal retaliation thus leading to an argument and arguing with my wife was not the best way to start the week.

I picked my head up and shouted, "Julie. I'm sorry, okay? I'm sick."

"Good luck getting better," was all she offered in a shouted response from the next room.

"Good luck?" I asked myself. "I'm getting over a cold; recovery is inevitable."

I moaned and groaned as I again rose from bed before stumbling toward the bathroom to ward off fatigue and sickness. Resting my hands on the sink for stability, I looked in the mirror and was surprised at the thickness of my unintentional beard. I had gone unshaven for days given my ailing health.

After an excessively warm and enjoyably lengthy shower, I lathered up my face with shaving gel. The shave following days without was always the closest.

Across the hall, I selected a light gray suit with dark blue socks and a dark blue tie. I left the jacket on the hanger after modeling it in the mirror, knowing it was going to be too hot to look professional to that degree. Below the well-dressed hanger was a shoebox that I quickly examined then placed under my arm.

As I stood at the end of the short hall connecting our bedroom to the living room, I regarded Julie as she sat on the couch, her long brown hair still darkened and wet from her shower. She was watching what sounded like an idiotically scripted soap opera, which, I realized, was a redundant label.

The lights were off, but the tiny apartment was radiating with sun entering through the well-placed small window. It beamed onto the exposed brick wall where Julie had affixed two mirrors, helping redirect, spread, and share the light.

The mirrors made the diminutive apartment feel larger than it was which, in turn, made me feel more successful than I was. They changed the floor plan, the angles, and corners of the room. But, ironically, when I looked into them, I saw the reality of life which was exactly what the mirrors were helping me avoid.

Despite their dichotomous message, the mirrors were a comfortable break from the abstract art Julie frequently displayed on our sparse wall space. She spent much of her time helping (for free) her friend Isadora, who had opened a living artists' gallery downtown. The two of them felt that living with the art they displayed in the gallery was the most effective way to experience it and understand its beauty. I found no value in that theory or in the decision to take one's unpaid work home with them.

I leaned against the hall wall for a few moments watching my wife. She was truly beautiful. I could mistake others for her at a distance, but I would never mistake her for another.

Julie's attention, directed by her beautiful brown eyes, was on her perfectly soft hands as they decorticated a banana. My eyes drifted downward past Julie's effortlessly fit body and arms to the wood floor beneath the couch. We never actively exercised because there was no need, in the city we walked almost everywhere we went. All of our furniture had long slim legs, just as did Julie, a method used by interior decorators to create the illusion of space, but that was all it was; an illusion. Our apartment was small. A studio converted to a one-bedroom with illegal dividing walls that shake when Julie slams the door after I send anger down her spine.

"Nick?" she asked, having heard the creaking of the old wooden floors as I switched my weight to my right foot.

"Morning, dear. Can I borrow this?" I asked as I held up the shoebox with an Italian name in an illegible script on the side.

I walked toward the galley kitchen as she squinted in thought before responding, "Sure."

I then opened a drawer, took out a knife, and began to stab my newly bequeathed shoebox, twisting as I pulled out the blade so the wounds would not heal. It was a murdering technique I had learned in my youth, watching the normally broken TV on the normally garbage-filled floor in one of our many eviction-notice-served apartments on the city's outskirts. Growing up with little or nothing had led me to spend rather frivolously in my adulthood which has led me to again having little or nothing. Now, I can only wish I had not internalized those youthful lessons because it only affected me negatively. And Julie.

"What are you doing?" Julie shouted angrily.

"You said I could have it."

"I said you could *borrow* it. Now you've destroyed it." She appeared dissatisfied with her decision to give to me the shoebox.

"Okay fine." I tossed the mangled shoebox in her direction, the top flying off and toward the floor during the trip.

"I don't want it anymore. It's destroyed." She leaned off the couch to pick up the two pieces and threw them back in my direction dramatically.

"Thank you," I said as I retrieved my prize from the floor.

"Why did you do that?"

"Sorry, I can't tell you," I said with a smile on my face.

She shook her head angrily and mumbled something under her breath.

Despite withholding information from her for good reason—doctor-patient confidentiality—I began to feel guilty. From Julie's perspective, this was just another malicious act from an obnoxious husband.

I attempted to make amends by changing the subject. "Did you hear those birds this morning? I couldn't stand it."

"No. What birds?"

"The birds. They were right outside the window. They just kept going and going. I wanted to kill them."

"No, but I did hear some people shouting," she said.

"People shouting?" I questioned. "No, the birds, Julie. They're driving me crazy."

"It was disgusting," she continued. "I heard some men shouting profane things back and forth down on the street. I wish people talked the way they did during Shakespearean times."

I found it difficult not to laugh aloud at the glaring flaw in Julie's knowledge of history. "People didn't walk around speaking in cryptic metaphors and talking to a nonexistent audience using iambic pentameter in some kind of Shakespearian old English! Ha!" I laughed directly at her. "People were just as dumb then as they are now. Degenerates were just as crass, probably even more so because it was more socially acceptable due to their more distinct class system. That was just the way Shakespeare wrote!"

"I was *just* saying it would be nice. You don't have to make fun of me. Why do you think you're better than everyone?"

"Because I am!" I responded confidently.

"Well, you're not. You take a distant second."

"Second to whom?" I asked, piqued.

"Second to everyone."

Feeling as though she had won, she swaggered victoriously toward the kitchen to dispose of her banana peel.

"Oh, by the way, thanks for fixing the chair," she said, moving on from her perceived win.

"What chair?" I asked in confusion.

"The chair by the table." As she walked back to the couch, she pointed toward one of the two chairs at the small half-circle table against the exposed brick wall.

"I didn't fix it. I told you to throw it out," I said.

"Well, you must have fixed it because I didn't," she argued.

"Hmm, when did I do that?" I thought aloud, rubbing my chin with my right fingers.

"Maybe on the seventh day while you were resting?" she offered.

"Must have been… Maybe some breakfast for the carpenter?" I inquired.

Begrudgingly, she complied; rising from the comfortable place she had just found on the couch, moving at a glacial speed, she silently fulfilled my request.

"Me and Jesus," I whispered as I hesitantly lowered myself onto the recently fixed chair.

"My cousin is coming into the city from Connecticut today," Julie informed me as she prepared breakfast.

"Okay," I answered, caring in no way for her cousin or any of her family members. They hated me just as I hated them and none of us troubled to conceal our feelings of mutual dislike. The only mystery was why Julie seemed to expect that we would one day play nice.

"She's taking the bus so I'm meeting her at the station."

"I don't like that area. I don't want you going there alone," I said with authority.

"Then come with me."

"I have work, I can't. Can't she take a cab?"

"No. I told her I would meet her and we would go shopping. Why don't you like that area?"

"It has all the city's transportation terminals—the train stations, bus stations, the tunnel. Those kinds of places are where bad people spend time. Why do you think the bad guy always goes to the bus station in movies?"

"Well, I don't think any crooks are going to be robbing banks and hightailing it out of town today," Julie prophesied. "I think you've been watching too many old movies."

I frowned before informing her, "I'm still uncomfortable with those places."

"Okay," Julie began. "Maybe, to avoid waiting around that area, I'll wait here until she rings me from a phone booth. She can use the pay phone."

"Was that supposed to be a joke?" I asked.

Julie smiled. "Yes. Yes, it was."

As we spoke, I could hear a quiet, light tapping at the door and the break in our conversation amplified the sound. We looked at one another for confirmation of the sound's existence.

"It's the downstairs neighbor's loudmouthed beagle loose again," I hypothesized.

Ours was one of the fortunate buildings in the city that allows pets, an appealing point for any animal lover. Unfortunately, I did not fall into that category.

"Can you take her back downstairs?" I asked Julie. "You're closer…"

She reluctantly left her post in the kitchen after decreasing the flame under the pan. "It's not the dog, Nick," she said as she peered out of the image-distorting peephole in the door. She opened it and the three-year-old twin sons of our neighbors rushed in.

"Doc, Doc! We need your help!" Darren shouted. Malcolm had his arms up, little hands waving around in the air, as he ran around in circles to emphasize the seriousness of the situation.

"Now, boys, say hello to Mrs. Thesiger," I instructed despite the fact that they had trouble pronouncing our last name; the reason they called me "Doc."

"We need help. Come!" Darren shouted while Malcolm began pulling at my left pant leg.

"Not until you say hello to Mrs. Thesiger," I insisted again.

"Hi, Julie," Darren forced out.

The audacity of this three-year-old, referring to an adult by her first name, but that was the state of the world. I decided to accept what I could get from him and attribute the rude behavior to his inability to pronounce the name. Julie loathed being referred to as "Mrs. Thesiger" anyway.

"How can I help the two of you?" I asked.

"We need you to help! Chip is hurt!"

"Is something wrong, boys?" Julie asked, her voice moving toward frantic far too quickly.

"Yes!" they screamed hysteria rising.

I arose somewhat lethargically and stretched, knowing that neither their father nor mother was named Chip so there was likely a less alarming explanation. Julie appeared to be tearing up as the boys led me out of the apartment.

"Calm down," I told her. "It's probably nothing."

She smiled a sad smile and nodded in compliance.

"You know, boys," I explained as their little legs whipped back and forth on the walk out of my apartment and across the hallway toward theirs, "I'm not a medical doctor. You call me 'Doc' like 'doctor,' but it doesn't quite mean what you think it does."

The boys either did not understand or were not listening because they gave no response, physical or verbal. They pulled me through their door and into their front hallway. There, on the floor, in a small shoebox, was a tiny bird chirping quietly.

"He's sick," Darren suggested with a caring tone in his little voice.

"This is Chip?" I questioned.

"Chip is sick," Malcolm said quietly as he stroked the little bird in the shoebox.

I gave the boys a look indicating how stupid their problem was, but I quickly wiped it away when I saw their concerned little faces.

"What's wrong with him?" I asked as I strained to crouch down toward the box on the floor.

Unable to articulate it properly, they created a chorus of "ummm" until their mother, Alicia, chimed in from the end of the hall where she leaned luxuriously against the wall, her long light blond hair fluttering in the breeze from the open window behind her.

"We found him outside. He was on the sidewalk fluttering around. The boys wanted to save him so we guided him into the box and got him some sugar water and rice. Birds eat rice, don't they?"

"Yes, they do," I assured her. "Most people think it will expand in their stomachs and kill them, but that's just a myth. Did he eat any?"

"Yes!" the boys responded proudly, assuming the nourishment would ultimately save the bird.

I smiled at the boys before looking back down at the creature who had stumbled onto his side and was slowly attempting to right himself. I knew very little, if anything, about birds, but I knew this one was on his way out.

Frowning, I said, "Let's make Chip as comfortable as possible, boys…"

"Yay!" the boys cheered. They took my words to suggest that Chip would be fine. Their mother, however, understood perfectly what I was trying to convey after she looked into the shoebox to see the weak, struggling bird.

"Boys, I don't know if Chip is going to be okay," she told them.

"Mira mira," Malcolm said in Spanish. The bird had lost its balance again, still chirping quietly but no longer attempting to find his way to his feet.

"He's going to sleep! Let's make him comfy!" Darren said happily.

"I think he's as comfy as he is going to get," I responded.

"Yay!" they cheered together as they danced around, performing what appeared to be their Happy Dance.

Chip's eyes began to close, but he was fighting it; the lids slowly came together then quickly opened seven or eight times. He began to flap his wings rapidly causing his feather-weight body to bounce around the box.

"Look, Mama, Chip is okay!" Malcolm said happily.

Their mother looked away, large mug held in both hands, the string to her teabag dangling off the side.

Chip stopped fluttering his wings after a dozen seconds, ending their last attempt at flight. His eyes closed slowly for the last time before opening wide. He stretched out his legs and his neck to their full extent, the elongation process slowing in speed toward its end. The muscles never returned to their resting positions.

"Yay!" the boys cheered, jumping around, waving their little hands in the air. "Chip is sleeping! Chip is sleeping!"

After checking the inevitable by shaking the shoebox only to have the lifeless bird bobble around, I stood from my crouching position on the floor and looked at Alicia. She was as sad as they should have been. I took salvation in the fact that I did not have to explain to the boys that their newest friend was not going to wake up.

As Alicia approached to explain the bad news, she gently scooped up their curious calico cat with the top of her foot and moved him three feet away, facing another direction. The animal appeared unfazed and continued walking its new path.

Not wanting to witness their adorable little faces drop, I began backing out, leaving the stench of death behind, but it would soon return to me despite my attempts to escape its grasp.

Alicia instructed the boys to "Thank Doc for his help."

"Thanks, Doc!" they sang before running to me and grabbing my legs in two small bear hugs.

"Good-bye, boys." I rubbed their little heads, messing up their soft, well combed blond hair.

"Come back anytime," their mother offered as I made my exit.

I reentered my apartment, breakfast awaiting my return; but somehow already cold.

"What happened? Is everything okay?" Julie asked, grasping the towel with which she was drying the pan.

"Old man died," I said looking at the scrambled eggs, bacon, and orange juice in front of me on the small half circle wooden table.

"What? What old man? What happened over there?" She was genuinely concerned which, as much as it should not have, tickled me.

"The boys' grandfather. Heart attack." I had the distinct tone of tragedy in my voice as I silently questioned my motives. I decided my drive was likely sourced in some justified desire to get back at her, retaliate for something she had done days earlier, perhaps weeks. I did not know what it was or from when it lingered, but it was there, underneath. My retaliation felt right.

"That's horrible. What should we do?" she asked.

"Nothing we can do really…" I responded, shaking my head as I ate.

"Whose father is he?"

"He *was* Alicia's father. Chip was his name. Chip Holloway."

"That is so sad. How are the boys? Did they see it all happen?"

"She's talking to them now," I responded, cold eggs in my mouth.

Julie paused for an extended period while I ate. I could see she was quite bothered by this. "I'm so sorry, Nick," she finally said, tears running from her eyes.

I, as I often did, took her tears to be my cue to exit. "I have to go; morning sessions. Enjoy your day." I took a last quick swig of the orange juice then grabbed the perforated shoebox while hurrying through the door, moving quickly enough to not give Julie a chance to gather her thoughts for a response.

Chapter 3

En Route to the Bar

Descending through four floors on the dark winding stairway, I hoped, as I always did, to not run into another tenant with whom I would be obligated to converse about some useless current event or the unpredictable state of the weather.

The lobby leading out of our Brownstone on the Upper East Side was brightly lit by the sun beaming in through the glass door decorated tastefully with horizontal and vertical iron bars, but the silhouette of an elderly woman was blocking my exit. I quickly identified the shadow to be that of Joanne, one of the tenants on the second floor.

I opened the door and held it at its widest position to facilitate her entrance. She slowly shuffled her way in then informed me that she was more than capable of opening and holding the door for herself.

Some New Yorkers, those who live in large apartment buildings, never get to know their neighbors. They nod hello and rarely speak. Names are a mystery unless mail somehow turns up in the wrong box. I envied them.

It had been our great misfortune to settle in this small but overly social Brownstone. We assumed it would only be temporary, just until my practice became successful and we made enough to move to a larger apartment, maybe even buy something. Two decades later, we were still there.

Joanne resided alone in her dusty one-bedroom apartment, identical to ours but three floors below. Definitively convinced that she was as self-sufficient as a woman half her age, she requested my help with suspiciously great frequency.

Each time a chore presented itself, a blown lightbulb or a finicky stove knob, she would slip a note into our mailbox asking for someone to "perform a repair" in her apartment. Each of her deliveries; usually a week's worth of groceries or some unidentified unnecessarily heavy package; somehow became my responsibility to carry up the stairs as I allegedly had no regard for the long-term health of my vertebrae and no wish to disturb the building's full-time super.

Seven years earlier, I had installed grab bars in her bathroom for her husband. Before his death, Joanne had been a sociable pleasant woman, baking cookies and cupcakes for all the tenants for no particular reason other than to be friendly. She and her husband were the resident grandparents of our building with whom many would play board games on Tuesday nights.

After his rapid degeneration led to a quick passing, Joanne became quietly withdrawn, interacting only with her cats. She owned maybe ten or twelve. And she dressed like a woman with a feline infestation. *Can't own any nice things because the cats will just ruin it.* She was, by every description, the stereotypical Cat Lady.

Not long after, it became quite clear to me that she was purposely breaking things in her apartment so she could steal a moment of human interaction, something even she knew was necessary, but I helped her despite the deceit. Had I not, her nagging would not cease until she joined her husband; assisted or due to natural causes.

I turned to watch Joanne slowly disappear up the stairs toward her cat cave before continuing on my way through the large door. Her relevance in my life was nonexistent, so as I moved through the doorway she went out of my mind. Descending the front steps, I turned to glance up at the Brownstone I had just exited. After a handful of unsuccessful years, the reality of this building as a permanent dwelling had set in, but my pride could not take the blow.

What had begun as a whispered lie, a stolen salvation, led me to repeat it to a growing group. *Our* Brownstone. It began as a reflexive defense to a rudely worded observation posed by one of Julie's condescending male society friends at a cocktail party. "Must not be doing too well if you're still renting a little one-bedroom."

"Well, we own the building," I barked back. "We just rent the apartments to low-income New Yorkers. It's like charity. But it's *our* Brownstone." I had expected to feel guilt, remorse, but I felt relieved, proud. I told the lie once or twice more at the same party, but, on the third time, Julie was within earshot.

What bothered me most was that she said nothing. Part of me wanted to be reprimanded. Part of me wanted her to tell the truth, correct her husband's *misspeaking,* but she did nothing of the sort. She smiled and let it continue, let me continue.

As I looked up at the structure wedged between two others, I felt dirty and was disgusted at myself for the years of lies, but still it was she who had let me continue down this despicable path. I blamed her for everything from that first step right through to the horrific crash; it takes two to tango.

But by now the lie had become not just my own, but hers as well. And I could not understand her reasoning. Julie was the most honest person I had ever known yet she maintained this mistruth. Maybe she was punishing me; she knew I had no way to stop myself, no control, and she knew I hated myself for it. Or maybe she liked the idea of her friends thinking that she had married a successful, generous, philanthropic man. Whatever the reason, she just let it continue.

As I walked up the road toward Fifth Avenue, Brownstone behind me, my mind wandered toward the likelihood of the lie being uncovered. On paper, the building was owned by someone's shell company. Despite years of searching, I had never been successful in revealing the actual owner's identity. This made it that much easier for us to continue the lie; no one else was likely to discover the real owners either. Also working in my favor was the fact that the building had been purchased only weeks before Julie and I moved in. If a suspicious party checked, the dates matched up perfectly. But still I lived in fear of someone uncovering the truth; that I was nothing but a liar.

Fifth Avenue was unfortunately busy for the time of day. I found slight salvation in the fact that city dwellers are impressive in their ability to negotiate the mayhem, heads down and arms at their sides.

I heard the sound of a balloon popping in the distance; it was faint, far afield, but I heard it. Seconds later, I heard another.

It must be intentional, I thought. *Preplanned.*

Seconds later, I saw its rubber remains scattered across my path. Blood red.

Ahead a slow moving obstacle threatened my pace. As I drew nearer, I made out a woman who appeared to be walking her dog. I made my way around her then turned in order to pronounce my harsh judgment only to find that her dog wore a sign that read, "Please don't pet me, I'm working."

Suddenly smiling, I rewarded the good-humored dog by patting its head with my right hand before resuming my previous pace. I thought about the woman's dreams and if they could be explained in terms that I could understand.

I laughed. "I don't have dreams anymore," I said to myself.

My cell phone proclaimed the time to be 11:43 a.m. and that I had three new messages since I had checked the previous night. My thumb gently touched the message indicator to reveal two newly arrived e-mails from patients and one from an address with which I was unfamiliar.

Probably my new patient e-mailing to confirm her appointment, I thought. I quickly tapped out a reassuring message confirming Monday at 1 p.m. to indeed be the time of our in-office session.

I knew I needed to create the atmosphere of a caring mentor. My fee was far too high for patients to justify a therapist who did not create a comfortable environment, but most negotiated lower payments anyway; a cascade of falling fees. I tried not to let the degree to which I cared follow.

Over the years I had become effective in conveying my false empathy. I cared for many of my patients, but the line had to be drawn somewhere. Sympathy on some level was acceptable, but empathy was forbidden. Had any kind of empathy been real, I would not have lasted as long as I did in this field. Feeling for and with so many different people with so many different problems would have destroyed me by now had I not drawn a line beyond which I would not allow myself to be emotionally invested.

I dismissed all thoughts of sympathy or empathy as the remainder of my walk passed without a vibration or chime from my pocket, thus categorizing it as somewhat relaxing. I paid little attention to much of anything as I moved swiftly toward the restaurant.

Chapter 4

Monday's Drinks

Pushing the door in to enter, I shook my head at the blatant fire code violation, but feared for my own safety in no lasting way. It was more comfortable to push in when arriving and pull out when leaving anyway. I suppose I prefer comfort to safety.

I noticed half a dozen patrons before I descended the handful of steps and walked confidently toward the back of the restaurant to the empty bar.

Before sitting on my regular stool, I placed the murdered shoebox on the seat to my left and then I swiveled 180 degrees to survey my noontime sanctuary. One server was attending the six patrons; extremely light for the time of day in that part of the city because they offered only a very limited lunch menu. Their money was made during dinner hours. This was why I spent an hour there every weekday; to be with as few people as possible.

After looking around the small restaurant, I swiveled back and pulled my cell phone into my visual field. 12:07 p.m.

"Late," I said to myself disapprovingly. Bill was coming from The Institute so there was very little consistency in his arrival time.

He and I had first met in college where we shared the same room, major, most of our classes, most of our friends, and thus most of our time. The only thing we did not share was background as I was there on much needed scholarship while he, like most others, simply was not. The two of us stayed in touch through graduate school, both in the city; and continued meeting to vent our frustration over our chosen paths in our shared discipline. Initially we acted as psychologist to the other, a necessity for any practitioner; but, after years of the same complaints, our time degenerated into a hazy hour each weekday; two friends having a couple of beers. We jokingly referred to ourselves as fellow nut-crackers.

On paper, Bill was a very lonely man. Never married; he never found the particularly right woman, or rather women never found him to be the particularly right man. His parents had passed years earlier, as had mine. No children, no siblings, several cousins, but they lived thousands of miles away toward the other side of the country. Bill never found them to be the kind of family to reach out to or rather they never found Bill to be the kind of family to reach out to.

I broached the subject with him on a morning during which he appeared particularly depressed. "You lonely?" I had asked bluntly.

There was no response for a while then finally, "I'm not lonely, Nick... just alone."

Despite his status as lonely, or alone, he did have the great fortune to work at one of the most prestigious and well-funded psychiatric research facilities in the city.

Subjects were treated like royalty; the cafeteria was run by a professionally trained chef, there were field trips to Broadway shows, museums, and more, and many of the subjects were compensated for their involvement with the research. Most of them, however, were too troubled to realize the amazing treatment they were receiving in exchange for years, even lifetimes, of being lab rats. Longitudinal studies were truly in-depth and comprehensive.

Highly respected published papers were prevalent, hundreds came from The Institute each year, but Bill was yet to make any significant breakthroughs. I searched his name in the databases regularly but uncovered nothing to speak of; his name was always sixth or seventh on mediocre articles. He was never the Principal Investigator on any research projects. And those years of hard work wore on him, never achieving quite what his colleagues did, never quite doing what he wanted, never receiving the recognition he believed he was due. Whether he deserved it or not was irrelevant because he believed he did.

Eventually he lost his drive, telling me one day that he "would rather go through life near the birds than waste it wishing for wings." Work turned toward a passionless pursuit guided without motivation. That feeling among us was mutual. So we met every weekday at noon to break up the workday. "Sharing a drink we call loneliness, but it's better than drinking alone," I mentioned once, knowing he used to be a Billy Joel fan.

Four of the patrons at the restaurant were regulars. They too enjoyed the quiet seclusion and small meals. They sat alone and ate quietly, never acknowledging one another, never looking up to connect over the shared desire to not be bothered in a quiet space.

The two that were new faces sat closest to me; a small pretty young woman with blond hair and a very large man with short brown curly hair. He was eating as if he was homeless and being served his first real meal in years. And it was clear that he had ordered five or six meals; a handful of plates with small serving sizes were bunched together on his half of the table, spilling over onto hers.

His size would have been merely a footnote had he acted with more class, but the crass manner with which he behaved forced his size to define him. I could not bear to watch him devour his food so sloppily so I swiveled back around to face the brick wall behind the bar. My mind considered informing him that eating with his non-dominant hand would slow his intake and result in weight loss, while maybe even decreasing his obviously high probability of choking or having a heart attack, but he would likely not take kindly to that sort of unsolicited advice.

I waited quietly for the server tending to the tables, turning toward the door repeatedly thinking I heard the sound of it opening.

"What're you looking for?" the server, suddenly behind the bar, asked while she made drinks for one of the tables.

"My friend," I answered rubbing my tired eyes.

I assumed she was new given that I had never seen her before and I was there with more frequency than anyone. She did, however, know her way around the bar quite flawlessly. My deductive reasoning led me to the conclusion that she was the weekend or dinner bartender covering the daytime server's shift.

"That's all you're looking for?" she asked, attempting to converse her way into a larger tip.

"Yup. That and what the future holds," I responded, indulging her.

"Oh, well no one sees that," she replied playfully.

"You just have to look hard enough, wait long enough," I said, smiling.

"How much of human life is lost in waiting?" she asked, surprising me with her appropriate use of Emerson's words.

"Too much, my dear. Too much…" I responded, leaning in.

We then turned together and looked toward the doorway, suddenly filled by Bill. He wore a light tan suit with a dark brown bowler hat. He took off the hat as he made his way down the steps and toward us, uncovering his balding head.

The server smiled at me then walked away toward a table with the drinks she had just poured.

"What'll it be?" she asked as the distance between us grew.

"Two beers, tap. Second from the right." I touched the tap I desired with my right hand so she could identify it when she returned. "Thank you," I added.

"Two?" she questioned.

"Yes, please," I responded.

"Sounds good." She nodded as she walked back over to one of the men at a table waving for assistance.

My hand then extended toward Bill as he placed his hat on the stool to his right then sat on the one to my right.

"Doctor," I said, addressing him formally.

"Doctor," he responded, equally formal.

"Late?" I declared of his tardy status.

"You know what they say; early is always late if you make your tomorrow your yesterday…"

I paused for a moment to consider his words while he continued.

"How are you doing? Feeling any better? How did the weekend treat you?" he inquired solicitously.

"Not too well. I'm feeling better, but still a little sick."

"How's your stomach?" he said, referring to the aftereffects of two days spent vomiting the week before, bad sushi.

"That's not the problem anymore. Just this cold now. And I keep thinking about that patient, the dead one," I said.

"Well. That's to be expected," he replied.

"True…" I agreed. "It's like he's in the background of every scene of my life."

"Courtland was his name, wasn't it?"

I nodded to Bill's past tense as the server returned and placed a mug of freshly tapped beer in front of each of us.

"And she said to thee… I shall provide," I said, prompting her to smile and wink.

"Ah, you read my mind, sweetie!" Bill said, leaning toward her and smiling wildly, never looking at the beer.

"Y'all doctor?" she asked with an unclear and unexpected Southern accent making it difficult to determine if she was addressing one or both of us. "I heard y'all say 'doctor.' "

"Yes, Ma'am," Bill answered, leaning farther over the bar, almost falling off his stool.

I nodded in agreement.

She smiled back and raised her eyebrows flirtatiously before quickly rotating her head, sending her dark thick hair twirling to catch up.

Bill turned toward me with a huge smile on his face begging me to acknowledge his perceived connection with the comely server.

"I ordered the beer," I informed him.

As Bill desperately wracked his brain for his next suave line in his fantasized flirtation with the server, I looked down to notice that she had poured the beer too quickly, resulting in an identical height of foam and beer. So dark was the beer, that the bottom half of the mug looked rather empty. It appeared to be a mug with foam suspended over darkness.

How can this mug be half full or half empty? I thought.

"Carly," Bill shouted, swiveling his stool toward the server as she tended to the tables behind us. "Want to finish filling up my mug so I can fill up your life?"

I looked at him and shook my head.

He turned back toward me with the same smile as before. "I read her nametag!" he exclaimed, generously revealing the secret behind his seemingly incredible powers of name divination.

Carly and I both ignored Bill's idiocy.

"What's the story with the shoebox?" he asked, leaning back and peering around me.

"Systematic desensitization with my phobia patient at 2:45," I answered swiftly.

"Oh. Made it to the fun part!" he exclaimed. "How are the rest of your patients doing?"

"Eh," I replied. "I don't actually pay attention too often these days. Laughing and crying sound the same when muffled through the indifference of the absence of attention."

"Poetic," Bill remarked.

I nodded and said, "They're all presently troubled or they're on their way toward a relapse. No one is ever cured..." I tilted my mug to almost horizontal, forcing the liquid to fight through the foam before running into my mouth.

"It's not that bad, is it?" Bill asked, sounding concerned.

"No, no... I'm just venting some frustration."

After responding with a nod and sipping through the foam from his own mug, Bill said nonsensically, "Eureka this wallet outside." He held up a brown leather wallet and then placed it onto the counter.

"I'm sorry; what?" I said, having no clear idea of what he was attempting to convey.

"Eureka," he said, knowing full well which word I was questioning.

"I'm sorry, Bill, but I can honestly say that I have absolutely no idea whatsoever what it is that you are talking about."

"It means 'I found' in ancient Greek."

"Well, thanks for the ancient Greek lesson, Professor."

He smiled and nodded.

"When I was young," I began, "before my father died, he told me I should look out for myself. He always said that people who ask for money are con artists and that I should not give a found wallet to the closest store. 'They'll pocket the money, max out the credit cards, then use the wallet for themselves.' You're better off keeping it."

"That's pretty cynical," Bill replied, laughing as he slipped the wallet into the left front pocket of his pants.

"You know me," I informed him before taking another sip of the bitter beer.

Carly returned and took Bill's mug to continue filling it as my leg began to vibrate.

"Sorry," she said, I assumed referring to her pour job.

"Yes," I said into my phone after retrieving it.

"Hello," Julie's voice responded.

"Yes," I said again with less enthusiasm.

"Oh, hold on just a moment…" I heard before the phone went silent. I looked at it to check if we were still connected; duration indicator counting up and up. My thumb then found the "end" button and the phone found its way back to my pocket.

It was not ten seconds before my right leg again experienced the vibration of interruption.

"Yes," I said for a third time to Julie.

"Hello?" the judging, angry, questioning tone of an accuser shot back.

Again I repeated myself. "Yes."

"Why did you hang up on me?" she asked.

"If you call me then ask me to hold on, I'll hang up. If you don't have the attention to talk to me, then don't call me."

"That's rude, Nick, and I don't appreciate it."

"I'm sorry, you'll have to speak up. I'm wearing a towel," I told her.

"Where are you?" she asked.

"Lunch with Bill," I responded.

"You're always with him. Why do you only have one friend? Why can't you find other people to spend time with?"

I was unsure if Julie called me to criticize my selective choice in friends or if she had something constructive to say.

"Hello?" she said after waiting for a response that never came.

"I was just thinking," I said.

"Sometimes I don't think you care, Nick."

"Care about what?" I asked.

"About me," she said.

"Really?"

"Yes," she said, sounding frustrated.

"Well, why would I spend so much time on the phone with someone talking about absolutely nothing if I didn't care about them?" I argued.

"There you go. You don't say that you actually care about me. You just question me questioning that you don't."

"Now, Cinderella," I said calmly, but condescendingly. "Let's keep our priorities in the correct order. We both well know that 'falling in love with love is falling for make believe.' I have to go. I'll see you tonight."

"Wait!" she shouted, trying to keep me on the phone.

"Yes?"

"I just wanted to let you know that I'm going to the opera so I won't be at the apartment when you get back tonight."

"See? That's all you had to say and now the conversation is done. Good-bye."

"Wait!" she said again, still struggling for power. "Don't you care who I'm going with or what I'm seeing?"

"Not really, no," I responded before pressing "end" and placing the phone onto the bar.

The conversation brought a queasy feeling to my stomach so I picked the phone back up and deleted the call history, which immediately relieved me, as if the conversation had never occurred.

"Sinatra?" Bill said of "falling in love with love."

"Among others," I responded.

"How's the wife doing?" he asked a moment before taking a sip from the mug hovering inches from his lips.

"Not too well," I said.

"What's wrong?"

"I mean to say, well, she's fine, but she's been acting strange and oddly argumentative recently."

"Did she want to join us for a drink?" he asked, trying to pry.

"No, no. I think she knows this is my time to spend away from her, away from things."

Bill pried further. "You explained that to her?"

"No, not exactly. It's hard to explain that kind of thing. 'I don't want to be around you and I hate you.' That's what she'll hear. You know that. There's something beneath it too. She has something going on in her head, some problem."

"Why don't you ask her what the problem is?" he asked.

"Because it's hard bringing something like that up," I said with a tone that held increasing frustration.

"I suppose you're right. So you'll just let it build up then? Let it eat away at you and her till you murder her in your sleep?" The level of sarcasm in his voice was also increasing.

"I live life one way," I told him. "That's not lying down or on my knees… it's standing up straight. I'm not bowing to her passive-aggressive behavior!" I drank from my mug aggressively after declaring my perceived dominance.

"How is she being passive-aggressive?" Bill asked.

"She just is…" I began before drowning my answer in another mouthful of beer.

"Maybe you're the passive-aggressive one?" he suggested.

"What are you inferring?" I asked defensively, but with the intention of having the conversation rerouted toward a grammar lesson which I knew Bill could not resist teaching.

"You mean 'implying,' " he corrected predictably.

"What?" I asked, despite the fact that I knew well the difference between the two words.

" 'Imply' is to suggest while 'infer' is to deduce," Bill instructed, confidently and condescendingly.

I nodded as he took a lengthy victory swig from his mug. "You know, Nick, if the queen bee isn't giving you any honey, you've got to shake the hive a little bit."

"That actually sounds like horrible advice," I said before quenching my own absent thirst.

Bill smiled and nodded, sticking his nose in his mug once again and allowing his previous accusation to simmer in my mind.

The short silence that followed felt uncomfortable, prompting me to blurt out my thoughts without much consideration. "You know when you're with someone for so long, the little things, they start to bother you. Then you start retaliating with other little obnoxious things; not responding when they ask a question, ignoring them, asking them to repeat themselves when you heard what they said the first time, that kind of thing. It's just all starting to get to me; I'm starting to hate who she's become, who I've become."

Again Bill smiled and nodded, smug nose in his mug. This time the silence between us felt less awkward before being broken by the buzzing sound of my vibrating phone.

I slid it toward myself, screen flashing "JULIE."

"Yes, dear," I said into the phone after lifting it from the bar.

"Are you sure you can't meet us?" she asked.

"Sorry. I have to go and get my teeth cleaned," I replied.

In the background, I could hear Julie's fictitiously red-haired and demonstrably insufferable cousin, Kathy. "We don't want him here anyway," she said obnoxiously loudly.

"You're not getting your teeth cleaned," Julie said. "Please. It would be nice."

"Absolutely not," I responded.

"He can't? Good!" I heard from the phone, muffled in the distance. I assumed the voice to be that of another of Julie's cousins, Abigail.

"And tell Kathy and Abigail that I can hear them," I added.

"Oh, sorry," Julie said. "We're having a few drinks ourselves."

"I thought Kathy stopped drinking," I responded.

"I don't drink anymore," Kathy slurred into the phone, then added, "I don't drink any less either!"

"Am I on speakerphone?" I asked. "You need to tell me when I'm on speakerphone, Julie." I then addressed Kathy. "Drunk in the middle of the day? Classic classy Kathy."

"Nick, stop," Julie said, raising her voice slightly.

"How's your divorce going?" I asked through the phone to Kathy.

"Nick! That's extremely rude," Julie shouted.

"Ask him how his is going," Abigail said, slightly muffled.

"Excuse me?" I questioned angrily.

Then Abigail, apparently holding the phone closer to her mouth, came through loudly with her crude harsh voice saying, "It's a shame your presence is absent, but your wife has to go." The call duration then began to flash on the screen of the phone. The call had ended.

"Great comeback. Hanging up on someone isn't juvenile at all," I muttered to myself sarcastically as I slid the phone back into my pocket.

"Everything okay?" Bill asked eagerly.

"Every single member of her family absolutely hates me," I told him.

Bill squinted and said, "Well, that never bothered you before."

"You're right. But things have been getting to me a bit more this week. I think it's the whole patient dying thing. I just can't get it out of my head. It's like I see him everywhere. I just can't see his face. I see him there, but his face is always obscured."

"You're seeing your dead patient everywhere? Nuttier than squirrel poop, huh?" he added with a smile.

"Ha," I said unenthusiastically. "That was so funny I forgot to laugh." I then thought for a moment and added, "Except for that first 'ha.' "

"I heard it in the clinic earlier today," he admitted.

"Real professionals over there…" I remarked.

"The jokes are one of the perquisites of the job."

Not wanting to give him the satisfaction of asking him what "perquisite" meant, I quickly and silently searched my brain for the answer. *Perk*, I finally realized. *Short for perquisite.*

"Here, I got another one," Bill began. "Ours is the only profession where we can have our clients do our job for us, at their own home, while we hardly lift a finger. Us and dentists, that is…"

The absence of a facial response prompted Bill to explain further.

"Because dentists ask people to brush their teeth every day…" he elaborated.

After some blank stares, our faces both found themselves against our mugs, drinking generously then sitting in silence until I spoke without much prior thought.

"When we first met, Julie asked her family what they thought of me, a second opinion. When you're asked to give a second opinion, you automatically look for the negatives to validate being asked in the first place; highlight the things the person clearly doesn't see for themselves. And her family had no trouble finding problems with me.

"Not prestigious enough… I wasn't anybody… I didn't have any money… My family was no one to speak of… She was obviously feeling unsure and they didn't reassure her. But somehow I managed to convince her otherwise, to go against their wishes."

Bill's response was delayed by ten or fifteen seconds. "Why are you telling me this?" he asked when he finally spoke. "What's going on with you?"

"Nothing," I said reluctantly.

We sat at the bar in the restaurant for a while longer before our silent relaxation was brought to an end by Bill's schedule. "I need to get back to work. You settling up today? I'll get tomorrow?" he suggested.

"Sure, buddy. Have a good one."

"Until tomorrow," he said as he put on his hat then walked away toward the door. "Same bat-time. Same bat-channel," he added as he made his exit behind my back.

I shook my head, smiled, and chuckled at his foolishness. I then swiveled my position to look around the restaurant once again. At one table, I noticed a man and a woman that I assumed had entered while we were facing the brick wall behind the bar. I watched them sign to one another with such vigor and beauty. It was something that amazed me every time I witnessed it, always wishing that I had taken that American Sign Language class in college.

They sat there, completely silent, but communicating with their hands more effectively than most hearing people could with their voices. No sound passed from one to the next, no sound passed between anyone in the restaurant. It was very quiet. My mind moved toward the metaphorical *silence is deafening*. I guiltily chuckled to myself when I realized how completely inappropriate that unintentional pun would have been had it been said aloud, or signed.

My thoughts then brought me to the words of Mark Twain. "Kindness is a language which the deaf can hear and the blind can see." I was living the opposite of the message. I needed to treat people with more kindness, treat everyone with more kindness. Head bowed in repentance, I decided that I would try to find something kind to do that day.

"What're you laughing at?" the large man sitting at the table closest to me asked.

"Oh, nothing," I said, somewhat apologetically.

"Ha! That's what I thought," he said with unnecessary confrontation in his voice.

I contemplated educating him on the maladies of such obesity, but I decided that ignoring him would be my one act of kindness, effectively reconciling the slight guilt about my lack of kindness that I felt for that handful of seconds.

I swiveled back around, took out my wallet, then left the appropriate amount of money under Bill's empty mug. Taking a deep breath to aid in the extreme physical activity of standing up from the stool, I picked up the shoebox and began to make my way toward the door.

Every day of your life, you're the oldest that you've ever been, I thought.

As I walked past the table pinning the large man to his chair—a chair held together by hope and partially masticated crumbs—I said quietly, "Food doesn't equal love. Don't try to eat yourself to happiness." The man likely did not hear my passively delivered insult because I was not hit and nothing was said to the back of my head as it exited the establishment.

Chapter 5

En Route to the Office

Walking toward and then up Fifth Avenue was uneventful. It was difficult to not think about the repetition of the journey I made almost every day of every week of every month of every year for the past two decades. From the apartment to the restaurant to the office. Sporadically I took a different route, but that choice was dictated by a closed road or a parade rather than made as a conscious premeditated attempt to change my unending routine.

Some filmmakers consciously choose to use only three different sets, only three separate locations, to evoke a feeling of claustrophobia in the viewer. Tight shots. Close-ups. They want the audience to feel uncomfortable. Somehow it adds to the film in some immeasurable way; atmosphere, ambiance. But, that is how I felt: claustrophobic, uncomfortable, closed in, anxious.

Work brought me to the office only the first four days of the work week, but I journeyed there the other three to shush the cries for escape that echoed in my head. Always demanding time together, Julie was vocal about her desire to have me around; to take walks or to go out to dinner, the opera, a show. It became overbearing, smothering, so work inevitably took up more and more and more of my time. I escaped every moment I could which led to spending every day in the office.

I mentally reconciled my stolen solitude by effectively surrendering control of my schedule, allowing it to organize itself. Patients sent e-mails all throughout the week and weekend to be viewed and returned within a day and those who lived close by were encouraged to drop in relatively unannounced, with only a short message or a call to check for availability.

My finger touched the screen on the phone to check the time. 12:45 p.m.

The frequency with which I had commuted up and down the same streets decreased my ability to notice the scenery. Practically nonexistent to me, I subconsciously negotiated the mass of individuals; some moving swiftly to work and others moving slowly, the luxurious members of society.

The phone, back in my left pocket, began to ring during the trip. I lifted it close to my face. "JULIE" was flashing on the screen.

"Yes, dear?" I answered reluctantly.

"Where are you?" she asked.

"On my way to work."

I caught a glimpse of myself in the reflection of the dark tinted windows of a building. Turning toward the glass, I slowed my pace to examine my appearance and straighten my collar and tie, I had no intention of hiding my vanity from my fellow pedestrians. The background displayed a haze of men in suits and ties on their way to lunch, jackets in hand, sleeves rolled; it was warm out.

My reflection was taller than the others with very few having a zenith higher than my own despite the fact that they had the aid of altitudinally enhanced hair while I kept mine rather short, close to my head with a strong youthful hairline, easier to manage and managing hair in addition to all else that I managed was simply not possible.

I was happy to see that I was taller and that my shave was close and smooth. I leaned in toward the building and lifted up my head to check my neck to be sure of the quality of the job. I stretched my face by way of opening my mouth wide and rotating my jaw before clamping shut and displaying my perfect smile. My movie-star quality dental endowment was a miracle given that my mother had been haphazard at best in her approach toward balanced nutrition, a deficiency not helped by her frequent lack of funds. But the enamel gods must have had a soft spot for the earnest youth I had been.

In addition to the genetic lottery prize of my smile, I was pleased to reaffirm in the reflection that my fit slim physique had also stayed with me over the years. I stood straight and pushed back my shoulders while tapping at my sides with both hands.

"Hello," I heard when the phone reached my ear after my bout of self-admiration.

"Yes," I said.

"I just wanted to call and check up on you," Julie said.

"Check up on me?" I asked before noticing that my left shoe had come undone during my preening dance with the building's reflective surface.

"Yes, I just wanted to see how you were feeling." Julie's voice sounded unconcerned, but the semantics of her words told a different story.

"I appreciate that," I said, lying without thought. The phone was wedged between my left ear, chin, and slightly sore left shoulder as I crouched down to tie the undone shoe. As I spoke my last word, the phone slipped, testing my reflexes as I grabbed it just before it hit the sidewalk.

"Fine then. I'll see you tonight," she said sounding increasingly disgusted.

I pushed "end" without replying and went on my way, shoe tied and tie straightened. My eyes were directed straight ahead, still oblivious to the surroundings and ignoring the plethora of people.

The door of the building opened quickly as I approached to reveal a smiling doorman. "Good afternoon, Dr. Thesiger," he greeted me.

I nodded and tipped my nonexistent hat.

The latest piece of "art" in the lobby was an obnoxiously obtrusive seven foot tall metal structure made of bent one inch diameter steel rods weaving in and out of themselves, together becoming bulbous then skinny, until two and a half feet from the top where it turned into a difficult-to-decipher analogue clock.

"Not your grandfather's grandfather clock," was how it was described in an e-mail from the co-op board to the residents and tenants. I pondered what that meant as I summoned the elevator.

The inevitable awkward silence of the suspended animation that is occupying an elevator with strangers is unavoidable. Elevators are the shared misery that brings residents of a building together in close quarters at frequent and tedious intervals. No one desires to converse with anyone else, but the ride is often just long enough that going without some form of acknowledgement of the other's existence would be awkward, even rude. And so, even though the encounters are quick and superficial, elevators serve as the building's social artery; gossip passes from one passenger to another and thence into the ears of family and friends and beyond.

Since I did not consider myself a real resident of the building, I stood motionless with a straight face as I blatantly ignored the other passengers as if they were just another button on the elevator display that I had no intention of touching.

Two older women, well dressed, and a young man who I assumed to be home from college for the summer, stood facing forward, making sure to look away from one another. The interior of the elevator was lined with brass, consistently polished so smooth that it created a clear clean golden-tinted reflection. This surface made the task of avoiding eye contact that much more difficult. These rides, as this one had, usually deteriorated into silently watching the numbers count up or down on the screen indicating our present position in the vertical space.

The two women exited on the 7th floor and the young college student on the 9th. I waited another two floors until the screen read "11." The floor was in reality only nine stories above the ground but, through the magic of elevator renumbering as a result of the desire for a more prestigious sounding address, floors 1 and 2 were labeled as 3 and 4. Additionally there was not, as there rarely ever is, a 13th floor to satisfy the superstitious.

I had been suffering from extreme optimism when I chose this location for my office, signing a fifteen year lease based on nothing but the fantastic view of Central Park. Several years later, I prematurely renewed, signing another fifteen year lease out of fright of losing the money I invested in renovations, sunk cost. Young and idealistic, I had assumed then hoped then prayed my practice would overflow with success based on the location alone. Time had proven me woefully incorrect.

I had soon learned that the prevalence of psychologists, social workers, and counselors and their much lower rates were the proverbial wrench in the gears of my practice. With my astronomical rent in addition to the rent for our small apartment and our other expenses, we just barely broke even, but I had decided long before that the appearance of success was more important than the balance in my bank account.

Chapter 6

Monday at the Office

After hearing the reassuring click of the door close behind me, I walked past the sitting area where most of the in-office sessions take place. The long soft tan leather couch and two matching love seats separated by the glass coffee table looked as clean as the remarkable light mahogany wood floors. The office cleaning crew that came on Saturday nights was pricey, but I justified it with my great desire to not clean myself.

I glanced over at the cliché psychologist's couch near the window in its perpetual reclined position like a chaise lounge with a small wooden chair behind it. This section of the office looked more like a small off-off-Broadway stage with stereotypical psychologist props for a one-man show than like a real-life modern-day psychologist's office. And those stereotypical psychologist props had never been used, yet there they still sat. I questioned their presence before settling behind my large mahogany desk, simple wooden armchair on the other side.

With these three different seating areas, new patients often had trouble making the decision. Each area lent itself to different methods of therapy. A face-to-face conversation. Lying down and staring at the ceiling with the therapist behind, neither heard nor seen. And the therapist instructing the patient from his perch.

Other than the elaborate seating arrangements, the office was decorated rather sparsely. Most patients expected art and sculptures from all over the world, pictures of me with the indigenous tribes of Africa or Tanzania to subtly demonstrate that I was accepting of different cultures and different people. A wall or two filled end to end, top to bottom with bookshelves holding thick heavy old books, spines with titles on the mind, the brain, behavior, therapy, mind control, dream analysis, and whatever else is associated with psychologists. Maybe even a painted portrait of me reading to the undernourished children of some developing country, all wearing tattered second-hand American clothing ironically emblazoned with gaudy expensive name-brand patterns and insignias. I refrained from that office façade because I did not want patients to assume my advice to be as cliché as the décor.

An analogy that I often made when explaining my decision to keep a simple office was the fact that a magician should not say "tada" after performing a trick. A magician who says "tada" is speaking for the moment when the moment should really speak for itself.

"Beige" described my surroundings well. Light and dark variations danced up and down the wallpaper. A soft hue radiated from the couch and love seats. A hard buttoned flavor across the chaise lounge like psychologist's couch and the large leather chair behind my desk. And countless other variations wherever else patients' eyes might find themselves as they searched for answers from within.

The oversized mahogany desk held the two large flat computer monitors, camera in between, through which I conducted most of my work. A wireless ergonomic half-oval keyboard occupied the space separating the monitors from where I sat.

There were only two other objects on the desk, intended to break the inevitable silence that would arise from the awkward situation of telling a complete stranger one's inner thoughts. An absurdly large jar filled with shining pennies was at the far end. The extreme wit and clever planning behind the visual gag was unfortunately lost on all but me: penny for your thoughts?

A short ceramic bobble head of a man in a white coat with a long white beard and glasses occupied the space next to the penny jar on the desk. A small placard across the front of his feet read, "Dr. Freud." I displayed it only for the sake of irony, also lost on all but me.

The dry air of the room forced me to blink several times and urged me to seek water. I opened the small refrigerator on the far side of the room, took out a large carafe of filtered water, and placed it carefully on the coffee table between the four medium sized glasses arranged upside down in a square. None of my patients ever drank the water, but I knew its presence made them feel more comfortable, more at home.

After quenching my thirst with half a glass, I cleaned it with the small square towel that separated the upside down glasses from the glass table and placed it back in its position. I then opened the bottom drawer of the large mahogany desk and dropped in the perforated shoebox before opening the top drawer. A framed photo of my wife and me taken on our wedding day lay inside. Years before, it had graced the desk's top, but was removed when I noticed patients paying more attention to it than to me.

She looked absolutely beautiful while I looked like a slob. I was unshaven; looking as if I had just come out of the woods and put on a suit. There was no excuse for my disheveled appearance. It was a day we would never forget and I never forgot it for the wrong reason: regret. Unfortunately, Julie remembered it in just the same way.

Knowing the right thing to say, that was how I won her. I always knew what she wanted to hear and said it in a way that only I could. But, to know the right thing to say is also to know the wrong thing to say. Over the years, the seemingly uncontrollable trajectory of my life and the resulting frustration led me to start saying only the wrong things to her. It began out of anger at myself and my lack of control over everything else, but then I got used to taking it out on her. She was the one thing I could control and controlling her in this way was eating me up inside even as I perversely enjoyed it. "I need to stop," I said aloud. "Before things get out of hand..."

Our wedding photo had been joined one week earlier by a photo given to me by a patient, Courtland. It was during our last ever session together. His mood was rather positive for someone who had been suffering from dysthymia, constant mild depression, since I met him five years before. "Ever-present," was how he described it. I said it aloud as I sat there.

His back was facing the camera. Beyond him was an expansive panoramic view of the Grand Canyon. His arms were in the act of being flung wide, blurring the bottom half of their silhouette, and his head was tilted back exposing a glimpse of his receding hairline.

Patients had given me presents before; wine, ties, cuff links, wristwatches, pictures, art; but I never accepted them. I did not want the relationship to become anything more than that between a therapist and his patient. Accepting gifts would blur the line between objective and subjective, in my mind. But, for an unknown reason, I had accepted the picture from Courtland. Maybe because he was so genuine in saying, "I want you to have this," his brown eyes almost tearing despite his seemingly positive mood. I could do nothing but take it from his trembling hand.

"This is a photo of me when I was younger," he told me.

"I'm fairly certain that all photos with you in them are of you when you were younger," I joked.

It was just before he left the couch as prelude to leaving the office. He said, "Excuse me while I disappear." Those were his last words to me and, I suspected, his last words to anyone. At the time, I took them to mean nothing more than a friendly good-bye. When I learned of his death the following week, I had spent the entire day searching through all five years of his file to find something to explain it. What was happening in his life that he felt so helpless? I was his psychologist. If anyone should have seen it coming, it was me.

Sinatra's last words on stage before he retired: "Excuse me while I disappear." Those five words haunting me. Why would Courtland have said that? It made no sense to me. Retirement is different from death. You can come out of retirement. Sinatra came back. But Courtland only returned at night while I was sleeping. More than once he had jolted me from a paralyzing sleep startled, confused, and slightly angry at myself, at him. I had even begun to see him walking around, following me, sitting at restaurants and standing in windows. His farewell, I suppose, was not as cryptic as once assumed. His exit had indeed been only temporary.

I rubbed the bottom of my nose with a horizontal left index finger. Despite the dry office air, a slight dampness met my digit; I was still slightly sick. Accordingly, I brought the tissue box to the top of the desk. It was often kept in the drawer because I did not want patients to see it and feel that they were being encouraged to cry. But taking that risk was necessary because my nose would not stop dripping. I lined up the corners of the box to the corners of the desk before commanding the computer to awaken, then watching as the dark screens flickered to life.

Then I noticed my right shoelace had come undone so I tied it in a knot with my right hand without even the slightest attempt to create loops. I could feel myself becoming increasingly frustrated with the world.

A short meditation session was necessary to calm myself; closing my eyes I concentrated on relaxing my body and mind. My patients expected me to absorb their problems and spit out positive direction. It would be an impossible feat to perform this service over and over, again and again, each day, week, month, and year without being perfectly calm and without keeping my own problems out of the office. Personal emotions, a therapist's worst enemy, needed to be absent in sessions.

After carefully examining the two pictures in the top drawer, I swiveled around in my large leather chair to gaze out the window. I had nearly forgotten how amazing the park looked in the summer, lush greenery spanning miles. I stood to look down, many stories below, wondering why, when people were on a floor above the third, they always experienced an overwhelming desire to drop or throw something. There is no word for this urge in English, but there is in French.

"*L'appel du vide*," I said aloud.

I thought about how it would be to soar through the air for those glorious seconds before exploding onto the pavement, horrifying passersby, possibly even landing on one. It was a strange and exhilarating thought.

I sarcastically recited words from Thoreau as I gazed out and down. "Go confidently in the direction of your dreams. Live the life you imagined." They echoed in my head as I again imagined flying through the air. My life was far from what I had envisioned. Listening to strangers prattle on about their own issues. Having their problems follow me around day after day, hour after hour, despite my attempts to forget. Being incapable of attracting enough patients to consistently pay the rent and my bills.

I thought about how I should have maintained better relationships with the hospitals and clinics where I interned and worked when I first started out. I was arrogant then, burning seemingly useless bridges in a whimsically luxurious manner.

I bent down and retied my right shoe tightly, correctly. It was time to work.

Chapter 7

Ms. Stewart

A sharp tapping at the door, the sound of metal on wood, pulled me from my thoughts. Slowly I approached and peered out the peephole. A short woman in a long gray and black skirt and a matching short-sleeved blouse stood pensively.

I opened the door. "Ms. Stewart, please come in. I'm Dr. Thesiger." I was sure to pronounce my name clearly so there was no confusion, emphasizing the short "e" and short "i" sounds. I extended my right hand in greeting, but she appeared to not notice the gesture. "Please, have a seat," I told her after she had stepped through the doorway and peered around.

After several more seconds of surveying the room, she asked, "Where should I sit?"

"Wherever you would like, Ms. Stewart."

"Is this a test?"

I rolled my eyes mentally and responded, "You can take a seat there, in front of the desk." I very rapidly determined that Ms. Stewart was not going to be one of my more enjoyable clients, but perhaps she would excel at making prompt payment.

"My apologies, Dr. Thesiger," she said sheepishly after sitting. Her head was down as she spoke. "I am a bit nervous."

Her appearance, accent, and mannerisms suggested that her childhood was spent in China, probably on the outskirts of one of the large cities. Immediately, I made countless assumptions about how she would behave, what brought her into the office, and how I should approach her treatment.

I assumed that Ms. Stewart came in search of advice, something that I, as a psychologist, attempted to avoid giving. Psychologists help patients understand themselves and their world and aid them in navigating through it in a better, more effective way. No decisions are made for the patient by the therapist, no advice is to be given; but that does not stop them from endlessly seeking it.

I lowered myself slowly into my large leather chair and spoke softly. "There is no need to be nervous, Ms. Stewart. Why don't you tell me a little about yourself to begin?"

She continued to direct her gaze toward the floor as she addressed my question. "Well, um, I am an administrative assistant in a law firm in Midtown, on the west side..."

Occupation is always the first thing patients discuss when they are asked about themselves.

"Do you like your job?" I asked.

"Well, yes," she answered, somewhat defensively, almost retaliating against the thought that I was analyzing her response. "I have been working there for six years. That is not why I am here."

It was clear that she was very uncomfortable with her presence in my office. She continued to look down while she spoke. It bothered me as this behavior was harmful to therapy; she was not able to see my eyes and I could not see hers. She was hiding her emotions, afraid of what I might stir up in her. In the culture I assumed she grew up in, it was customary to look down when addressing a professional, but this behavior was not appropriate in a psychologist's office.

I decided, before getting into her particular issue, to try to calm her so the two of us could look at one another and gain some level of rapport.

"Calm down, Ms. Stewart. Would you like some water?" I asked.

She shook her head quickly, nervously. No one ever accepted the offer.

"Tea? Coffee?" I continued.

"No, I'm fine. Thank you, Dr. Thesiger."

The offers were meant more to soothe her than as an actual suggestion of beverage.

"Ms. Stewart, I'm not sure how to fully and effectively convey this, but there is no need to be nervous, although I am also well aware that it is a difficult emotion to control."

She interrupted me with swift and rather frantic words and, for the first time, looked up. "Therapy is not an option in my family. Not taken seriously. Witchcraft. A waste of time, money. If someone has something wrong with them, they deal with it themselves, privately. We have to be strong, no weaknesses, but if there is a problem, we blame ourselves because that is who is at fault."

She paused and went back to her previous nervous sheepish demeanor. "I am embarrassed to be here," she continued. "I told no one. Will you be able to help me?"

I had found that new patients invariably ask this loaded question so I had long ago developed a standard response that I believed to be sufficient, although it did not really answer the question in any definitive way. "The answer to your question is extremely complex. What do you mean when you say 'help'? Do you mean to help you function better? Do you mean help you understand your actions more clearly? The truth is you could mean a number of different things when you ask a question like that. But, regardless of your meaning of 'help,' there are two main limitations that shape the ultimate answer to the question.

"Sadly, Ms. Stewart, there are some people who just cannot be helped. If someone has a condition that doesn't respond to therapy or if they're just unwilling to change, all that can be offered is support and some guidance."

"Can I not be helped?" she asked sadly.

"I don't know that yet, Ms. Stewart. We need to get to know each other a bit before I can make that determination.

"The second limitation is my own ability as a psychologist. If we learn that this is the case, I will direct you toward someone I think could more appropriately help you." I looked at her, still not looking directly at me for longer than a glancing squinty second. "You see, Ms. Stewart, there would be no reason for me to continue sessions with a patient if I didn't believe I could help them."

I explained these limiting factors because I sensed that she was the kind of patient who viewed psychology as a quick fix and that I would do the majority of the work. She needed to know that the process would include hard work from both the psychologist and the patient and that I would guide her through the process, metaphorically holding her hand as best as I could.

"To answer your initial inquiry, if there are no limiting factors present, then I can honestly say yes. I do think I can help you as long as we make a strong effort and work together through this process!"

At that she looked up and flashed a brief smile.

Encouraged, I continued. "Therapy in this office is about a personal journey, but with a helpful guide."

Ms. Stewart, apparently becoming more comfortable, blurted out, "I feel anxious sometimes... Actually, I feel anxious all the time."

As she spoke, I thought about how a medication prescribing psychiatrist would shut her up there, push anti-anxiety medication on her, and have her out the door without learning the source of her anxiety. But that was not my way.

"In what kinds of situations do you feel anxious?" I asked.

"Well, it is hard to say. I'm more anxious when unfamiliar people are around and I have to interact with them."

It was hard not to roll my eyes, but I held them steady. I really wanted to tell her, "Everyone feels anxious when they have to interact with unfamiliar people."

She continued. "And when I have to touch things that I do not know have been cleaned properly. Or if I think I forgot to lock the door to my apartment or return a call to a client or give a message to a partner at the firm." The pitch of her voice rose and its pace sped as she spoke. "Excuse me, Dr. Thesiger. I need to make a quick phone call."

She opened her purse and searched its contents with her right hand until she found and pulled out her phone. She then walked toward the corner of the room and talked into it quietly. I politely pretended to check something on the computer screen, bringing up my schedule for the day. Three in-office clients including Ms. Stewart, one internet client, and a check-up phone call to a client mandated by The Court.

I then lost myself in thought because I had already gleaned enough information for preliminary diagnosis. *Quicker than normal,* I congratulated myself, before considering for a moment that she was merely reciting a list of symptoms that she read online when searching for a close fit for whatever her issue may be.

When she completed her call she tiptoed back to her seat apologetically. "I'm sorry, Dr. Thesiger. I needed to check on a memo for one of the partners to make sure she received it."

"Don't worry about it. It isn't a problem at all. Please continue."

She settled herself before speaking; closing her eyes for a moment and breathing deeply. "It is hard to get through the days now. I spend a long time checking things. It used to help me during work, to ensure everything was correct, but now it has become too difficult and limiting." She stopped, as if suddenly realizing that she had been talking for a longer duration than she was accustomed and to a complete stranger.

"Many psychologists like to think of anxiety through the lens of existentialism," I began. "Because we live in a world that allows us so much freedom and choice to go about our lives in any way that we choose, the responsibility of our choices and our actions falls directly upon our own shoulders. The possibility of a negative outcome is manifest in the form of anxiety. But, contrary to logical assumption, sometimes we like to encourage anxiety in our patients, to explore it and allow it to become a well-respected and accepted part of our lives. If monitored properly, its power can be harnessed and used constructively to help guide decisions in a positive way. Instead of desiring and attempting to destroy that power, many psychologists like to encourage patients to embrace their anxiety and use that as a means to attain their full potential."

After I paused for her response, she asked, unintentionally mocking me, "Will you be analyzing my dreams?"

I knew from her question that I had chosen the wrong approach with Ms. Stewart. She had likely been to a handful of psychologists and was yet to find the right one. I decided to adjust and continue.

With both hands on the desk, I leaned in toward her in an intimidating swift fluid motion. "The vast majority of psychologists choose methods of therapy based on their and their colleagues' personal experiences rather than those that are scientifically proven to be effective. This bastardizes the profession and pushes it far from the scientific practice that it should unquestionably be. It gives us all a bad name!"

Her eyes widened as I spoke.

"I won't have you swimming with dolphins and playing computerized virtual reality games as therapy like some of my *peers* would. If you would like to talk about dreams, you are welcome to do so, but I have to request that you do not spend much of our time on them. Freudian Dream Analysis has no place in therapy given that the connections between dreams and the real world are inconsistent at best and completely unsubstantiated.

"What we need to do is approach your situation with some specific diagnostic tests followed by a strongly structured and scientifically proven therapy. Structure is what I would like to emphasize in our sessions."

Ms. Stewart looked at me with a slight smile as I said this, so I added, "I assume a strict structure would be appropriate for you given that you called and e-mailed to confirm three times over the past week and you arrived exactly on time. It is clear to me that you would thrive within a rigid therapy structure."

"Yes!" she said with some enthusiasm.

"First, I will require you to see your doctor for a full medical physical examination." Every word I said was more authoritative than the previous. Ms. Stewart was responding favorably to a strong swift calculating figure of authority.

"You will receive an e-mail from me after you leave this office. It will contain ten questions." I raised my hands to my head's level, palms in her direction, and forcefully displayed all digits when I said "ten." "You will answer them in three sentences each then e-mail the responses back to me at least two days before our next session.

"The questions will be as follows…" I felt strange speaking in that manner, but the patient was responding remarkably well to it so I continued, pausing only momentarily while I wracked my brain for appropriate questions.

"1. What brings you into therapy?

"2. When did the problem begin?

"3. How often does the problem occur?" After "three," I began to pick up pace, not thinking about the next question or even the one I was presently asking.

"4. When and in what situations does the problem occur?

"5. What tends to occur before the problem?

"6. What tends to occur after the problem?

"7. How does it affect your life?" After "seven," it dawned on me that I would have to remember all of these questions so that I could put them in an e-mail but it was too late to stop.

"8. What do you think about when the problem is occurring?" After "eight," I began to panic at the thought of recalling all of the questions in order; a difficult task when I was paying little attention to any of them. But then I relaxed, realizing that there was little chance that she would remember them either.

"9. What do you feel when the problem is occurring?

"10. What steps have you already taken to alleviate the problem and with what results?"

I let out a mental sigh of relief and patted myself on the back after somehow coming up with ten coherent, non-repetitive questions off the cuff. I wanted to smile at my amazing feat, but I knew a smile would have sent the wrong message to Ms. Stewart who had become comfortable and was clearly satisfied with my performance. This was a job interview and I was close to landing it.

I looked at her as she looked squarely in my eyes without looking away. I noticed that her arms, on the opposite sides of her elbow, were slightly discolored to a faint pink hue.

"Additionally, you need to start wearing your glasses when you work," I added.

Looking startled she asked, "How did you know I wear glasses? They make me look bad, so I don't wear them."

"You squint a bit when looking at me. And your arms, they're irritated there." I pointed down at her forearm. "You sit too close to the screen when you type so that you can see it, scrunching up your arms in the process. Since you do that all day, every day, your arms have become irritated. Straighten out your arms. Sit farther from the screen. Wear your glasses when you work," I instructed.

"Thank you," she said, looking a little embarrassed, but noticeably impressed.

"I have a standardized set of questionnaires for preliminary sessions I would like to go through with you, but I would first like to administer a visual exercise." I took out a pencil and tore a sheet of paper from the notepad in the desk drawer.

"Yes, of course," she agreed, her tentativeness gone.

"Draw a picture of yourself." I pushed the piece of paper, pencil on top, toward her. The pencil rolled off the paper, off the desk, and onto the floor. She looked at it and froze, eyes open wide. We sat there for several seconds.

"I apologize," I said unapologetically while reaching into my desk, this time handing her the pencil, a *clean* pencil.

"I don't know what you would like me to draw exactly," she said, holding the pencil as if she had never done so before.

"Draw yourself," I repeated.

"I am not a good drawer."

"It doesn't matter. Just try."

She drew a circle, looked at it for a while, then pushed it toward me.

"What is this?" I asked, legitimately confused.

"This is me?" she answered in question form, apparently equally as confused.

"Can you draw the rest of you? Maybe with a little more detail."

She drew some wavy horizontal lines then dropped the pencil and began to cry.

"What is the problem?" I asked, still in my authoritarian voice.

"I don't even know what I look like," she managed through the sobs. "I don't even know how I look."

Her head was down as she sobbed into her hands. I pushed the box of tissues toward her, a third of the box dangling off the edge of the desk. I always became uncomfortable when patients cried. It may have been cathartic for them, but I always preferred it to stop as soon as it began.

I glanced at the clock after several minutes of sobbing. 1:12 p.m. The session was far from over so I sat back and allowed the tears to continue.

She cried on, face in hands, as I held back my discomfort by imagining myself somewhere else, anywhere else. A dozen minutes felt like an hour. So did the next dozen. And the next. When the session finally neared its end, I slid the box of tissues off the desk and into her lap.

"Ms. Stewart, your time is nearly up; we must keep on schedule. We can pick up here next week."

I then watched as she suddenly ceased her sobbing, took a tissue from the tissue box, dried her face and eyes, folded the tissue into a rectangle, placed it into her purse, stood up, and began to walk out.

"Hold on a moment," I said as I rummaged through my desk.

She turned and stood silently. I walked over to her with a rubber band in my hand.

"Here. Put this around your wrist. We will talk about why next week. It's clean. Don't worry."

I intended for her to get accustomed to wearing the rubber band around her wrist because her future therapy would require her to snap it every time she felt anxious to remind herself of her therapeutic progress thus relaxing her.

She nodded her head, took the rubber band, and left, closing the door quietly behind her.

"Well, that was strange," I said aloud to myself as I shook my head. "I hope she'll be back…"

I returned to my large leather chair and opened a blank e-mail. I addressed it to Ms. Stewart, listed the ten questions, then sent it before swiveling around and leaning back as I gazed out the window at Central Park.

———

Looking out over the vast expanse of greenery, filled with trees and spotted with ponds, lakes, trails, roads, baseball fields, tennis courts, a reservoir, a museum; I lost myself for a moment in an empty daydreaming daze.

The words of an old advisor I had after graduate school came back to me. She warned us daily about the traps of feeding into patients' needs to better connect with them. "If you spend all your time trying to please patients by being someone other than yourself just to fit what you think they want in a therapist, you begin to forget who you are, start to lose yourself…"

In theory she was correct and I wholeheartedly agreed with her, but, when bills needed to be paid, the definition of "correct" became a malleable entity. The reality was that I needed to change my personality and my approach with each different patient to better relate to them and thus aid the process of therapy. Whether I have begun to, or have already, completely forgotten who I am or lost myself is somewhat irrelevant when survival is at risk.

After some time, I was jolted from my daze by the realization that there was work to be done. The large leather chair swiveled 180 degrees back to work position. I woke up the sleeping screens, and my schedule revealed an in-office session ten minutes from the indicated 2:35 p.m. I decided there was just enough time to respond to an e-mail or two so I exited my schedule and tapped into my inbox.

I very rarely saw the majority of my patients in person. Some had never even been to my office. Some had never even been to New York. After receiving my doctorate and completing my internship, passing the licensing exam, and getting through an apprenticeship, my private practice was slow to start. The thousands of existing psychologists located in the city were better established than I and, despite their tenure, were also struggling to get patients.

We were all in a competition with one another in which none emerged victorious. And the high cost of living certainly did not help. An income that seems high outside of this location places us into the category of poverty in New York City. Second, third, and fourth jobs in clinics, hospitals, research institutes, and schools were not uncommon in this field just to make a living or, in some cases, just to get by. This kind of complicated, complex, and rather rootless existence was unappealing to me so I concentrated on only the private practice.

In an inspired attempt to increase my patient base, I decided to market myself as specializing in guiding students transitioning from high school to college. This specialty was particularly appealing to the city's countless dual-income parents concerned about their children's adjustment during that fragile period, but too busy to take an active role.

With this branding, my practice began to pick up, but only temporarily. The success of the practice was based mostly on word of mouth recommendations and my short-lived surge in clients was credited to one set of parents recommending me to their children's friends' parents. After that generation of students graduated, my practice went back down toward nothing.

Sadly it was the irony of the practice of psychology that hurt the most; repeat business. Psychologists want the patient to continue coming back so they continue to get paid, but psychologists, by definition, are working to help the patient become self-sustaining and essentially without need of therapy. A balancing act between ethics and good business practices was constantly teetering.

When a former patient e-mailed me from college searching for advice, I replied without thought. When she e-mailed again, I decided to lend my services for a fee. This model worked well for her and for me, so I contacted the parents of other former patients and encouraged them to keep me as their children's counselor through the tough times of college and possibly beyond, preferably until the children were established enough in the professional world to independently afford a therapist.

For a reduced fee, I was receiving weekly e-mails from dozens of students with questions, concerns, and just to check in, to have someone to talk to with whom they were comfortable, someone who could give to them what they needed to keep them grounded and on track. I held video sessions with some through the computer while others e-mailed or even sent update videos.

There were still patients who came into the office, but most of those sessions were either with older patients or with new patients looking for a psychologist. And those new patients almost never ended up returning.

My practice, however, never thrived. With the reduced internet fee, it only brought in enough to cover the expenses of operation: rent, insurance... Most people wanted medication to get through their problems, not talk therapy, and my training did not allow me to write prescriptions. Even if it did, I probably would not prescribe it because the vast majority did not actually need it.

And, sadly, most of my peers offered similar interactive video-based therapy, so the competition continued, but with computer savvy psychologists all over the world, not just those in New York City.

It was a miracle that the practice broke even, but even that was merely an assumption. I had no knowledge of how much money was brought in because Julie managed all of our finances. I had lost the right to pay the bills and make decisions about our finances ten years earlier when I had spent our relatively meager savings, and taken out a huge loan, to purchase a custom sports car. She had been pushing for a baby and a move to the suburbs. I panicked and used up every ounce of our credit and cash on a car instead of the home of her dreams, the life of her dreams.

I went through one bout of refinancing followed by another and another to lower the monthly payments and avoid default, but this did nothing but extend the term of the loan; extend the term and drive a wedge between Julie and me, farther and farther apart we drifted. Ten years later and I still have years and years to go. And I will probably have to refinance again so I won't lose it.

Chapter 8

Tim

"Tim B." filled the subject line of the first e-mail. Timothy, who I had counseled all through his college years, was from Palo Alto, California, but, instead of his choice of college in that area, he was pushed into college in Vermont by his parents who wanted him to "experience different climates in life." He felt out of place and disdained being on campus so he kept to himself and was miserable most of the time.

—

(E-Mail from Tim)

Dr. Nick,

So I'm midway through summer classes and I'm realizing that I'm graduating in a matter of weeks. Such a weird feeling. I never thought this day would come. Looking back at the past four years just makes me sad because I realize that I was so unhappy for most of it.

Currently looking forward to the next stage of my life though... I'm just not sure where I'll be or what I'll be doing. That's a scary notion; not knowing what the immediate future holds or the distant future, for that matter. I forgot how this feels 'cause I haven't felt it in at least four years, or maybe I've never felt it. You know; Freshmen know they'll be Sophomores and Sophomores know they'll be Juniors and Juniors know they'll be Seniors. The same was true for high school and junior high and grade school. I always knew what was coming, what was next.

I heard someone say something earlier today, someone who's also graduating, that made me think. He was responding to a question about how he would remember college. His response, "Hard to remember... impossible to forget!"

"Why?" someone else asked him.

"Because I was so drunk I can't remember much, but the years were so good I can never forget."

All around me are reminders of how I missed out on so much without even realizing it.

You have no idea how happy I am to leave, but how depressed I am at the same time. Also, still no word from employers and it's not looking too good. And I realized, as you brought up two weeks ago, that one of the reasons I'm so unhappy is because I expected to have certain things accomplished in life by now.

Here are a couple, like you asked me to identify. One of them was having a steady girlfriend. Another was a job lined up; career path maybe. Some direction in my life would be nice. Maybe some good friends to spend time with... I have none of those really. And I thought that I would enjoy my college years much more than this. But that's something else. Whatever, I just want to get my diploma and get out of here.

-Tim B.

—

Tim's e-mail was painfully typical; dissatisfied with his present situation and craving to talk to someone about it. He was not even seeking advice, just someone to hear him out, hear his thoughts.

I decided to offer a fully fabricated story from my fully fabricated past as a metaphor for Tim's situation. I had few ethical qualms about lying when I felt it would aid the patient's growth.

—

(*E-Mail to Tim*)

Tim,

You're probably feeling a lot like a dog on the freeway right now…

When I was younger and lived Upstate, my aunt and uncle had this dog. It was a Dalmatian. Beautiful dog: strong, thin but muscular, spotted coat, a bit crazy—that's the way those dogs are—but it was only crazy around people it knew. Whenever a stranger or strange dog was around, it hid in the corner; a bit of a coward, but we loved her.

So somehow the dog got loose. It was usually tied up in the back, behind the house, but it wiggled out of its collar and, for some reason, no one realized that it had gotten loose. This dog, this crazy dog, somehow walked farther than I can imagine any dog walking in one day.

Down the freeway this dog walked, ran probably, for the entire time that it was out from behind the house. She must have felt lost and confused and scared and lonely… this poor dog. No one deserves that. Cars were whizzing by holding passengers that saw the dog, felt bad for it, but were too involved with their own lives to try to help it. They had their own problems.

Meanwhile, that same day, my mother needed to get to the doctor's office for an appointment and for some reason I went with her.

So we're driving and suddenly there was a road block ahead; some wires had gone down and we were directed around, through miles of congested traffic and backed up side roads. So we got off of one road and onto another and then onto the freeway. That's where we saw that crazy dog, just walking on the side, no clue where she was going. Scared, sad, uncertain what would happen next.

We pulled over, but the dog was on one side of the highway and we were on the other. As we called her name, she stopped and looked across to see that what she had been looking for all along was so close, but separated by a death march through speeding automobiles.

After a number of seconds of looking from side to side, almost as if she had been planning, she took off toward us, every car narrowly missing her. Some slowed, some took no notice and kept their pace, and one even appeared to speed up and aim for the canine.

But finally she made it. I picked her up lovingly and she licked my face until it hurt. "Happy" didn't come close to explaining this little dog's behavior, jumping all over us.

After that day, the dog was constantly happy, even when strangers or strange dogs were around. She would go up to them and lick them all over. She lived every moment as if it were her last, loving every minute.

Maybe you're a little like that dog, Tim. Maybe you need to find your hole in the traffic so you can start your new life as a person satisfied, even happy, with his life. This is the time for new beginnings and you need to grasp it, hold on to it. Be ready for whatever comes next and approach it in a manner that allows for success and greatness.

Congratulations on getting through your college years, Tim. The future holds only great things for you; the things on your list and beyond!

—Dr. Thesiger

—

I leaned back for a moment after signing my name to it and acknowledged mentally that my response was mostly irrelevant. The valuable part for the patient was the catharsis of thinking about their problem, making sense of it, and writing it down in a coherent manner. My response, of very little importance.

After spell-checking and leaving in the appropriate run-on sentences, incomplete sentences, and grammatical mistakes, the message was sent to Tim, automatically billing his account in the process.

Did I just tell him to run through fast-moving traffic? I thought and then tried to push the idea from my mind.

Chapter 9

Robert

The computer read 2:41 p.m. in its corner so I went on to the next e-mail which was from Robert, a forty-four-year-old man, married, no children, from New Jersey, just outside New York City. It was always enjoyable to read his e-mails because he was smart and his age was close enough to mine for me to accept his good responses as my own.

I often asked him questions that I wanted answered for myself and I always received well thought out, insightful responses that slightly brightened my day by making me think differently about the way I looked at the world.

—

(E-Mail from Robert)

Dr. Thesiger,

What am I thankful for, you ask? The last time I was asked that question was probably more than thirty-five years ago, around Thanksgiving in grade school. During that time, we would sit in a circle, what they repeatedly referred to as sitting "Indian-style," and go around the room telling the group what we were thankful for.

I remember doing it every year for a few years in a row. We would dress as either Native Americans or American Travelers. I realize that Columbus and his crew were not American per se, but I suppose historical accuracy was over my teachers' heads in those days. Tact was also over their heads considering I always was instructed to dress as a Native American because I had darker skin than the rest of the class.

The things people at that age are thankful for are all quite superficial and selfish. Even when family members and relatives are mentioned, they're only in the context of what they can do for the individual who is thankful. During childhood, there is not really much of a way to experience the world and look at it other than through one's own eyes and in relation to one's self.

So when I was sitting in a circle, "Indian-style," dressed as a Native American on Thanksgiving, I was only thankful for selfish and superficial things. I liked nice fast pretty cars and my parents' big house, swimming pool, tennis court, going on fun vacations, and so on. Everything centered on benefiting me.

Now that I am more than thirty-five years older and wiser, the answers are quite different. Even thirty-five years ago, when a family member was something I was thankful for, it was only because of what they did for me. Now family is number one on my list because I love them and because they are all good people.

Although, ironically I actually dislike my family more than I did back then because I know them better now—I'm sick of them really—but my relatively newly acquired ability to define and see their character styles has allowed me to accept them for who they are. Of course I still get frustrated with them, but that is unavoidable sometimes, as we discussed.

I would also like to extend my definition of family to include friends; not every acquaintance, but those truly good human beings with whom I am blessed enough to share friendship. Those selfless, generous, intelligent, challenging, and amazing people that I have connected with over the years. They are few, but I am thankful for them because they make the world a better place for all. They really do.

Next on the list is health. Health refers not just to my own, but to that of my family (same definition as above). We are all blessed to be healthy; all of our senses are intact and there are no pending illnesses… that I know of (knock on wood!).

Health also includes physical and mental abilities. I admit that I am not the smartest man in the world, but I am very thankful for the intelligence and drive that I do possess. The same goes for physical abilities, more specifically athletic abilities. Ever since I was young, I have excelled at sports. Much of my development has been shaped by this fact. During my youth, peers looked up to the ones who were the best at sports; the last man standing in dodgeball was king.

Business is going quite well and I'm happy about it; I know that we are a lot better off than many other people. I'm extremely thankful for that because I see how hard it is sometimes for others.

That is a key part of my list and a key characteristic that should be taken into account for all people. Everything is relative. Family, friends, health, financial security, everything. There are numerous people in the same position as I, yet they always want more. Who can blame them really? We live in a society that values excess and that strives for perfection. I am very proud of the fact that I am more than content with what I have; I am thankful. I am also very proud that my list of today contains little superficial content. I think that is something that I have been consciously and subconsciously striving for since I was a youth, even before I knew and understood the meaning of the word.

Thank you for helping me realize that I have reached this goal.

—Bob

—

I sat back in my chair after reading Robert's e-mail. I thought about my own life and if it fell in line with his enough for this to apply to me. There were similarities, but there were many more differences. I was unable to steal from him the benefits of this experiential exercise, but I thought deeply, if briefly, about my own self. My response was short.

—

(E-Mail to Robert)

Robert,

Good thought went into this one. I like where you went with it. I like where it brought you. How do you feel about your position in life? Do you feel guilty? What about those not as fortunate? How do you feel about them? How do you think they feel about you? How did inheriting a great deal of money make you feel and how does it make you feel now? Was there guilt about having opportunities that others without money did not have? Is there guilt now about the discrepancy between you and others?

I know you mask your wealth, never speaking of it with anyone. And I know you give generously to those less fortunate. We have not delved into the reasons why (not that you need reasons) and this might be a good place to do it. Let me know what you think and how you are feeling about it.

Be well, Robert, and keep up the fantastic insightful work!

—Dr. Thesiger

—

After quickly skimming my message for spelling and grammatical errors and finding none, I sent it and then decided staring out onto the park would be the most effective use of time until my next in-office patient arrived.

Chapter 10

Mark

Two or three minutes passed before a strong deep knocking, created by what I assumed to be a loosely held fist, filled the room and brought me back into the realities of the day. Without looking through the peephole, I swung open the door revealing Mark, a tall, strong, intelligent looking man. He had short black hair, wore faintly tinted thick glasses with dark black rims, and fitted tan pants with a tucked in light blue fitted collared shirt which matched his eyes just perfectly. All of his clothes were without wrinkles; I assumed he ironed even his socks. He had the kind of look and moved with the kind of whimsical swagger that suggested he had not a care or a problem in the world.

"Mark! Come in, Sir," I said.

"Doctor, it's good to see you! Lookin' good!" Mark was quite the flatterer.

I smiled. "And the same to you, as always."

He slid into the room and spun in a half circle before he collapsed himself onto the couch across the glass coffee table from the two matching love seats, the central seating area in the room and his usual seat, almost everyone's usual seat.

"How did the week treat you? How are things?" I asked as I sat across from him on one of the comfortable cushy love seats opposite the couch.

"You know. Same old same old. Wife. Kids. Work. Goin' through the motions."

When speaking about himself, Mark downplayed the enormity of his life because he believed its past was much more interesting and exciting than its present, a present that was not worth focusing on. He was the owner of a company that had contracts with many of the glass façade skyscrapers in the city to clean their exteriors. He started out "dangling off the sides of buildings with a rag," as he put it, but early success had led to a life behind a desk.

He had dealt quite well with his initial dissatisfaction with the move toward mundane. In fact, he had no regrets whatsoever. He filled the void of excitement in his life with dangerous, adrenaline inducing hobbies. Skydiving, bungee jumping, windsurfing, hang gliding, rock and ice climbing. The list went on. "Getting dirty is the only way to keep your head clean," he often opined.

His reason for therapy arose while climbing at Yosemite National Park when he was vacationing in California. He was slowly working his way up an incline when he settled his left hand into a crevice. Screaming out in excruciating pain, he recoiled his limbs back to his body, his weight caught by the safety harness which twisted him around and around as he dangled far from the ground below.

He looked up to see a long dark snake slithering out of the crevice. Out of fright he froze, and was stuck dangling for several hours before being saved by a rescue team.

Thankfully the snake was not poisonous and the bite marks healed after a week, but Mark felt as though he had been scarred for life. His resulting condition left him unable to put his hands anywhere that he could not see them. When Mark first came to me, he had been afraid to hug his children because his hands would disappear behind their backs. He was afraid to put on gloves. Even thinking about scratching the back of his head would send him into a fit of anxiety.

"How about you, Doc? How you doin'?" he asked, sprawling comfortably on the couch.

"Can't complain. No one would listen if I did anyway…"

"Ha! That's a good one," he replied.

Mark enjoyed the fact that I often played the beaten down, washed up, sad old man to his strong, successful, extreme-sports playing young man. It was clear to me that he liked feeling that he was better than those around him. I suppose everyone does, but his emotional response to feeling that he was better than others was an extreme elation that helped him in sessions so I complied. It was who I had to be to draw him in and help him improve himself. Like all other patients, he had shopped around for the right psychologist. I needed to be what he would respond to best.

There was a short pause which I broke with, "Okay, let's get down to work!"

"Let's," he agreed.

"So, Mark, we've spent a great number of weeks and months weaning you back into losing your hands from sight and dealing with the accompanying anxiety."

"Yes," he affirmed.

"It took us a long time to get to this point because we took a slow and steady approach, starting with imagining and breathing exercises and relaxation tapes…"

He interrupted me. "Yeah, Doc. So what's next? Am I cured?"

"Mark, I would like to try to get you over the next hurtle relatively quickly and I think you can do it if you remember to use your relaxation methods as you have been for the duration of therapy."

"Okay, but where else do we have to go from here? I feel like I'm cured. I can do it all without even really thinking twice." He put his hands behind his head to prove his recovery.

I then got up and walked toward my desk.

"What's over there, Doc?" he asked without a hint of apprehension in his tone.

I answered him with only a smile as I thought about how Mark was right. He was able to do everything that his traumatizing experience took away. He was truly cured to the highest level he could be. There really was not much more, if anything, that I could do for him. This meant that therapy, and thus I, was a success, but it unfortunately also meant that therapy, and thus I, would no longer be needed by Mark.

All the seminars and classes and talks that the institutions and licensing boards required psychologists to attend came rushing into my mind. The various speakers, videos, short educational skits; they were all suddenly swirling around in my consciousness.

I bent down behind the large mahogany desk, then began to shake my head vigorously to bounce out the bold capital letters E-T-H-I-C-S. I opened the bottom drawer and took out the shoebox then stood up, holding it carefully as I walked slowly back to where I sat earlier.

"New shoes?" Mark asked laughing.

"What's so funny?"

"That's a shoebox for ladies' shoes," he informed me.

"How did you know that?" I asked, momentarily distracted.

"They only make ladies' shoes." He pointed at the side of the box where the manufacturer's name was written in script. "Lisa loves them. Why are there holes all over the box?"

I placed the shoebox atop the coffee table between my seat and the couch then pushed it closer to him.

"Mark, there is a snake in this box," I said with a straight face.

Immediately he tensed up and began to push himself away, backing into the couch.

"Now, calm down, Mark. Remember the breathing exercises," I instructed.

He started to shake his head back and forth.

"It's not poisonous and it can't hurt you. It can only bite you like the one did at Yosemite."

"Where did you get a snake, Doc?" he asked, swallowing his words, still pushing himself away from the shoebox.

"It doesn't matter, Mark."

"Why would you put it in a box for ladies' shoes? How big is it?" He was speaking quickly and frantically.

"It's two feet long. Just a baby." I spoke slowly and calmly in an attempt to model proper behavior. I knew nothing about snakes. I was uncertain if two feet was long or short. It was the first measurement that came to mind as I glanced down for an answer.

I sat for a while hoping that Mark's anxiety would decrease, but he remained extremely uncomfortable and frantic as he continued to push himself into the couch and attempt to physically and mentally distance himself from the shoebox.

I then deliberately picked it up at which point Mark began to climb up onto the couch, scratching to get away. I slowly placed the box onto his legs as he squirmed and tried pushing his face away from it, closing his eyes tight.

"Try not to move around, Mark. Just be still and calm. It can't hurt you if it's in a box."

"Doc, please. My heart is starting to hurt. I can't take this kind of thing!" He began to clench his chest.

In fear of killing my patient, I picked up the box and brought it back to my desk, placing it atop. Mark's body immediately relaxed and he began shouting angrily.

"What are you doing, Doc? Tryin' to kill me?"

"How are you feeling, Mark?"

"I feel horrible, Doc. Like I just had a heart attack." He was no longer holding his chest leading me to believe that I should have continued the exercise longer.

"My intention here was to keep the shoebox on you for as long as possible until your anxiety decreased and eventually disappeared," I explained. "It's physically impossible for you to be so worked up forever. Eventually the anxiety would go away and you would realize that there was no reason to be anxious."

Mark had an angry and bewildered look on his face.

"Mark," I continued, "I have to tell you—"

"What?" he interrupted angrily.

I hesitated for a moment before telling him, "There's no snake in the box." I opened it and then showed him its nonexistent contents.

"What the hell, Doc? What are you doing? I'm out of here." With that Mark got up and walked out, slamming the door behind him.

My face dropped as I considered for a moment if what I had just done was unethical. Shaking my head in response to my thoughts, I placed the shoebox atop the desk before opening a blank message to compose an e-mail.

—

(E-Mail to Mark)

Dear Mark,

It appears that my exposure method of flooding was ineffective in today's session. Be advised that, even though you have conquered the symptoms of your problem (inability to place hands in unseen places), the underlying problem is still very strong (your phobia of snakes).

We have successfully treated the symptom, but still have a great deal of intense work to do with regard to the actual problem. Without the focus being directed toward the underlying problem, your symptoms will return and all the work we have done for the better part of a year will be lost.

Feel free to share your thoughts with me via e-mail before your session next week.

—Dr. Thesiger

—

After quickly scanning for errors, I sent the e-mail then opened the billing program to manually bill Mark for the session.

Again, I briefly debated the level of ethics present or absent in the short session, sided with myself, and then used the computer to research a restaurant from which to order. Chicken Teriyaki with brown rice and steamed vegetables. My credit card information was carelessly stored in the computer for a rapid check-out process. If someone accessed it somehow, I felt that it would be difficult for my financial situation to get too much worse than it already was. What was the point in being safe with my credit card number?

Feeling almost as if I had accomplished something, I thought about rewarding myself by turning my chair around to observe the great outdoors, looking through its beauty and losing myself in mindless thought. I chose instead to keep my eyes on the screen so I could reply to the last two e-mails before my inevitable staring match with the park would commence.

Chapter 11

Samuel

The next e-mail was from nineteen-year-old Samuel who had been complaining about relationship problems for weeks. His ex-girlfriend, who had acrimoniously ended their romance months earlier, had recently been hired as a waitress at the restaurant where Sam had been waiting tables for more than a year. Sam suggested in previous e-mails that she had been acting cold toward him, even a little obnoxious at times, all while sending him mixed signals about their long-ended relationship.

During our last three or four correspondences, it was uncovered that Sam still harbored feelings for his ex, but was hiding them because of fear of rejection. The last response I wrote to his message was unfortunately when I was feeling quite sick from the sushi incident so it lacked much substance. I was curious to see what

Sam's reply would be.

—

(E-Mail from Samuel)

Dr. Thesiger…

Sir, you are brilliant. I don't know how you do it, but you always manage to say just the right thing to get me going, get me thinking, then I come up with the answer even when I don't know there's a question. But, I know it's you; it's all you. You say what needs to be said for me to think and then I come to the conclusion that you wanted me to. You are a genius!

"Better to have loved and lost than never to have loved at all."

Why would you even say that? That's what I thought. I actually got a little bit angry at you for it. I'm pouring my heart out for pages, angry at the world and everyone in it, especially Maggie, and that's what you say to me? That's it? Just that cliché and one other line? Oh, I was mad. I punched the pillow then stomped around the room for a while before reading it again.

"Better to have loved and lost than never to have loved at all.

"Think about it…"

Ohhhh… I thought about it and got even angrier. Then I thought about why you would say that (which I'm sure is what you actually wanted me to think about). I asked myself, Has Doc T ever even loved and lost?

Like you told me a while ago, "It's not about the right answer, it's about the right question." *Have you ever loved and lost?*

That's when it really hit me. This is life! Living life. And that's what you wanted me to see! You wanted me to realize that the reason this is a good thing is because I actually did it, went through with it, lived it. Like you told me a while back; life is experiencing it!

You're a genius, Doc. And now I feel a heck of a lot better about the whole situation and I actually appreciate her even though she's treating me badly now. But, that brings me to the problem. I need a way to get her to stop. I appreciate her now, but I want to be able to have her as a friend, not just an annoyance. You know what I mean?

What should I do, Doc? Maybe a little manipulation is in order? Give me some more genius wisdom of the ways of the world. I will be grateful.

—Sam

—

Samuel's e-mail was refreshing. Being called a genius (multiple times) was something of which I would never grow tired. And it always amazed me how much some patients will interpret and read into even the shortest of messages and come up with something that, in the end, helps them progress. I wrote merely one line from Alfred Tennyson then one more.

Smiling as I thought about how to respond, his flattery encouraged me to step somewhat out of my role as a therapist and into the role of the aged looking to impress the youth.

—

(E-Mail to Samuel)

Sam,

Fantastic that you saw through my attempt to guide you toward the correct conclusion with some simple yet infuriating words! Your reasoning and logic come together to create an intelligent young man.

So let's apply those attributes to the problem at hand. Ask yourself this, Sam: Why is Maggie treating you like she is?

I'll answer it myself: It's about power. It's always about power. She wants to make you feel like you really lost something important when you lost her. And you wonder why she has been dressing up for work so much… she wants you to see what you've lost.

And her mean behavior toward you? She wants to see you squirming, wants to see you angry at her, and you're playing right into her trap by mirroring her behavior; acting hostile toward her. She then convinces herself that your anger toward her is a result of your desire for her and the fact that you don't have her anymore. She ignores the other factors, like her mean behavior toward you. And now she feels she has the upper hand, the power.

Now, while I don't condone manipulation per se, what you have to do is stop mirroring her behavior; stop behaving in a hostile manner toward her. Treat her kindly, but act somewhat timid around her, like a dog that gets beaten by its owner.

She'll feel like she's won, she's broken you; then she'll start to feel bad about how she treats you. She will then start to act more civil and civil will lead toward acting nice. Once that happens, you can safely go back to being yourself around her. You'll have a friend within a week or two!

I look forward to hearing about the success of this coming week, Sam. You have a good one and remember, don't make eye contact. Would a battered dog look its aggressor in the eye? I think not!

—Dr. Thesiger

—

A short and quick spell-check later, the e-mail was sent and Sam's account was charged. I decided to allow myself to turn toward the park and relax for a moment.

Sometime later, I was dragged out of an unexpected slumber by a sharp knocking. I rubbed my eyes with my right thumb and index finger as I stumbled toward the door. A glance   out the peephole revealed a below average height man holding something oddly shaped.

I opened the door.

"Delivery!" he informed me. This announcement felt like an insult to me. It suggested that I was incapable of deducing his purpose from his attire; a previously white and currently dingy chef's coat, apron and pants of the same material and color, and a chef's hat matching the wear of the other articles of clothing. At the same time, I did enjoy his pronunciation of "delivery," his accent appropriate for the food he was holding.

He handed me the bag with the receipt stapled to the side.

There was a pause, as I was still waking up, before I finally said, "Thank you," but he had begun to walk down the hall toward the elevator before I even had the chance to express my fatigued gratitude.

I watched the man as he walked and could not help but wonder if he had been the one who prepared the food weighing down the bag in my right hand. I hoped not, noticing that he had the hands of a man who had recently changed a tire. Luckily, I was hungry enough to convince myself that he changed the tire after preparing my food.

I placed the bag on my desk, then I took a glass out of the cabinet and filled it with filtered water from the carafe on the coffee table. I pushed the keyboard to the side as I selected a news channel on the computer; just something to have in the background as my mind wandered between bites.

After throwing the empty containers into the bag before its trip to the garbage chute in the hallway, I returned to the office and lay down on the couch. It was then that my running nose reminded me that I was still sick.

I retrieved a tissue from the box on the desk then returned to the couch.

Chapter 12

Barry

A slow knock, each rap separated from the last by twice as much time as was customary, woke me. It was dark in the room. The sun had gone down and only the flickering streams of light, an echo of the street lights below, were available to guide me to the door and light-switch beside it.

I peered out of the peephole then took a moment to adjust my matted down, wrinkled, and clearly slept in clothing before opening the door.

"Barry!" I said loudly with a voice that was scratchy and half an octave lower than its normal timbre.

Barry worked in finance, previously out of Boston, but now New York after he requested a transfer due to his suspicion that someone was watching and following him. He trusted nobody and kept mostly to himself. He had no spouse or friends or family to speak of. He initially came to my office because he began to have trouble at work and his company's human resources personnel suggested that he try therapy instead of going through with another transfer.

"Dr. Thesiger," he replied with an accent that was hard to place, elongating his "r" sounds and sharpening his "e" sounds. Barry normally had no accent beyond that of an average American, so the fact that he was affecting a different speech pattern was strange. Also strange was the fact that he called me "Dr. Thesiger." He had always called me "Nick" because ours was a less formal relationship than what I shared with most of my patients. Since he had a healthy distrust of authority figures, it was one small step to making him feel comfortable.

As he made his way toward the couch with a slight limp, I put the oddities out of my mind, assuming the meanings behind their presence would be uncovered in minutes.

"Happy birthday!" I said to him as I closed the door.

"Aye, aye… me birthday. Avast, ye matey! Ahoy, strangest thin' happened t' me just now, outside ye' building." He paused for a moment then added, "Garr."

"Oh," I responded, ignoring his odd word choice. "Is the homeless man outside bothering you? If you give him some change, he'll stop asking you if he can touch your feet."

Barry laughed and said, "Narr. Ye comely wench broadside ye' building be smilin' at ye old scurvy dog."

"And this is strange why?" I probed.

"T'was a fair maiden and I be a barnacle covered seaman. Somethin' was amiss with it. Somethin' was amiss…" He paused again, before adding, "Garr."

"Ah, Barry… May I ask why you're speaking like that?"

"Arrr, me matey! I thought y'eed never ask! Tis International Talk Like a Pirate Day…"

Before responding, I thought about why Barry was doing this. All my patients with diagnosable psychological disorders adored Halloween. Every one of them would dress up, attend parties, go door to door trick-or-treating. There was something very appealing to them about having the abnormal suddenly become accepted and celebrated. International Talk Like a Pirate Day was similar enough. I decided to explore this with Barry by challenging his thought process.

"Isn't International Talk Like a Pirate Day September 19th?" I asked.

"Tis true!" he said rather enthusiastically with upward inflection.

"It is not September, Barry."

"Tis true," he said sadly with a downward inflection as his strong posture and lifted head slowly fell.

"Why then are you speaking like a pirate?" I asked.

"I don't know, Nick," he said in his normal average-American voice. "I suppose I thought it would make me feel better."

"You're feeling down?"

"Not really. No."

"Okay," I said, taking him at his word. I wanted to start the session with the structure that his condition required so I did not focus on the potentially low level of his emotional state yet.

"Let us start with the oriented times three assessment, alright, Barry?" I took a piece of paper off the notepad in my desk and brought it to Barry with the pencil that Ms. Stewart had left on the floor hours earlier. I then sat in the chair across from the couch while he leaned over the coffee table and wrote down the date, time, and where we were and for what reason in some detail.

"How'm I doing?" he asked as he handed me the paper and pencil.

The remaining part of Barry's orientation assessment was that of his awareness of who he was and who the familiar people around him were and for that I was unsure of his status.

"That is yet to be determined, Barry, but I think you're doing fine so far. Let's get back to how you feel on this particular day."

"I feel fine," he replied, obviously not wanting to share his feelings in depth.

"Why did you behave as though it was a different day than this day, your birthday?" I asked.

"What's with the shoebox?" he asked, noticing the box on my desk.

"Oh, I keep crickets. Their chirping calms me," I responded. Barry was a bit of a quirky man and he seemed most comfortable around a bit of a quirky psychologist, the kind that would keep crickets. I tried my best to keep up with his quirk, but I often found our sessions to be a bit disjointed.

He looked up and thought for a moment before saying, "Good idea…"

"So why are you ignoring the day of your birth, Barry?"

He became noticeably uncomfortable so I quickly changed the subject. "How was your week? How is work going? Let's start there."

"You talked to them at my work? My boss? He's a liar and a blabbermouth! Don't listen to him." Barry spoke quickly and stopped abruptly. He scrunched his head down toward his shoulders and began looking side to side rather frantically.

He continued. "They're sending me secret messages on my work phone number now. You know that? They found me, even here..."

"Please tell me about it, Barry." I arranged my features into an appropriately interested display of concern and then sat back in the cushy chair, placing my right ankle atop my left knee, hands together with fingertips of each touching their corresponding tips and with palms apart.

"It's in the phone call. It's hidden, you know? The line is tapped by some government agency. FBI, CIA, something like that, you know? But these people are sending me messages; they get them through undetected. They're smart, you see? They found a way around it all, around the tapped phones."

"How?" I asked wrongfully strengthening and feeding his delusion.

"They do something with the phone system. They cross the lines, you know? They redirect someone tryin' to call someone else. Then the call comes to me, comes to my desk. I pick it up, you know? 'Barry here,' I say. 'Oh, ah, I think I dialed the wrong number. Sorry, Barry.' Something like that from the other end. And it's legitimate too. It's from a real number and a real person tryin' to get somebody else. So then the people tapping the phone, they just delete it from their files like it's a wrong number 'cause it is, you see?

"But the message, it gets through. I knew something was happening so I set up my computer to record my calls. Then I go to the file and I listen to the short call. In between me sayin' 'Barry here' and the person on the other end sayin' whatever they say, there's silence, but it's only silence to the human ear. Humans only hear sound in a certain range of hertz, certain frequencies. Like, you know, dog whistles; dogs can hear 'em, but we can't.

"So this silence. I isolate it on my computer. Then I adjust the levels, the treble and bass and mids and stuff. Then I move the hertz levels out of what humans can hear normally. When I do it, you know, it pulls the secret message back into what humans can hear.

"Then I turn up the volume, play it backward at 1/16 speed, and I get the message out. They've been sending me messages and I figured it out! I figured out how to receive 'em!"

I could see that Barry was very impressed with himself. Actually I was pretty impressed with him too. It always fascinated me that his paranoia could come up with these elaborate delusions that sounded so intricately intelligent and complex. *I* never could have come up with something so clever if I tried.

"What do the messages say?" I asked before I could stop myself.

"That I don't know, Doc. I can't understand them yet. They're in some kind of language I haven't cracked yet. And it's all fuzzy sounding. I need to work on the method a little longer before I perfect it." The complete conviction in his face was ebbing.

I knew I had to, but I did not want to tell him. *Ethics,* I reminded myself. "Barry, I don't think anyone is sending you messages. I think you just stumbled upon background noise or static on the phone. That's why it doesn't resemble any kind of decipherable speech."

"If you say so, Doc. I don't think you're right though. I'll bring in some recordings for you next week. You can judge for yourself. You'll see."

"That sounds good, but don't preoccupy yourself with this too much. If somebody really needed to get secret messages to you, they would find a more efficient and foolproof way."

"Hmm, I guess you're right on that one."

Barry, for some reason, trusted me and allowed himself to see my advice as worth considering without much hesitation. At least it seemed that way in session, although I often wondered if he treated everyone like this, then scrutinized them behind their backs, assuming they were all out to get him. I hoped I was different. He told me I was. Being different in his eyes was the only way I could help him.

"So back to today as your birthday. Why did you convince yourself today was the 19th of September?" I asked.

Barry looked at me for a moment. He was thinking of a way out, a way to change the subject without answering.

Finally he spoke. "Something funny happened to me in the office today. Want to hear it?"

I allowed him. "Sure."

"The people in the office, they knew it was my birthday. So at lunch they all got together and brought me this cake. The cake was ice cream!" His speech turned from words to laughter. I smiled, mirroring his jovial mood.

"And, in this ice cream cake, they had candles burning for me to blow out." He let out an infectious laugh. I chuckled along.

"Some of those guys are funny, you know?" He continued laughing.

Still smiling, I continued to politely chuckle along with him, but the chuckling needed to stop. Barry's emotional responses to everyday events were often exaggerated, which was one of the things we were addressing in therapy.

"Why is this so very funny, Barry?"

"Come on, Nick. You know. Fire melts frozen things! The ice cream cake is made out of ice cream! Ice cream is frozen! It melts! Don't you get it?" He laughed even harder as he explained, not waiting for me to agree with the presumed hilarity of the situation.

"But did the cake melt?" I asked.

He thought for a moment. "No, it didn't," he responded in a sober tone.

"So then it really was not that funny, was it?"

"I guess not." He was no longer laughing and his face was deep in thought. "You know," he continued, "they gave me a drink with ice in it. They're always trying to find ways to get rid of me."

"What do you mean, 'get rid of you'?" I pressed.

"You know, they lull me into a false sense of security with the party and the singing and the cake for me to laugh at, then they give me a poisoned drink." Barry immediately smiled, knowing what my next question was going to be. He enjoyed explaining his conspiracy theories; probably because I obviously enjoyed their clever nature.

Asking the obvious question, I said, "How did you know the drink was poisoned?"

"Well," he said as he put his hands behind his head and leaned back, "you see, I never drink anything but the water from my thermos that I get from my tap then filter thoroughly. My colleagues know it, but they tried to get me to drink their soda anyway. 'The office paid for the cake and the soda so we have to finish it.' That's what they told me when I turned down a filled up cup.

"You see, they already knew I wasn't going to eat the cake. They think I have every food allergy out there so they don't even offer; it was just a symbol and something for them to eat. So, you know, they couldn't hide the poison in the cake; instead they tried the drink. They thought I would have some soda because it was my birthday and because the office paid for it.

"And they knew, even if I took the soda, I would test it before drinking it. You know, have somebody else taste it first and see if they drop dead; something like that. I looked around in everyone else's cups. Do you know what was there?"

I was unsure if this was a rhetorical question or if he wanted me to answer. A moment of silence indicated the latter. "No, what was there?"

"The soda!" he shouted, as if to declare the climax of his story.

"Why is that surprising?" I asked.

"My cup had ice in it, but nobody else's did. If I had somebody else test the drink, they would be fine. Then, when I drank it for a while, I would be dead."

"I don't follow, Barry."

"The poison, Nick, it was in the ice. They're pretty smart there in the office, but I'm smarter. If I tested it when it was handed to me; all would go well. Then the ice melts, releasing the poison into the drink. I drink it and die!" Barry was clearly elated with himself and his deductive powers and my reaction only further pleased him.

"Oohhh! That *is* smart. I never would have thought of that one." I stopped myself, realizing that I was encouraging Barry's extreme paranoia. "But your co-workers were most likely *not* trying to poison you. They were probably just trying to cool down the birthday boy's drink. They have no reason to try to kill you and, even if they did, they probably wouldn't try to poison you at your birthday lunch party in the office. That's too obvious."

Barry's delusions were much like a murder mystery or a who-done-it, where you have to guess how a crime was committed before being given the answer. I often allowed my own interest in the guessing game of real-life fiction to get in the way of meaningful therapy.

"Too obvious?" he questioned. "I guess you're right. They would do something else, something that couldn't be traced as easily."

"That is probably true, but it is extremely unlikely that they are actually trying to kill you," I told him.

He paused for a moment appearing to give it some thought. "I think you're right, Nick. That makes a lot of sense. I'm still going to keep on the lookout though. You can never be too careful."

Whenever Barry said, "You can never be too careful," I always heard, "You can never be too crazy," which brought a smile to my face every time; a smile that, I was sure, he interpreted as silent agreement.

Recalling the intended topic, I attempted to steer the conversation back toward what Barry was trying to avoid. "So today was a good birthday for you then. With the party and everything?"

"I suppose."

"Are birthdays normally like this for you? Are they good or bad? Do you do something on your birthday usually? Tell me about your past birthdays."

"Normal day. Nothing special really. It's just the day I have to start saying that I'm one year older than the previous day. That's about it."

It was clear that Barry had nothing to say about pretending it was a different day, so I decided to move on.

"Let's get back to how you're feeling, Barry."

"Oh, you would be proud of me, Nick! I did something you would be proud of." Again he seemed pleased with himself.

"Please, tell me."

"Do you remember when you were explaining the 'misattribution of arousal' *paradigm* to me last month?" He pronounced the word "paradigm" slowly. "Saying how I think that I am happy because of one thing, even though it is actually something else makin' me feel that way?"

"Yes," I responded before trying to explain it in more specific terms. "You are physically excited, your heart rate is raised and your mood changes, because, for example, I punch you in the arm and shake you every time I see you." I leaned out of my chair and punched him in the arm then shook him, right hand on his left shoulder and left hand on his right shoulder. "Then, because these specific feelings occur every time you see me, it is interpreted by your mind to be a result of your positive feelings for me."

"That's right," he agreed. "And you were saying how I should try to think about if that happens to me, you know, if I'm all worked up about something then I attribute it to something else."

"Yes." I was happy to hear that he understood what I meant when I was explaining the paradigm to him.

"Well, I applied that earlier. I had a dream about living in this really nice apartment and then Sandy, she works in my office, she came in and I had this amazing feeling about her. My first thought was that I was in love with her, but then I thought that maybe I was feeling so good because I was comfortable in this great apartment and it had nothing to do with Sandy." He ended his story with an appropriate title. "Misattribution of Arousal," he repeated, head up slightly, appearing to read the words in the space between us.

"This was a dream?" I asked.

"Yes, of course," he replied, still proud of himself.

I did not want to hurt his feelings, so I tried to be as delicate as possible. "This method of identifying the true source of emotional arousal is most commonly used for only waking situations. So using it to explain a dream really isn't quite the way it was intended to be used."

His face began to drop. I did not want to discourage Barry from applying what he learned in sessions to his everyday life, so I added, "But, that was a great new application of the paradigm! Nice job, Barry!"

His facial confidence returned.

"Keep it up!" I added.

I then got up from the cushy couch and walked toward my desk. "Barry, I would like to teach you a new skill today."

His eyes, head, neck, and shoulders followed me around the room. He always seemed uneasy when I stood up while he was still sitting.

"This is something that will help you relax." I took an ancient cassette tape out of my desk. "I made this tape of the instructions of a relaxation technique for you. It basically just instructs you on how to concentrate on and then relax parts of your body separately in a specific order."

I slid the tape across the coffee table toward him. He picked it up as he stood up. I sat down then he followed my example.

"What is this? I don't have a tape player."

"I know. I was just kidding. I thought it would be funny to give you an antique tape and pretend I thought it was current."

The expression on Barry's face suggested that my joke had painfully missed its mark.

"Anyway," I continued, "I have the audio file on my computer. I'll send it to you tonight."

"Oh," he started. "I know why you gave this old tape to me. So it would remind me to check my e-mail for the file! Clever…"

I decided to take the credit. "Guilty," I said with my hands up, palms toward him. "I thought maybe we would try a preliminary test run at it right now. What do you think?"

"If you think it's best." He seemed a bit reticent to try something new, but he always was wary of new things.

"You can lie down on the couch, if you'd like. You should try to get as comfortable as possible for this."

Barry lay down slowly, watching me as his torso descended and as I walked toward the light-switch next to the door.

"When you do this at home, make sure you're in a very quiet place without any distractions or random noises. If that is too difficult to find, you can put on headphones with the instructions playing. Dim or turn off all the lights and try to get comfortable." I dimmed the lights as I spoke.

Barry was becoming increasingly uncomfortable, squirming around on the couch. He was behaving as though someone told him there was a snake on his lap.

"Next you should close your eyes," I said.

"I can't do it, Nick!" he shouted. "This isn't relaxing me at all. I need to hear and see what's going on around me. You know that. I feel vulnerable. Remember I used to have problems sleeping 'cause of it? I get too paranoid about what I can't see."

"I suppose you could do this with the lights on and your eyes open, but the idea is to not have any distractions. What if you did it in your bathtub with the door locked?"

"I guess that could work," he replied reluctantly.

"Okay, then make sure to put some pillows and blankets in there. Make it comfortable."

"That sounds like a good idea," he said, getting up from the couch.

I tightened my face and said, "Maybe we were moving too fast in here anyway. How about we try to work toward doing this in the office? That can be a short-term goal."

"Sounds like a good goal to work toward," he said enthusiastically. Then he added, "I should be off. I want to go make my tub comfortable." We both laughed at his crazy sounding sentence.

"Don't say that to too many other people," I instructed as Barry and I moved to the door. I opened it with my left hand and stood at attention, ready to see him off.

He stood there for a moment before saying, "You know, they have a machine that can see into your little peephole in your door." Barry appeared genuinely concerned for my well-being.

"What do you mean?" I asked. "The peephole here?"

"Yup. They have this thing that they can put on the outside of the door and it flips the image right side up, reverses it, and undistorts it. They do it so they can see you coming and catch you."

Again, it was necessary to highlight the flaws in his logic. "Catch me in my office? But they would already know I was in here. Why wouldn't they just wait outside until I come out? There is only *one* door…"

"Well they have it; the machine. You need to outsmart them, you know? I put a piece of tape over my peephole. Think about it, Doc."

I smiled and said, "Have a good week, Barry, I'll send you that file right now."

"Arr, me matey!" he replied. "Be thee well!"

With that he was gone, down the hall toward the stairs. He never took the elevator. Something about not being in control of the direction of locomotion made him uncomfortable.

"Garr!" he shouted before disappearing into the stairwell.

I closed the door and walked over to my computer on the desk, opening a blank message to which I attached the relaxation file.

—

(E-Mail to Barry)

Good day, Barry,

I promise there are no hidden messages in here so don't waste your time looking for them!

—Dr. Thesiger

—

Entering the billing program showed that Barry had been billed automatically based on his permanent place on my schedule. I then buried my hand into the top left drawer of my desk to find my black electrical tape and went over to the door to save myself from potential ambush.

"Barry," I muttered to myself as I shook my head.

———

As I fell back into the large leather chair behind the mahogany desk, a glance left, to the lesser used screen, informed me of the time. 7:38 p.m. I had seven minutes before the next session, a video session.

I intended only to rest my eyes with a quick blink but was roused from a comfortable slumber by the loud pinging tone of an incoming call on the screen ahead.

Chapter 13

Gus

"Gus" the screen proclaimed in red letters flashing frantically from bright to dim to bright to dim. I stood up slowly and stretched before returning to the seat and checking my appearance in the camera on the adjacent screen.

"Good enough," I said aloud.

Gus's face and upper torso filled the session box with the door to his closet and the bottom half of a poster of Mohammad Ali and the same half of a Bob Marley poster, top halves out of frame, on the wall in the background. I scrolled over to the green answer button.

"Gus! How are ya, buddy?" I said loudly toward the computer.

Gus, a doctoral student in philosophy, had been a patient since he began his undergraduate studies. Sloppily dressed, short, and stocky, he wore a hairstyle of long brown hair that was balding at the top; what he referred to as his Reverse Mohawk. Gus always had the appearance of an unfortunate fellow who had just recently been defeated in battle.

"Dr. Thesiger," he said slowly with an affect suggesting I was a superhero and he was my arch nemesis. "How be thee on this glorious summer night?"

"Thee be glorious!" I said mockingly, but Gus interpreted my dialect-mirroring to be more complimentary than derisive. "And yourself, laddy?" I adopted a Scottish accent for the inquiry; I was unsure where it came from.

"You know; same old same old. A perpetual circulating existence of the three R's of being a graduate student."

"And those are?"

"Reading, writing, and research!" he exclaimed.

Without thought, likely due to my fatigue, I glossed over the fact that "writing" begins not with an "r," but with a "w," and asked, "You're nearly done, right? How is the dissertation moving along?"

Gus had completed all of his classes and credits and had only to revise his dissertation before presenting it for a second time. If accepted, he would receive his PhD.

"Its movement is much like that of my hand right now." He lifted his hand in front of the screen, flat, palm down, motionless. I forewent asking him to decipher the meaning of his visual aid and instead asked, "Why do you think you're not working on it? Anything going on you want to talk about?"

"No," he said quickly. "I'm working really well, almost done actually." He paused, waiting for my face on the screen to display a confused look. When it came, he continued. "I was talking about my other hand."

I searched the screen, but his other hand was out of sight. He was laughing so I did the same for his benefit. "Funny guy! Well, congratulations! Continue working hard and I'm sure they'll accept it this time around."

"Ehh, I was just setting up the joke," he said reluctantly. "The dissertation is actually going pretty bad. I haven't been able to do anything but open the document and stare at the screen all day."

"Oh," I said trying to think of a helpful response. "Well, at least your joke was funny!"

"I'm glad one of us is positive. I haven't been positive about this for a long time." He paused for a while. "What was it that William Butler Yeats said? 'Education is not the filling of a pail but the lighting of a fire.' Sometimes I just don't think I have it in me."

"Why not, Gus? How do you feel about things? Take today for example. Tell me what you've been up to, what's held you back."

Gus enjoyed having open-ended questions posed to him because he enjoyed going into depth about his emotional state and how it affected his life in the most poetic and metaphoric of ways. I knew I was in for a speech, so I sat back in my chair and got comfortable as I adjusted the camera to keep myself in frame.

"Well, I'm sitting here, late afternoon, night, noir, nuit, in my room, dark, death, somber, mort. Morning. I awoke quite late, later than expected, later than planned. Wanted to, yearned to awaken early, but no. It never happened, never came about, fruitionless aspiration.

"The alarm clock, the beeping, spitting, twirling teller of time wanted to pull me from my bed, but it was powerless in the absence of concrete plans in my day, the long ago fond farewell to a schedule. Not mandatory? Why leave the sweetness of slumber? I did nothing short of turn over, turn it over, turn it off, roll over, roll back to sleep.

"I woke hours later feeling exhausted, fatigued despite the abundance of hours added to my sleep log. I knew showering offered little helpful to my journey so another hour was spent contemplating the stumbling trip down the hall to stand under the indoor rainstorm of saltless tears. It was skipped; yielding to the environmentalist within.

"Now I sit, here sitting, sit here in a chair in a room on a computer obsessing over the future, the present, the past. Questions about them; all different. Yet questions about them; all the same."

Gus observed a moment of silence before asking, "What do you think, Dr. Thesiger?"

"What do I think?" I asked. "Very poetic, but you sound like you're falling into a bit of a slump…"

"Slump?" he questioned. "A slippery slope to the slump… I emote a locomotion of slow motion."

I often spent time searching for poets with which Gus would not be familiar so I could use them in conversation. Keeping Gus as a patient for all these years was based on the premise that he always had something to learn from me, that I knew more than he on topics important to his life. Casually turning him onto an unknown poet was what Gus needed so that he would feel his time with me was not wasted.

So I attempted to do just that. "I believe it was the philosopher/poet/thespian who goes by the nomenclature 'Common' who once wrote 'slow motion is better than no motion.' "

Gus froze for a moment with an inquisitive look on his face before nodding and smiling. "Right on, Dr. Thesiger."

I nodded back, the knowledge of keeping Gus impressed bringing to me a smile.

He continued, "This feeling of emptiness, I have this overarching undying undulating feeling of emptiness filling me up inside. I'm standing in the corner of the room looking cross-eyed asking, Where does it go from here?

"The bed, the bed in the corner, the bed in the corner of the room is not made."

He then picked up his laptop and turned its built-in camera toward his bed to prove his statement. On the trip back, I noticed a giant stuffed-animal polar bear sitting at a small table opposite a life-sized inflatable skeleton with a large plastic pink flamingo looking over the shoulder of the skeleton. I assumed they were playing chess.

He continued. "Not made this late in the day is true and direct; it is my life as I know it. All should be different, should have been put together, should be made much earlier, a long time ago, but it is not... Now I sit, knowing something should be done, but can I get up off this chair? No! Not to do it, to do anything about it. I can sit here obsessing over it, but I know it won't ever get done and it will force me to sleep on it, sleep in it, that bed, tonight and the next. Again and again messy, not made, disorganized, going nowhere, no future.

"Will there be a day, a day when I make that bed? And, if so, will I make it the next or the next or the next? Doubting, I am.

Doubting. My bed'll be made never in this state of my life, I don't think, I don't believe.

"But, for now, I sit here looking at the pillows on the ground, all but the one on the bed; left, center, soft, inviting; only visible because the sheets hang down, hang low, tucked into the end, but draped over the floor, over my dirty clothes and dirty carpet; my dirty life; in my dirty messy room in this dirty messy dorm.

"Why do it to myself? Why stay? Why continue? Why go on? Good questions, all good questions, but where are the answers? Do they exist? Who knows? Who cares? Why is the sun going down, but I am just beginning my day, just rising? Where did the day go? Where did the days go? My life… Will they ever return to me? Will I ever catch up?"

There was a long silence during which I realized Gus had completed his rant and was awaiting my response.

"Procrastinating, Gus, will only fill the time that you give it," I said poignantly.

Gus peered at me through the computer with the same inquisitive look on his face as earlier, followed again with nods and smiles. "You're right, Dr. Thesiger. I need to just get down to it and do my work. No more lollygagging."

"Lollygagging?" I questioned, preempting the inevitable lengthy soliloquy.

"Yes, Sir! No more; for no longer. It stops here; it stops now. I work until I finish; I work until I am content!" He stood up as he preached and began using his hands and arms to gesticulate, but I could only see from the middle of his chest down given that the camera was affixed to its position.

"Great to hear, Gus!" I said to his crotch.

"I thank you, Dr. Thesiger; transferring your drive, your compassion, your motivation to get the job done, get it done right, to me. I'm rejuvenated and ready to work. I bid thee adieu!"

With that, his hand traveled toward the keyboard. I managed to fit in, "Best of luck to you, Gus," before it went dark.

Chapter 14

Kevin

After exiting the session box on the screen, I navigated back to the e-mail inbox. It revealed the last e-mail of the day, the sender was listed as Kevin L., a middle aged man who had been arrested for an indecent exposure infraction and disturbing the peace.

After going through trial and the subsequent court-ordered treatment, he ended up heavily medicated by a psychiatrist, and was further ordered to see a therapist regularly. Thankfully, I was not that regular therapist. I was, however, recommended to his sister by a former patient as a psychologist that he could e-mail or call at any time.

After his brief brush with potential incarceration, he moved in with his sister and her husband and their two children far downtown. He was able to get a job in the transportation business driving a bus for the city. When I learned of this, I was happy for him, but rather alarmed that a heavily medicated individual with a past of psychotic behavior and no relevant work experience could become a city bus driver.

"---(: tO tHe DoCtOr :)---" the subject read. I knew immediately that Kevin had gone off his medication.

—

(E-Mail from Kevin)

Mr. Dr. Sir Nicholas Thesiger AB MS PhD!

What is going on in your world, might I ask? The days go by, one by one, and the day when you return approaches swiftly despite the intense anticipation and lack of other happenings.

How have things been? How is your mother enjoying the deep deep South? Winter is a bitter mistress, but her kiss is soft and light. Unfortunately, her bite is hard and heavy. Of course, I speak of your trip to the shallow shallow north for your skiing excursion. How, or should I merely say, did it go? Obviously I hope the answer to be well and good. And, by that, I mean you enjoyed your time and you saved an injured fellow mountain rider. Respectfully and respectfully and respectfully, of course.

And that, that is when I came to the important realization; how could they know when the world was going to end down to the date and time? What time zone would it be in?

I have been further mentally exploring your suggestion of a very small, sans common living area, place for the two of us for a short period of time in the Nevada area to aid in my rapid acclimation to said area; you know, taxes, but don't you get me started on taxes. I believe it to be an even better idea than I had originally understood it to be, an investment even. Bravo, Sir, bravo.

As decided a while back, we should have little trouble identifying and acquiring a place fitting the above description.

If not overtly apparent, I am extremely enlightened at the moment. I don't want them to go away. I'm too lonely without them. And they warn me, warn me of impending danger danger danger! I think I'm going to get caught. Everywhere I go, I look up and I see vultures circling.

I subconsciously know I'm in my own little world, but I like it because I'm understood here.

It's humorous how such an insignificant thing as a subconscious thought can throw off one's days. Days spent doing... dot dot dot... the spaces in between. Dot dot dot. Those are the actions of late. Things to do have run away and are long departed. Dot dot dot. It would do me some good to spend this time doing something productive. I just have not discovered this "something."

Dot dot dot.

—

When I hit "reply," I added Kevin's sister, his other therapist, and his psychiatrist to the list.

—

(*E Mail to Kevin*)

Kevin,

Please begin taking your prescribed medication as instructed by those in your life who care about you and seek to help you.

—Dr. Thesiger

—

I sent the e-mail, closed the window, then billed his account.

Chapter 15

Derrick

The corner of the monitor read 8:14 p.m. I opened Monday's schedule to verify a missed appointment, that of Derrick, a recovering drug addict.

After being released from prison and completing his community service, he was required by The State to meet with a therapist for a certain number of hours over the course of two years. He was then required to check in with a therapist once every week for a progress report.

Derrick was a true con man in every sense of the word; really born that way. He often talked about childhood recollections of stealing his mother's jewelry and money from her many boyfriends' wallets when they spent the night. This behavior increased and was honed over the years until it became something he felt he simply could not change about himself.

When I first saw him, it was clear that, upon entering my office, he had already identified what he could take, how he could take it, and what he would have to do to distract me. Luckily my own youthful experiences helped me recognize him as what he was and I made certain that he knew that I was more like him than he suspected.

The first thing I did when he entered my office was hand him a file to hold while I straightened up some pillows and papers so he could sit down. Later I informed him that con men such as himself often hand items to people they are trying to con to see if they are gullible, trustworthy, easy to manipulate. It is also to keep them in the immediate vicinity. And just the act of holding whatever the con man handed off predisposes the individual to trust the con man and thus they are more willing to fall for whatever the con man is trying to pull off. I then explained how this relates to the Benjamin Franklin Effect: if someone does a favor for someone else, the person who did the favor is more likely to do another favor for that person than if they had received a favor in the first place, as opposed to doing a favor.

It was something that he did instinctually, without any thought, but it was important for me to demonstrate that I understood him on a level that he could not yet comprehend. After I had explained the Benjamin Franklin Effect and we talked for a while, Derrick was stunned when I pointed out that he was still holding the file. He was also quite surprised when I handed his cell phone back to him at the end of the session; surprised because he had never given it to me.

I had manipulated and conned him without his knowledge— something he was accustomed to being on the other side of—but it established our relationship. From then on, he trusted me and took seriously what I had to say, my critiques, suggestions, analyses.

I suspected he was drinking again, but without proof or confirmation I could do nothing except listen to his progress reports, as full of air as they obviously were. My cell phone had no voice messages and no missed calls.

Locating his number in his file, I called. It rang and rang before going to his voicemail.

Angry screaming, what he referred to and interpreted as music, played loudly before its volume lowered just long enough for Derrick's voice to say, "It's Derrick. Leave a message." The "music" continued at a higher volume before cutting off with a beep and then a digital voice instructed, "Please leave a message."

"Good evening, Derrick. It's Dr. Thesiger. Please call me back when you get a chance."

———

I closed Monday's schedule, billed Derrick, and guided the computer screen to blackness. I looked down at the shoebox and decided it needed to be torn up and disposed of so the destroyed remains found their way into the garbage. The filtered water in the carafe on the coffee table was then poured out in the sink and refilled with more filtered water from the dispenser on the refrigerator. I placed the carafe inside before closing the refrigerator door then the pillows on the couch received a quick straightening as I made my way to the door. I removed the electrical tape from the peephole to check for danger.

"Nothing," I said aloud.

I turned off the lights and locked the door behind me, allowing myself the satisfaction of experiencing the reassuring click.

The elevator was empty. So was the lobby, other than the doorman, always quick to open the door.

"Have a fine night, Dr. Thesiger."

I tipped my imaginary hat to him as I passed. "And the same to you, Sir," I said.

The summer night was warm and humid, sticky and damp, smelling of buds and bees and buses. I walked quickly, working up an uncomfortable sweat between my skin and clothes. There were few others on the streets. Cabs and cars headed down Fifth Ave were moving quickly, deliberately. I watched them pass as I ignored the drooping trees and magnificent detail of all the surrounding architecture.

My phone began to vibrate in my pocket so I took it out to see an incoming video call.

"Hello," I said, holding it in front of my face as I walked on, answering despite the ambiguity of a blocked number on the caller ID.

"Dr. Thesiger?" Derrick's voice inquired. His head, black hair and sharply groomed black mustache, bobbed around in the frame just as mine probably did; we were both walking.

"Yes. Derrick, is that you?" I asked politely.

"Hey, Doc. Yeah, it's Derrick. Sorry I missed your call. I was in the shower."

"Well, it's good to hear you're keeping clean," I said before I nodded and smiled at my pun.

Derrick smiled and laughed a somewhat forced laugh. "Ah, I see what'chya did there, Doc. That's a good one."

"So what happened today? You were supposed to call."

"Well, I was gunna call after I got out of the shower. I'm going out tonight. Got a date."

I stopped walking for a moment, centering my head in the frame. Derrick did the same, seeing that my attention was now fully on him and not on negotiating the dips and potholes in the street. I caught a glimpse of the now stationary background; he was in what I assumed to be his apartment; and his shoulders were bare and rather hairy with thin black hair; it appeared that he had indeed just got out of the shower.

"Oh, I see," I responded. "Where are you taking her?"

"We're gunna go to dinner at this Italian place downtown. I know the owner. Said he could hook me up."

"Hook you up with what exactly?" I asked, concerned.

"Just food, Doc. You know me. Haha!"

"I *do* know you, Derrick." I paused for a moment to contemplate and to watch for his reaction. When he smiled nervously as he watched me watch him through the phone, I continued. "Well, have a good time then. I won't keep you. You're sounding well so we don't have anything to talk about, do we?"

"No, Doc. Nuttin' at all. We're good." He sounded and looked relieved at the reprieve, exhaling the anxiety he had been holding in.

"Keep your mind in the game tonight, okay?" I said, pointing at him with my right index finger. "I know how hard it is when you're on a date, but try to stay away from excessive alcohol consumption. It will lead down a bad path."

"Hey, Doc, like I said, you know me, eh?"

I smiled. "Have a good night, Derrick."

"Thanks, Doc."

With that, I pressed "end" on my phone, ending the call and ending the workday.

Chapter 16

Monday Night

I found myself walking up the steps to the front door of our Brownstone, fumbling with the key ring in my pocket. Only three keys on it, yet I always confused which fit where. The front door I was about to enter, the door I would enter soon after walking up the steps, or the office door I had locked twenty minutes earlier. It was a dark walk up and up and up.

Four failed attempts resulted in my flat hand slapping the center of our apartment door several times. "Julie!" I shouted loudly. The fatigued sick feeling was coming back to create a less than ideal night. Julie's slow response time frustrated me leading to an overwhelming anger; I pounded again and again, but nothing.

I tried my keys for a fifth time and finally found the fit. "Julie!" I shouted again as I triumphantly flung open the door, expecting either a response or a recently deceased corpse; either would have sufficed.

I walked around the apartment flipping switches, triggering violent explosions of indirect lighting—Julie's preference—and then mercilessly bombarded the paintings with direct track lighting, also Julie's preference; the size of the space allowing my dramatic search to take up very little time.

Hungry, I huffed my way to the kitchen and opened the refrigerator. Julie was not there to make dinner, so I pushed containers of leftovers and condiments around hoping something edible would appear, but to no avail.

"Nothing," I announced to nobody. "Where is she?" I said angrily, getting increasingly worked up over her absence. I had expected dinner and she was nowhere to be found.

I settled on a bowl of cereal, cut up a banana then mixed it in, took a glass and filled it with water from the kitchen sink. My back found the couch and my finger found the power button on the remote.

The channel and program were irrelevant considering I paid no attention to either. The cereal and water went quickly, as did I, sprawled out on the couch in an uncomfortable position, but too far from consciousness to adjust or move elsewhere.

"Nick." I heard a muffled, delicate voice, trying to wake me slowly, carefully. "Nick."

"Where have you been? I'm hungry," I responded, still mostly asleep.

"Nick, I told you this morning and then I told you on the phone; I went to the opera."

"You didn't tell me on the phone," was the only reply the functioning parts of my brain could come up with.

"You're sleeping, Nick. You should go into the bed."

"I'm not sleeping," I shouted, not fully awake. I shook myself until I was sitting up on the couch, feet on the floor, elbows on my knees and head bobbing in my hands. I knew standing would be a chore after such a duration of being a twisted and contorted mess.

"I told you this morning and on the phone that I was going to the opera tonight," Julie said, defending herself. "You have no right to be mad at me because you forgot. I told you I would be back to the apartment late."

Julie called it "the apartment." She had not referred to it as "home" for fifteen years. Each time she said "the apartment," it cut into me, but I had learned to ignore the pain.

Before addressing her, I picked up my emergency snack, a jar of peanuts, from the coffee table and contemplated our respective positions: I, cranky and angry from my broken nap, and she, putting up a defensive front.

Still in a fog, I spoke calmly to her. "It angers me that you spend so much of what is hard earned money on tickets to the opera and a hideous dress and ridiculous shoes that you'll only wear once."

The lid of the peanuts was stubbornly resisting my turning and twisting.

"Would you prefer to spend that hard earned money on another wasteful extravagant car? Maybe that would make you happier? And I've worn this dress more than once. And it's not hideous!"

"Oh, you've put me in my place," I said as I stoically endured the excruciating pain of standing then made my way to the kitchen to put the unopenable peanut jar in the cabinet.

"You need some help with that?" Julie asked in an attempt to emasculate me.

I stopped, looked at her, and asked angrily, "Do *you* need some help?"

"Please don't talk to me like that, Nick."

Quietly and calmly, I said, "Sorry *you* took it the wrong way."

"Just because you're not raising your voice, it doesn't mean you're not yelling at me, Nick."

"What? That is actually exactly what it means."

She thought for a moment then adjusted her initial statement. "Just because you don't raise your voice doesn't mean you're not being mean." She appeared content with her revised statement.

I took a carton of ice cream out of the freezer and a large spoon from the drawer before making my way back to the couch and collapsing, saying nothing to her in the process.

But Julie was unwilling to allow the conversation to end. "You think you're the smart one, making all the right decisions while I make all the dumb choices."

"Yeah, that's pretty much right," I said obnoxiously. "Maybe if you wouldn't waste money, there would be more to go around and I wouldn't be stressed all the time."

I took the top off the ice cream carton and attempted to retrieve a spoonful. The metal utensil gave way to the solid block of frozen ice cream, bending it back until the tip was touching the handle.

"What are you making for dinner?" I said as I brought the ice cream back to the freezer and discarded the mangled spoon in the garbage.

"I didn't make anything for dinner. I've been out all day. I called you and told you I wouldn't be home. I invited you to join me. When you refused, I assumed you would make arrangements for yourself."

"If I had known you would never cook for me before we got married, I wouldn't have married you," I told her with a slight smile, but I was turned so all see saw was her husband's back as he made an obnoxious statement, not that the smile made it any less obnoxious.

"Charming," she responded sarcastically.

"Do you know what 'caveat emptor' means?" I asked.

"No, Nick," she said angrily. "What does it mean?"

"Oh, nothing…"

She clenched her fists furiously. "You don't have to be such a jerk, you know that? I don't need you to talk down to me."

"Right." I used as few words as possible, adding to her frustration.

Letting out only a portion of her anger, she asked, "You'd rather I acted like an intellectual? Is that it? So we could share ideas instead of emotions?"

I said nothing and stared blankly at the television as I monitored Julie's increasing anger out of the corner of my eye.

"Are you even listening to me?" she asked with a loud but shaky voice. Looking in her direction was not necessary, I knew that she was tearing up.

Still facing the television, I said, "You know, in ancient Sparta, important matters were decided by those who shouted the loudest."

"That's completely irrelevant, Nick."

"Did you know that 'non sequitur' means 'does not follow' in Latin?" I added.

Disgusted, she stormed off toward the kitchen and grabbed a large empty glass in her right hand. She stomped back toward me and dramatically hurled it toward the television. It crashed into the wall, shattering into countless pieces, large and small.

Surprised, shocked, I wrenched my neck around and saw her frightened, scared, startled, crying, as broken as the glass. She ran into the bedroom.

"You can't just throw a glass against the wall and then storm off like that," I shouted. "This isn't a movie. Someone has to clean this up and it's *damn* sure not going to be me. Julie! Julie!" She did not respond.

After shaking my head in disgust, shaking the disgusting situation out, I continued to stare at the television for half an hour before she tiptoed back in, wearing her pajamas. She sat next to me on the couch, saying nothing, just sitting there silently for several minutes.

After the silence between us became sufficiently palpable with emotion, but still looking straight forward, I asked, "What do you want from me, Julie?"

I was fully disinterested in the answer, but knew the question needed to be asked.

She said nothing for several more minutes. Then in a quiet, defeated voice, "I just want to be able to talk to you, Nick."

"What do you mean, 'talk to me'?"

"Can I ask you how your day was?" she said.

"It was fine." I hoped my short response would send a message more complex than its length would normally allow.

"That's it?"

"We've been over this. I can't tell you details about my day. Doctor-patient confidentiality. I can't divulge information about my day because information about my day is information about my patients."

"Fine, Nick," she said, voice more defeated than before.

She looked at me, eyes bugging out, lips curled, coaxing me to speak. I knew what she was expecting so, reluctantly, I gave it to her. "How was your day?"

She began a story about walking around, shopping, and eating with her cousins. I stared into the screen, aimlessly waiting for the end.

"Are you listening to me, Nick?" she asked, rightfully assuming that a blank stare not in her direction meant I was indeed not listening.

"Yes, of course," I responded while still staring at the TV, paying even it no attention.

"So then, what do you think?" she asked.

"Think of what?"

"The paintings, Nick. I brought them from the gallery earlier in the day."

I looked up to where the mirrors had been on the brick wall above the couch. Flat against the wall was a rustic metal frame with thin metal sticks protruding randomly and ending in a metal slab upon which small oil paintings were affixed.

"Stand up," Julie commanded.

I stood up, still a little shaky from sleep, and took a step away from the couch to take a proper look at Julie's latest "find."

Each painting was unusually small, averaging about the size of my hand, but with no consistency in size between them. Each was filled with color, many of which clashed and had no business being next to their adjacent pigments. None appeared to resemble anything in the real world; just colors floating and swirling around.

"They don't look like anything. What are they supposed to be? Should I cross my eyes or something? Unfocus them?" I asked.

"They're not holograms and they don't *need* to be anything or represent anything, Nick. But look at this one." She pointed toward the center of the compilation. "What about the larger one in the middle?" she asked. "You can see what that one is, right?"

I looked at it for a while, deeply, but I saw nothing but smudges of browns, reds, oranges, and some greens, and noticeable brush marks in different diagonal directions.

"I don't know. What is it?"

"It's autumn!" she exclaimed proudly.

I looked again and saw nothing. "Okay," I agreed, attempting to end the conversation.

"And look closer at the rest of them. Maybe take a couple steps back."

"I don't know," I said. "The rest of the seasons?"

"No!" she responded, ready to enlighten me. "The title of this series is *Le Fait de Crier en Automne.*"

"Screaming in Autumn?" I asked.

"Oui!" she responded, showing off all her knowledge of the language in one three-letter word.

"I still don't get it," I confessed.

"Look deeply at them. The artist hid a face in each of them, screaming out."

"If they're hidden, how are they screaming out?"

"Just look," she instructed.

I looked and saw nothing resembling faces or any cohesive whole. "Oh yes, I see it!" I exclaimed. "It's there with the contour of the head and the lips." I pointed toward the general area of one of the small paintings and moved my finger around rather randomly.

"Yes!" Julie was understandably excited, believing I was admitting to be on her level with something.

"What if someone wants to buy one of them, for a postcard or something?" I asked in a tacitly mocking manner.

"They're not for sale individually. This is all one piece, Nick. Not many. Guess the price."

"I don't know," I said. "There seems to be a good amount of metal back there; maybe two hundred dollars or so?"

Julie laughed, assuming my educated guess to be a joke. "Over a million, Nick."

"What?" I exclaimed. "I don't think this thing is worth much of anything, let alone more than a million dollars."

"That's not nice. The artist spent years creating this and a lifetime dreaming it up."

"But for a million dollars?"

"So you think it's worthless?" she said dismissively.

"That's not what I'm saying. I'm just saying I think it's worth... less..." I trailed off and looked at the paintings for several seconds. Then, assuming the conversation to be over, I said, "I'm going to sleep."

As I brushed my teeth, I caught a glimpse of myself in the bathroom mirror. I looked disheveled for no good reason, as if I had been carrying something heavy all day or performing some kind of manual labor.

I heard the television turn off as I washed my face. Then I found the bed in the darkness. Julie was not in it, but I dropped to sleep immediately just the same.

"You're talking, Nick." I kept hearing. "You're talking. Stop talking. Turn over." Julie was shaking me. "Nick, you're talking in your sleep."

I was fully unaware of anything other than the fact that I was being shaken awake from a deep sleep. I mumbled something before trying to regain my absence of consciousness.

"Nick, there's something that's been bothering me lately," Julie said, still shaking me in an attempt to keep me around. "It's just been really hard. Everything hasn't been going well. I'm sorry for throwing the glass, but earlier it would've made me feel a lot better if you had just sat with me. There's just been a lot of stuff going on in my head."

Absolutely exhausted and experiencing a dark blurry fuzzy woozy world, I asked her to "Give me a second so I can wake up."

Several minutes later, I felt a shaking sensation as I lay on my back with my eyes shut tight. I knew she was not going to let me simply fall back to sleep until I spoke to her, so I pulled together all the consciousness I could and told her what I felt she wanted to hear.

"Sorry, Julie," I said slowly. I then began to drift off.

"I love you, Nick," I thought I heard her say as I slipped away, but it was more likely a figment of my imagination than actual words leaving my wife's mouth.

Chapter 17

Tuesday Morning

I fought for what, in reality, was likely close to an hour to both wake up from and to fall back into the restless state of sleep I had tossed and turned through for most of the night. My mind was fully present for that presumed hour, begging to start the day, but my body had no intention of giving in and allowing itself to be dragged from the relative comfort beneath the covers. The night was spent like too many were; barely able to remain asleep for longer than thirty or forty minutes at a time before spending at least the same duration awake and alert, yet physically and mentally trapped in bed.

I detected Julie's presence, her silhouette under the covers. She was still sleeping deeply and I had trouble determining if I was too. The room appeared to be the same shade of black when my eyes were open as when they were closed. The process of waking was thus made more difficult, being unable to determine the length of time I had allowed my eyes to rest. I might have been dead for all I knew.

Firmament at last, I thought, biblical meaning.

Consciousness confusion, I mentally labeled my conundrum.

The thick wooden overlapping window treatments let in not a shimmer of light, accomplishing their goal without the slightest gap in purpose. My mind focused on the fortune we wasted on them; purchase price and equally expensive installation cost; but they had performed their function only twice, the previous day and the present one.

Quietly, I made my way to the bathroom for my morning routine. After stubbing my toe on an anonymous misplaced hard object on the floor, what felt like a large stray rock taking up residence in our bedroom, and after silently screaming out in pain, my left hand found the door handle.

Miraculously, the door silently opened just wide enough to slip my body through. Had our positions been switched, Julie's door open would have creaked wildly and let light pour in uncontrollably, waking me and keeping me from the state of unconsciousness I tried so hard to maintain through the night.

As I squeezed the shampoo from the bottle into my hands, warm city water bouncing off my body, the instructions, back of the bottle, were recited in my head. "Lather, rinse, repeat… lather, rinse, repeat… lather, rinse, repeat…" I thought about nothing else while blindly obeying.

More times than not I drifted off in the shower, thinking of nothing at all, losing myself in this mantra of circular unending destinationless direction. I forgot how many times I did it, lost track of the frequency of its occurrence. I was unsure of the appropriate number of repetitions, so I did it once more and put the thought behind me.

The motions were completely automatic. There was no need to think about it. Never did I think about what I was doing until I got caught up, lost, stuck in this cycle. Life had become this repetitive behavior. It was something of which I was well aware, but I chose to ignore. Just repeat it once more and go on to the next step which, unfortunately, happened to be the same.

[Note: The following is what I, after much retrospective thought and consideration, believe to be the most accurate representation of both sides of the conversation.]

"Are you awake?" I heard muffled through the door, over the water wastefully rushing from the faucet as I brushed my teeth.

"Yes, of course. Can you make breakfast?" I asked with my most articulate toothpaste-filled-mouth pronunciation.

"I would love some breakfast," Julie responded, happy to hear me attempting to make amends.

"Scrambled eggs and bacon, glass of orange juice?" I continued, hoping not to push my luck, but knowing that the reward would be worth the risk.

"Sure, that sounds great!" she exclaimed. "Can you also put in a load of dirty laundry downstairs?"

"I just have the clothes I slept in," I said. "Do you want those?"

"Yes, clean those too," she responded.

"And can you put some water on to boil?" I inquired, realizing a good cup of tea would round out the meal quite well.

"I would love some tea, thank you, dear," she said, ecstatic at my presumed newfound desire to wait on her hand and foot.

"Thank *you*, Julie," I responded with a toothpaste-filled smile.

Crossing the hallway to the bedroom, I heard Julie in the living room, television on. I threw my dirty clothes toward her, where I assumed the laundry basket would be waiting to be brought down to the basement laundry machines.

The wooden blinds were pulled up, brightening the bedroom. "Let day in and let life out," I said aloud, quoting Shakespeare, but consciously misusing his words.

Lather, rinse, repeat. I dressed quickly, readying myself for what I knew was going to be a long day. A light tan suit with an off-white collared shirt. I chose to forgo the tie and jacket and to leave the top two buttons undone, sleeve cuffs rolled up three times. Dark brown shoes and a dark brown belt.

My summery style was admired in the mirror for an extended duration during which I congratulated myself on how well I was aging. *Distinguished*, I said in my mind. I then slid down the hallway to the table in the main room, by which time, I expected to be greeted by the sweet aroma of my morning scrambled eggs, bacon, and a nice glass of orange juice. But, as the hallway shrank in front of me, I smelled nothing but the somewhat clean dampness of the recently used shower.

"Why aren't you making breakfast?" I asked Julie as I entered the living room. She was lying down on the couch with her computer opened on her lap.

"Because you're supposed to make breakfast," she responded, noticeably perturbed by my inquiry. "Are you going to make breakfast?" she asked.

"No. Of course not. Are you?" I ask, beginning to become a bit perturbed myself.

She looked up from her computer, the sour expression on her face was her only response.

"Whatever…" I said, giving up on my dream of ever having a good full breakfast. I picked up my clothes from the floor and tossed them toward her. "Here's my dirty laundry."

"Why are you throwing those at me?" she asked, genuinely surprised at my gesture of goodwill (helping her with the laundry).

"So you can do the laundry?" I said, more as a question than as a statement.

Again, she glared at me with a sour look. I then forced myself to retrieve my dirty clothes from the floor and walked toward the bedroom to deposit them in the laundry basket, all the while confused and a bit angry.

Upon returning to the living room, I again decided that the risk would be worth the reward. "And my tea?"

Looking at her computer screen, she pointed toward me and then toward the kitchen.

"Why does she play these games?" I asked myself aloud.

Still looking only at the screen of her computer, Julie said, "I've decided I am going to stop nagging you about spending time with my family when they're in the city."

"So you read my letter to Santa?" I asked mockingly.

"Seriously, Nick. I understand you don't like them so I'm not going to try to force you to spend time with them anymore."

"Thanks," I said coldly. Julie was clearly expecting me to deny her claim, but I had no intention of doing so. Disregarding her obvious dissatisfaction with the direction of the conversation, I assumed everyone was a winner.

"Well," I said as I walked out the door, "off to the salt mines."

Julie's attention remained on her computer screen while she spoke no words in my direction.

The alarming sound of barking echoed up and down the dark winding staircase, loudest when passing the third floor. Amy, one of the neighbors, had five or six dogs for an unknown reason.

They must play a lot of poker, I thought, bringing a chuckle to my mind. "I'm hilarious," I said aloud as I rounded the corner.

I then drifted into a daze as I mentally slid into autopilot for the trip, which I took day after day after day. I was awoken from this blissfully unaware state by the vibrating phone in my pocket. "JULIE" flashed across the screen.

"Yes," I answered, more aggravation in my voice than I had realized was inside.

"Oh, Nick! I'm glad I got you."

"What is it, Julie?" I asked rather impatiently.

"I just wanted to remind you not to forget about the wine tasting I signed us up for. It's today at twelve."

"Yes, yes. I didn't forget. I'll meet you there at twelve," I responded, having not only forgotten, but also having no recollection of ever being informed in the first place.

"You won't be late, will you?" she asked, knowing I would show up late or not at all to something in which I clearly had no interest. "Oh, and don't forget about dinner tonight with the Lowerys."

"Julie, I really don't like them at all. Do we have to do this?"

"Oh, they're delightful people!" she defended. "Isabella is always smiling."

"That means she's deranged, not delightful," I argued. "And she's always smiling because she can't not smile; her plastic surgeon made sure of that. She looks like a badly drawn caricature of her former self."

Julie was silent for a moment, a moment spent trying to ignore my comments. "Come on, Nick."

"I'm still not feeling too well, Julie. Think we could postpone until next week?"

"No, they're going on vacation next week and through the rest of the summer. It's tonight or never."

"Well, if those are my only two choices…"

"We're going, okay?" she asked, question rhetorical. "I'll see you at the restaurant for wine tasting at twelve."

"Fine," I said sharply, hanging up before I fully pronounced the word.

No sooner did I end the call than I found myself in my office. I questioned how I had stayed on the phone all the way up the elevator without losing the call or even noticing that I had entered it, but I allowed the inquiry to drift from my mind. Inconsistencies of this nature were best ignored.

As I came off autopilot, I quickly opened the e-mail inbox on the computer perched atop the large mahogany desk. Three messages, but I was expecting more throughout the day. The corner of the screen read 10:16 a.m.

Again, my phone began to vibrate. Julie had sent the address of the wine tasting; all the way across town.

At my request, a blank message expanded on the screen and I typed in Bill's e-mail address and then "important" in the subject line.

—

(E-Mail to Bill)

Can't make drinks today. Apparently Julie made plans for some kind of wine tasting. Until tomorrow, old-timer.

—Nick

Chapter 18

Mr. Williams

After taking the carafe of filtered water from the small refrigerator to the coffee table, my chair rocked me back and forth as I stared out the window and imagined floating aimlessly back and forth. My body sank deeper and deeper; back, head, arms, and hands all engulfed in the cushy chair while rocking back and forth. Thoughts began to escape my conscious mind, brain becoming blank as I drifted off by way of the slow smooth comfortable rocking sensation of back and forth and back and forth in the chair.

Following what felt like very little time staring, the wired phone which I kept in the mahogany desk's left lower drawer began to ring loudly, startling me from my hypnotic state.

"Yes, Jeffery," I said, knowing the caller could only be the doorman because the phone was connected only to his post.

"I have a Mr. Joseph F. Williams down here to see you."

The building employed only four doormen who had very strict and repetitive schedules. They thus knew the faces, schedules, friends, and family of all residents and, in my case, they knew my regular in-office patients.

"Thank you, Jeffery. Please let Mr. Williams up."

"Yes. Good day, Sir," he said before hanging up.

I assumed Mr. Williams was a large intimidating looking man. I had found that the doormen rarely stopped unfamiliar women or unfamiliar harmless looking men, but always stopped large unfamiliar men.

I carefully placed the phone back on its receiver then placed the receiver back into the desk's left lower drawer. I straightened up the room, arranging the pillows on the couch to line up with one another.

Based on his very specific, very direct e-mail, I knew Mr. Williams would be difficult to hold as a client. He was interested in meeting with me because he was "shopping around for a good psychologist." In very few words, he informed me that, after his wife quietly asked around, their friends recommended a few psychologists, but he could not stand the thought of any one psychologist knowing what his friends said about him and what he was saying about himself. "A psychologist in that position would be biased," he stated clearly. He had no intention of starting without a "clean slate."

Tabula rasa, I thought as I opened the door after aligning the objects in the room. I left it slightly ajar and walked down the hall toward the elevator doors which opened only seconds before I reached them.

"Mr. Williams," I greeted him. "I'm Dr. Thesiger." I extended my left hand to shake his, but he either did not notice it or it was intentionally ignored, leaving my hand unshook, hovering there for a moment before I pulled it back toward my body and swept it in the direction of my office. "This way," I said, seamlessly gesturing with my still open hand.

As we walked down the hall, he spoke with a gruff authoritative tone. "I didn't want to give the idiot doorman my name. He was a pushy little bastard. Wouldn't let me in without calling you. Why didn't you tell him you were expecting someone?"

Mr. Williams was, as expected, a generally large man, intimidating due not only to his size, but also the perpetually angry expression that lived on his face. His eyebrows appeared to grow in a furious angular arch. He spoke with a raspy voice; years of cigars with the other highly compensated executives, no doubt. His suit was dark blue and he wore a sharp white collared shirt with a dark blue tie. The jacket hung from his right hand before being slung over his right shoulder as he menacingly walked the up the hall toward my office in front of me.

"My apologies, Mr. Williams. It's the building's policy that visitors not recognized by the doorman show an ID and be logged into the books."

It was easy to deduce that he was a man who treated everyone like an employee. Performing an action against his wishes occurred so infrequently in his life that he forgot how to comply. He was yet to tell me his reason for seeking a therapist, but I assumed this to be at its core. I made a mental note to ask Jeffery to have Mr. Williams show his ID each week.

"It's an idiotic policy. I'll have it changed," Mr. Williams declared. "I'm sure I know someone on the co-op board..." He was quite confident in his vastly reaching connections and felt it necessary to convey his presumed clout before we even reached my office.

He entered through the slightly open door before I did, dropping his jacket onto the couch then sitting down next to it. With a light blue check in his left hand, he gestured toward one of the chairs on the opposite side of the coffee table; the chair he had apparently just assigned to me for the session.

I debated following his silent directions or standing up to his obnoxious bravado, setting a stern precedent for the rest of our sessions. I then took the check from his hand and slid it into my right pants pocket as I sat where he had pointed.

"Thank you," I said.

I reconciled my passive behavior with the thought that having him feel that he was in control was essential to his comfort and his comfort was paramount to therapy. He had made it clear from the moment of his arrival that he was the one paying for me to jump when he said jump or sit when he said sit. It was the control he needed, so I gave it to him.

"So, Doc," he began. "I'm not some freakin' crazy guy. I'm totally sane. Not a crazy bone in here. Got me?" He paused, awaiting a response.

"Yes, sure," I said.

"What do you mean, 'sure'?" he asked contentiously. "You mocking me? You think I'm crazy just because I'm sitting across from you?"

"No, no, of course not, Mr. Williams," I said. "I was only agreeing with you. It seems pretty clear that you're a little uncomfortable being here?" I added an upward inflection at the end of the sentence to allow for him to indulge himself in the sound of his voice going further into the topic.

"I'm not uncomfortable, Doc. I just don't want you to think I'm one of your crazies." He shifted rather uncomfortably on the couch as he spoke, indicating that there was more behind his words than he wanted to convey.

"Okay, Mr. Williams. That's fine," I said. "I feel like we got off on the wrong foot here. Maybe I can tell you a little bit about what I usually do with clients. That might help us start out better?" Again I added an upward inflection to my declarative statement to allow for him to respond, thus giving him the illusion of control and power.

"Alright, Doc. That sounds good. Why don't you go ahead and tell me what usually happens here with you people." By seemingly dictating the direction of the session, he felt that he was in control. I smiled at his false perception of power over me.

"I have helped individuals such as yourself deal with many, many different kinds of issues in their lives, ranging from marital problems to anxiety issues to an inability to function properly, whether it be physically or mentally." I watched him as I spoke to gauge his reaction to different scenarios. He looked away and shifted uncomfortably during "inability to function properly."

I continued. "Depending on your specific needs and preferences, we may focus on methods to learn new ways to perceive yourself or your environment. Or maybe we'll introduce new skills to cope with others and ways to interact with others in a productive fashion.

"Sometimes, when a client's issues are thought to be primarily related to longstanding relationship problems and unresolved emotions, we may include in therapy some conversations about the client's past, focusing on their childhood.

"If a client's current problem is presumed not to stem from their past experiences, we may explore their thoughts and feelings about their particular situation so we can understand it more fully and possibly discover new strengths within themselves. This newfound respect for oneself and one's ability often allows for clients to look at the world from a less subjective perspective."

Mr. Williams appeared to be paying full attention to me, but his expression remained in its perpetual angry configuration so judging his thoughts was difficult.

I forged on. "Sometimes personal mental health problems are related to problems in family relationships so other family members may be directly involved in treatment in order for it to improve efficacy. In these situations, a client may be seen for treatment with another family member, such as a spouse, a sibling, or their children."

Reacting to his still unchanging facial expression, I tried appealing to Mr. Williams's obvious propensity for running things. "Or therapy doesn't need to be as structured as all of that. We could just start talking and see where it leads us. That method often deteriorates into the client talking around their specific issues as opposed to directly about them, but it's less stressful and can even be quite enjoyable. And I will do my best to keep us on track and keep the conversation at least tacitly therapeutic."

Then I added, "And we can always do a combination of any number of methods. It's all up to the two of us, but mostly you. You decide what the best route is."

Mr. Williams sat quietly while I spoke and, surprisingly to me, did not interrupt. I then sat quietly, waiting for a response as he thought.

"What do you think?" I asked after an extended silence. "You're free to think aloud."

"So what orientation are you?" he asked in a forceful confident voice, chin between his right index finger and thumb and elbow on his left hand as he crossed his left arm over his midsection and leaned back into the couch. He had done his homework about different kinds of therapy and he wanted me to know it.

"Well, I like to think of my therapeutic orientation as my arsenal of therapeutic techniques," I answered swiftly. I made the assumption that he was a gun owner so I chose my words accordingly.

"That really doesn't answer my question," he said.

"Oh, but it does. I'm an eclecticist."

"Which means…?"

"I take parts from all therapeutic methods according to the patient, issue at hand, time frame, biases, and other variables."

"I see… Can I choose the method?" he asked, indicating the obvious; that he needed always to be in control.

"If you so desire," I answered, "but, if I believe it won't be or is not being effective, I will let you know."

"Fair enough," he said.

Mr. Williams continued to sit quietly for several seconds before standing up, leaving his jacket on the couch unattended. He walked around the room, touching chairs, running his finger across the top of the desk, spinning my large leather chair around, inspecting the unused coffee maker and sink, and opening a cabinet. His behaviors were all confidently executed; his walk was solid, without a bounce, just straight, deliberate, stern. He moved like a king or warlord. I wondered if Napoleon walked like that.

"What's this?" he asked of a small model on one of the built-in shelves; a head with smoothed over features on the nondescript face. The top of the head was sliced off revealing not a brain, but a number of scattered filing cabinets and little monkeys. Some were sitting at desks, some getting files out of the filing cabinets, and some were sitting at computers.

"That's just a clever metaphor for the personification of the thought process," I answered.

He smirked, then continued walking around, judging everything in the room with his hands. I glanced down at the check he handed to me while his back was turned. The amount was small, but it was my full quoted rate. Every other patient negotiated a lower fee, but Mr. Williams had too much pride for that, too much money for that. I always wished that my income reflected my talent, but it simply did not.

"And this?" he asked, pointing at a picture frame in his hands.

I squinted to help focus my eyes on the pictures of me with two monkeys, one on each side. "Oh, that's from when I went to South Africa on safari years ago. I'm the one in the middle there."

Again he smirked then continued his trip around the room, looking, touching, judging. The picture had been taken at the zoo. I had never been to South Africa. I had never left the country. I had never left the Northeast.

Mr. Williams began to speak, still with his back facing me, but my mind was not attending to his words. Rather, it was working on what I believed to be his problem. I presumed that he had experienced some kind of setback at work, maybe a botched business

165

deal or maybe a subordinate undermined him in some way and, for some reason, he was unable to respond appropriately. That experience resulted in some kind of panic attack. Anxiety followed him around ever since, affecting his performance in every aspect of his life.

The most appropriate treatment for him would be to explore the experience verbally, but he had likely first started on an anxiety medication regimen then found it to not treat all of his symptoms and his psychiatrist was ill-equipped for talk therapy. He then began his search for a psychologist with whom he felt comfortable, someone that he felt was capable and worth his money. I did not need to listen to his words to hear his story.

Something about not feeling that he was reaching his potential was said followed by silence. He was sitting on the couch again. I turned to him and straightened up my posture, firmed up my expression, and looked him in the eye. I replied with what I believed to be the type of response that would appeal to him most.

"One can sit and wonder what would have been long enough for what would have been to become what is not happening and what will never be."

Mr. Williams looked at me for a while with an inquisitive look on his face before I continued.

"What I mean by this is we spend close to our whole lives wishing we had done this or had not done that. This is just us unknowingly letting life pass us by."

He began to nod while I spoke.

"Or are we really *knowingly* letting life pass us by? Maybe because we know our goals take effort to reach, we have created this mechanism, this passive absence of action, to ensure that we never even attempt to attain them; dwelling on the past and the likely absence of a satisfying future. It's an endless cycle of sitting idle and complaining but that's where I come in."

I leaned forward in the chair and gestured with my hands forcefully as I spoke with a sharp tone. "I help people realize this cyclical counterproductive thought process, then guide them away from it and toward a more fulfilling fruitful life. Mr. Williams, I can help you with your problem and, yes, it is a *problem* and it is *your* problem and a problem that you are going to soon take responsibility for and conquer shortly thereafter."

He smiled at the thought of personifying whatever his issue was and taking control over it and thus his life.

"Soon you'll be living the life that you want and you'll be genuinely happy with yourself, your choices, everything around you. It's going to take some hard work, but I'm assuming you are capable of a little hard work, eh?"

At my inquiry, designed to challenge, Mr. Williams smiled large, the smile of a powerful man acknowledging his equal in another whom he had previously questioned. I knew I had him. I was to be his therapist for whatever he believed his problem to be.

I knew well Mr. Williams despite this being our first interaction. He needed someone who knew how to help him, maybe even through manipulation. He needed to be led to feel empowered and in control over the changes in his life that were going to take place during his time with me. He needed to feel that he was the one changing himself, not me. He needed to know I was capable of guiding him, but he needed to believe he was doing the real work. Mr. Williams would not be happy until I made him believe he was happy.

But, just as I was about to finish up my speech, smug at what I believed to be a new full paying in-office patient, he stood from the couch and grabbed his jacket with his right hand. My confidence dropped.

"This session is over, Doctor," he said as he walked toward the door.

I cursed my failure in my mind before standing to walk him out, maybe shake his hand, never to see him again.

"So this is my time slot then," he said as he opened the door.

It was difficult to determine if his statement was declarative or interrogative, but I was simultaneously surprised and pleased with it nonetheless.

"Yes, Mr. Williams."

"Call me Joe," he commanded. And with that he closed the door behind him.

I took several steps backward until I fell into the chair in which I had previously been sitting. I spent two or three minutes reliving the short session so that I could commit to memory some of the tactics that worked with people of Mr. Williams's character. Every session I learn something new to use in the next.

I went over to the computer, sinking into the large leather chair, and added Mr. Williams as a client, taking note of his rate, his payment method, and his regular time. I then deposited the check by taking its picture and loading it into the banking system. I smiled as I rocked back, both hands behind my head.

———

Not until that short moment of reflection did my body remind me that I had gone without breakfast and without a proper dinner the previous night. The computer screen suggested the time to be 10:49 a.m. The hour and eleven minutes I had before being expected at the wine tasting across town was more than enough time for breakfast so I left the office in search of food, closing the door without taking care to consciously lock and check and recheck for confirmation. The door was designed to securely lock automatically upon closing, but it was part of my routine to check the knob regardless; a part of my routine I carelessly omitted.

Each step toward the elevator exponentially increased my discomfort with my cavalier choice to forgo the lock-check procedure, but I chose to press on, assuming the anxiety would subside. The elevator doors opened almost immediately when I reluctantly depressed the down button, but my mind was still on the lock and if I should go back to check it. Facing me as I boarded were three individuals in full uniform. "The help": two maids and a butler most likely for residents far above my office.

Owners on the top floors often kept smaller apartments on the lower levels for their servants, equipped with one window and the absence of a proper view or any semblance of natural light.

I frequently found these lackeys on the elevator with laundry bags on their way down to the basement washing machines. Some late nights, I found them looking tired, riding down to their cramped rooms after a full day's work. A mere phone call at any hour of the night was all it took for them to quickly dress before going up to deliver a warm glass of milk to a wealthy individual having trouble sleeping.

Their presence did not bother me in the least, but I always wondered why residents did not complain and force these people to take the service elevator.

I smiled and nodded to them and they smiled and nodded back. They were fully oblivious that each one of them made far more money than I did. Part of me wanted them to know, but it was a very small part.

The elevator stopped three floors down and opened to reveal a woman, well dressed and wearing more jewelry than was prudent. She waved us on quickly, looking away rather disgustedly. As the doors closed at her gestural request, I questioned if that was the proper protocol when faced with a butler or a maid on the elevator.

My discomfort increased as I realized my repeated faux pas. For years, I had thought nothing of joining these servants, but, as I stood there, it became remarkably clear that this was not appropriate behavior for a gentleman who aspired to the higher levels of society.

The elevator felt hot and stuffy. *How had I missed this? How could I not have known the appropriate behavior?* I questioned. Then my mind went quickly to the potentially unlocked door of my office. I began to sweat and move around uncomfortably during my painstakingly lengthy descent. I thought about pressing the button for the floor below the current position, but I feared running into a resident and having no explanation for exiting on their floor.

When the doors finally opened onto the lobby, I walked briskly away.

"Done for the day, Dr. Thesiger?" Jeffery, the doorman, asked politely.

I ignored him, my mind bouncing between my societal faux pas and the office door's lock.

It took three blocks before I stopped covering my face with my left hand and another two before my muscles began to relax. After an additional block of obsessing over my recent unacceptable behaviors, I calmed fully, realizing that my hunger was causing me to react to an inappropriate degree.

Every time I shouted at Julie when I had not eaten for an extended duration, she condescendingly suggested that I had hypoglycemia. That only made me more angry and encouraged more shouting and, of course, denial of the validity of the diagnosis. Her medically-untrained theory went through my mind as I looked around and realized that I had been walking in the wrong direction.

At the next intersection, I crossed the street and walked back in the direction of the small café at which I had intended to stop for a quick meal.

Chapter 19

Melanie

As I passed building after building of varying heights, I looked ahead to see a woman in a wheelchair in front of one of the many ornately beautiful and architecturally stunning Brownstones of the Upper East Side. She was peering up the steep stairs leading to the front door with a distraught and defeated demeanor.

As I approached, I thought about jaywalking to the other side of the street to avoid the awkward, obnoxious, but increasingly necessary *New York walk*; head down, accelerated pace, glazed-over look on my face to indicate ignorance of her situation, all while praying not to trip or draw any of her attention to myself thus requiring me to acknowledge her acknowledging me.

I looked both ways, but cars were approaching. Trapped. Closer and closer became analogous to sadder and sadder judging by her face and unfortunately more and more empathy welled within me.

When I was mere feet away, my emotions overwhelmed my better judgment.

"Excuse me, Ma'am, is everything alright?" I asked without my conscious knowledge or physical control.

She looked up at the generous man standing before her and began to weep openly. She was about thirty years and she had likely been in the wheelchair for no more than a couple of weeks or days. I determined this when she let go of the wheels to cover her tear-soaked face and, unbeknownst to her, began to roll toward the street.

I stopped her momentum with one foot behind her right back wheel as she stammered, sniffled, and cried. Between sobs I caught something about her parents' house and coming back from vacation and not knowing what happened to her.

As she blurted out words to reluctantly attending ears, I gathered that she had been injured on vacation and lacked the confidence to explain the situation on the phone to her parents. When she returned to the city where she lived mere blocks away from her parents, she was still unable to find the words so she decided, after avoiding them for weeks, that she would show up unexpectedly.

I took out my phone to check the time while she wept. 11:16 a.m. I considered my options and made a decision.

"My name is Nicholas Thesiger," I said. "What, may I ask, is yours, Miss?"

She looked up at me, still very sad, her face overcome with tears. "Melanie," she managed.

"It is nice to meet you, Melanie. Would you like to have brunch with me?"

She looked at me for a moment, a moment that had the potential to be very awkward, then agreed to brunch. I took a step behind her. "May I?" I asked politely.

"Yes, of course, Mr.... What did you say your name was again?"

"Nick Thesiger. Doctor actually," I said as I began to effortlessly walk with the chair, comfortable with something I could lean on as I moved along.

"It's nice to meet you, Dr. Thesiger." Her words were clear as she became less and less overcome with emotion the farther we moved from her parents' Brownstone.

I decided to stop at the closest place that was wheelchair accessible, but that proved harder than someone not in a wheelchair would assume. We ended up traveling around for quite some time looking for an appropriate place to dine.

"I was on vacation alone," she began. "The plan was to meet my parents in Paris after I spent a week in London, traveling and relaxing. I own my own business so I need a little time to unwind sometimes." She was delightful in the smoothness of her voice and the confidence with which she spoke once the proximity to confronting her parents was decreased.

"I know how that can be. I haven't taken a break for years from my practice," I said, trying to relate.

"Oh, what kind of doctor are you?" she asked.

"I'm a psychologist."

"That has to be a hard job!" she exclaimed. "Sitting around all day listening to other people's problems? That has to wear on you after a while."

"It doesn't take all that long to wear on you…" I said. "But, it's my job and I enjoy it very much. It is probably one of the most trying professions, but the one that has the potential to be the most personally satisfying and rewarding."

She smiled at the description. I had not allowed myself to think about my life in a positive way for a long time and it felt good; I too smiled at my words.

"So what happened in London?" I asked.

"Well," she began. "Long story short, I slipped and fell. Spent some time in the hospital. I told my parents I wouldn't be able to make it to Paris, that I was having too much fun in London. They just assumed it to be the truth."

"Why did you tell them that? Why not the actual truth?" I asked.

"It was too hard. I didn't know what they would say, how they would react. I got back to the city weeks ago, but I've been telling them I was still in London so they wouldn't come to see me. I wanted to tell them, but I just couldn't. I just couldn't…" She trailed off thinking about how her parents would react.

"So you decided to surprise them?" I asked in an attempt to show her that her choice of how to reveal the information was probably the hardest on all parties.

"I guess I just wanted to be there for them while they go through it. You know? To help them accept it instead of just making them deal with it by themselves and not really know the whole story until they saw me." She started to get a little teary as she spoke.

"I can understand that," I said, admitting that maybe her choice was a formidable one. "What have you been doing for the past weeks in the city? Just avoiding them?"

"I've been in my apartment. I've been trying to adjust to this new life. I told everyone I was still in London, my friends and employees, family. I was trying to run my business from home. It's falling apart without me. I'll have to go back. Everyone will have to see me like this."

"So? What's so bad about that? It will be a little harder to get around, but you're still the same person, right? Still capable of everything you were before. Listen, you're obviously a very driven woman to have made it as far as you have. Don't let a little thing like this stop you now."

"Thank you. That is all very nice of you to say, but life is much harder now. Even a kitchen cabinet can be an insurmountable challenge when it's too high to reach, or a sink or shelf. I can't use my toaster or microwave. I can't use one of my closets. I may be able to get the wheelchair in, but I can't get it out. And the locks are too high on my windows so I can't use those either."

"So have them redone, your bathroom too," I said, trying to encourage her to keep her life on track. "It may cost a little bit, but I'm sure your parents won't mind helping out if you don't have the money and I think there are government programs that help with the costs of those kinds of conversions."

"It's not the money," she said. "I don't want to have to change things. My apartment, where I go, how I get there. And I can't imagine how my friends will react. When I talk to them on the phone now, they try to get me to come over and go to parties and restaurants. But when they see me in the wheelchair, I'm afraid what they'll think. They'll stop inviting me out. It's too much trouble for them. Look at us, we can't even find one place to eat that I can get into."

"Well, I don't disagree that this will be difficult for you. And it is rather frustrating that the city is so horrifically wheelchair unfriendly. Someone should really do something about that, really." I then saw a café that appeared to be wheelchair accessible. "Look, there *is* one!" I said, happily proving her fears to be unfounded.

I opened the door and she moved herself inside. Dining with her was one of two things; either extremely boring or amazingly interesting because, before I knew it, we were parting ways and she was smiling, waving, and shouting her thanks. Her voice faded as I walked south.

Chapter 20

Wine Tasting

I then felt my phone vibrating in my pocket. Pulling it out revealed several missed calls. The recently delivered voicemails consisted of somewhat distressed greetings from my demanding spouse.

They began with short messages of "where are you?" and ended with "since I don't know whether you forgot or you're intentionally standing me up to make some obnoxious point or if you were in a horrible accident and you're dead, I am uncertain as to how I should respond emotionally. Please call me back and let me know if I should be angry or mournful. Thank you."

After looking at the phone to see that it was already 12:12 p.m., I jumped into a cab and directed the driver to get me to the restaurant where the wine tasking was taking place "as quickly as possible." The maniac behind the wheel drove as if I had a gun to the back of his head and he desired to die in a spectacular automobile accident as opposed to by a bullet.

We were across town and in front of the restaurant faster than I had imagined possible. A waving of my credit card across the payment box in the cab and a dash through the restaurant door landed me in the empty seat Julie had saved for me.

"Sorry I'm late," I said rather nonchalantly.

She gave me a simultaneously angry and disappointed look. I gave her a contradictory exaggerated smile; all my teeth showing, eyes wincing shut.

"Where the hell were you?" she whispered as the man wearing a large tag that read *Wine Master* lectured pompously; something about champagne from the region of Champagne.

No good deed goes unpunished, I thought, but dared not say aloud. I just continued to smile like a Cheshire cat.

"Fine. You'll explain later," she whispered authoritatively.

Julie, hopeful as she was, had made sure to save me my tasting portions at the empty seat adjacent to her own. There were thus six small paper cups, two filled with vodkas and four with white wines.

"Are these mine?" I whispered to Julie.

"Yes, I had him pour them," she whispered back. "I figured I paid for two of us so I might as well get the drinks."

"Aw, thank you," I said. I then picked up one small paper cup in each hand, vodkas first, and commenced throwing the contents of each past my teeth and tongue and directly into my throat in impressively quick succession. Those were directly followed by two of the white wines, then the other two white wines; all done like a

179

seasoned college grad. My face puckered up as I shook the bitter out of my head with three vigorous left-rights. When my eyes opened, I was faced with blank stares from everyone at the table and The Wine Master.

Looking back at them with a smile, I nodded as if my behavior was completely appropriate, but made a mental note to pour very little for myself for the remainder of the tasting. The Wine Master continued with his detailed descriptions of what we should be taking note of while tasting the alcohols I had just downed like a pro.

"Please, everyone, talk aloud about what you are experiencing, how this one tastes to you," The Wine Master encouraged.

One woman spoke endlessly about "bouquets of earth" and "finishes of acidic perfection with tart overtones." After the next wine had gone around, another taster went into detail about his experience with a completely different wine years before when he dined with the former mayor. I suspected he only spoke to inform us that he had dined with the former mayor.

"What about you?" The Wine Master said in my direction. The whole class looked toward me for my own nonsensical description of the drink or story of dining with a head of government.

"It's a little bitter," I said with honesty on my tongue.

"How can you even tell?" asked a man sitting across from me who had obviously sauced up before he had arrived. "You're pouring almost nothing for yourself!"

Immediately I liked the man because he had the audacity to arrive at a wine tasting already drunk.

I then stood from my chair and said, "Hi, my name is Nick and I'm a recovering alcoholic." I expected laughter at the joke, but everyone just looked at me stunned before a scattered "Hello, Nick" came out.

Still standing, I again attempted to get a laugh out of the crowd. "My sponsor said I shouldn't even be here, but I decided to just keep the portions small. It's not drinking if you don't get drunk, right?"

Not one laugh.

Julie pulled on my left arm, jerking my body down onto the chair. "What are you doing? Stop it. Just be quiet!" She was less than impressed with my jokes.

Despite everyone's discomfort, The Wine Master continued instructing us on how to experience the wines. A quick glance at Julie was all that was needed to see that she was fully embarrassed and clearly did not see the humor in the situation. I smiled at her as I had been doing since I arrived. She looked sadder than I had seen her look for a long time.

"You're practically making me cry, Nick," she whispered.

I had a chance there, right then. I had a chance to turn everything around. To apologize. To tell her how I wanted things to change, to be better, to save us. But all I did was get defensive. "It's always my fault, isn't it," I whispered. "Everything has to always be my fault."

Her eyes started to tear up. "No, that's not what I'm saying at all," she pushed out in a low whisper.

I continued down the path that should not have been taken. "If I make you cry, why do you even want me here?"

"If you don't want to be here," she whispered to me, "then just go."

"Really? I can go?" I asked, knowing that I had gone too far, but also very aware that there was no turning back, so why not take advantage?

"Just go, Nick."

"Okay. I'll see you at home!" With that I kissed her on the forehead, stood up, and exited, checking my phone for the time as the door smoothly closed behind me. 12:28 p.m. I decided to hurry across town in hopes that Bill was manning our bar stools solo, despite my cancellation.

Serendipitously, a taxi was passing upon my exit. I threw up my left hand and, unbelievably, it came to a screeching halt. I got in and commanded the driver to get me across town "as quickly as possible" then, remembering how horrifying the ride had been when I previously used those words, I corrected with "as quickly as reasonably possible."

As the driver moved in and out of traffic, thrusting me forward and backward, side to side, over and over in the backseat, I began to feel a bit nauseous. I credited my squeamish feelings to motion sickness, but I had never experienced it before in my life. My undulating mind then went toward my emotions, very mixed and confused at the moment.

I had trouble making a clear decision as to how I should have been feeling. Happy because I did not have to sit through the wine tasting, but sad because I knew it would have meant the world to Julie. I knew I should have handled it in a better way, but I also wished that she had not told me that I could leave. My mind then briefly went to my office door, which may or may not have been closed properly. Anxiety began to increase.

Then it hit me; my justification and thus my release from this frustrating nauseating confusion. It was really all Julie's fault. She was the reason that I was confused about my emotions. She was trying to make me sit through the wine tasting. She told me I could leave in that passive-aggressive manner knowing that I would go and then feel bad about it. I decided I would not give her the satisfaction of making me feel guilty. I did not want to let her win.

The cab came to a skidding stop in front of the restaurant. My emotional state had been decided; I was angry at Julie. After waving my credit card across the payment box in the cab, a spot of gum on my pants created some resistance to my exit. I may have acquired it at the café earlier, at the tasting, or in one of the two cabs I had ridden in. Whichever place was irrelevant. My anger toward Julie was immediately transferred onto the gum on my pants.

Chapter 21

Tuesday's Drinks

Bill was visible through the front window of the restaurant, sitting at the bar by himself. The cab skidded away behind me. I was beginning to think that all cab drivers drove like that all of the time. Shaking my head with dismay, I entered the restaurant.

"Sorry I'm late, Bill," I said as I sat down on my regular stool.

"You said you couldn't make it in your e-mail." He was pleasantly surprised to see me, something not obvious from his words.

"Let he who is without sin cast the first stone," I said as I extended my hand in greeting. "Julie let me off the hook, but only after I sat there for a while and listened to some pompous Wine Master drone on for a while about Champagne the region and champagne the sparkling wine or some such nonsense." I turned to the bartender. "Barkeep, a round on me for everyone. And by 'everyone,' I mean me."

She smiled. "Coming up, Doctor." She clasped a mug and pulled down on the tap. The ratio of beer to foam was much greater than the previous day, but still a good portion of the mug fizzed and popped; continuing to learn.

"So," Bill said, "what's the eulogy?"

"What? Did someone die?" I asked, realizing only after the words passed my lips that Bill only used that morbid expression to allow himself the chance to explain.

"Eulogy," he responded. "It means 'good word' in Greek." He had obviously learned the word earlier in the day and was excited to teach me something new.

I gave him the satisfaction. "Oh. I didn't know that."

He smiled victoriously, then looked at me. I was shifting around as I remembered the gum which was adhering my pants to the stool.

"Everything okay? You feeling alright?" he asked.

"Ehh, I think I sat on some gum earlier. It's been following me around all day, shellacking me to everywhere I sit, and leaving bits and pieces of itself on all surfaces with which it comes into contact in the process. I feel bad for the next guy who sits in that cab."

Bill seemed unamused. He was wrenching his neck, looking all around the restaurant.

"What are you looking for?" I asked.

"Where is that wench?" he demanded. "Another new girl."

"Really, another one? What is going on around here? They're replacing everybody." I also began to look around.

"You saw her," he responded. "She poured your beer."

I stopped looking around the room and settled my gaze on Bill. "That is the same girl as yesterday."

"Is it?" he asked, still searching the restaurant with his eyes.

I began to search again, believing that if two of us were looking, we would be more likely to find what was not there. A woman sat alone chewing gum on a dedicated side of her mouth at the corner table closest to the entrance. Her chewing made her appear ten years younger than the handful of faint wrinkles around her eyes suggested. Her hair was in two loose pigtails at the back of her head and she wore a short plaid skirt and a white collared blouse; also taking about ten years from her aesthetic age.

Bill caught me eyeing the woman. "Who's that?" he asked.

"Oh I don't know her," I said. "What's she wearing? Who does she think she is?"

Bill looked in her direction then winced at me. "What a mistake," he said. Then he pondered for a moment before saying, "or maybe she's a stripper?"

The woman looked up when Bill said "stripper."

"Yup," I confirmed. "Stripper."

The bartender walked up behind us, the sounds of her footsteps prompting Bill to turn on his stool in her direction. He asked for a refill while I continued looking at the woman wearing the stripper school-girl uniform. I thought about her delusional thought process. "People will think I'm younger if I dress like I'm in grade school. That'll work."

"Now *she* is a pretty one," Bill said of the bartender after she had walked to the back of the restaurant where the kitchen was.

"A little young for you, isn't she?" I asked.

"Well, I suppose," Bill responded, noticeably hurt by my implication that he was an aging single man interested in women far too young. As we sat for a moment, I took a pen out of my pocket and began to write on a napkin.

Bill turned toward me, trying to position himself to see. "What are you doing there?" he asked.

I said nothing until I finished. "Here. Read this to her." I handed him the folded napkin.

"To whom?" Bill asked, utilizing his consistently correct grammar.

"The bartender. Go for it," I encouraged.

She was walking toward us at that moment so Bill jumped in without looking over my words. He read, "Excuse me, Carly. I know you think I'm a little old for you, but here is the way I see it; age is just a number and the number I'm thinking of is two hundred dollars…" He trailed off at the end as he realized what was being suggested, then quickly turned to me with an angry embarrassment.

"Maybe you could get my friend here some coffee?" I asked.

"Sure thing, Doctor," she said, completely ignoring Bill, assuming he had drank more than he could handle.

"Why did you do that?" he asked, clearly not happy with me, but also clearly acknowledging the humor with a barely concealed half smile.

I laughed. "You didn't have a chance anyhow."

"Oh no?" Bill challenged.

"Of course not!"

"You don't know," he said in a less confident voice.

"Oh yeah? How about you see if you can get the number of any woman of your choosing in this restaurant? I'll pay today if you can pull it off." I spoke assuming Bill would not take on the bet.

He thought for a moment. "It's your day to pay anyway, but you're on."

We looked around the room for a suitable target.

"The stripper?" I questioned.

She looked up again at the word. Bill and I then looked to one another and shook our heads simultaneously. Sadly, aside from the bartender, the stripper was the only other woman in the restaurant.

Then, almost by magic, a woman we both had not previously noticed appeared at the end of the bar swiping away on her phone. Bill gave me a look and I nodded. With that confirmation he left his stool to take up the chase. On the trip toward her, he leaned over to pick up a small rectangular packet of sugar from a container on one of the tables.

"Excuse me," he began, holding the sugar packet toward the woman. "I think you dropped your name tag."

She looked up at him, then to the packet of sugar, forced a smile out, then looked back down to her phone.

"I like your blouse. Where did you get it?" he asked.

The woman looked at Bill again. "Thank you for the interest, but I'm just here to relax and enjoy my lunch break. I don't mean to be rude, but I'm not in the mood to be hit on." She looked back down at her phone.

Bill looked back at me. I displayed to him two clenched fists, thumbs pointed straight up, encouraging him to push on.

He turned back and tried a different tactic. "I'm sorry, Ma'am. I was just trying to be nice. I didn't mean to bother you. Have a nice day." He turned very slowly around and began to make his way back toward me.

Feeling quite bad that she may have been too caught up in her own life and was thus rude to a stranger for no good reason, the woman answered Bill's previously posed question. "Wait. Sorry. I got it from a place in SoHo. Great deal too; 30 percent off actually."

Bill smiled wildly as he turned back toward her. "If you give me your number, maybe we can see if I can get it 100 percent off," he suggested as he leaned against the bar, left foot crossed over right.

Disgusted, the woman got up, picked up her plate and glass, and moved to a table at the other end of the restaurant.

"I hate to see you go, but I love to watch you leave," Bill offered as a parting gift.

He shook his head and, defeated, he lugged himself back toward his stool.

"That was almost as smooth as you were with the bartender," I informed him. "Luckily I'm wearing an 'I'm with stupid' T-shirt under this one." I laughed loudly at my clever quip.

Bill merely looked at me and took a long gulp from his mug, finishing up what was left over after the foam from the bartender's sloppy pour had settled. The bartender, who watched the whole ordeal, brought a large cup of coffee with a dish that held four different kinds of sweetener and two small plastic containers of milk.

Bill placed the other woman's "name tag" on the dish then thanked the bartender as she smiled at me and nodded.

"So," Bill said, desperate to change the focus of our conversation. "How are you doing? Been thinking about that patient at all?"

Effortlessly, I forgot what a fool Bill had just made of himself and my mind went directly to Courtland's recent death. I answered him honestly, "Yes, actually. I've been having a good deal of trouble getting this one out of my head. And it's not just in my head." I stopped talking abruptly. I said nothing for a while as Bill waited for me to continue.

He broke the silence. "Well, what do you mean 'it's not just in your head'?"

"Sorry, I was just thinking about the whole thing. It's been hard. Sometimes, I think I see him. You know, like walking around."

"Well, that's a pretty normal reaction to something like this. It'll pass." Bill was trying to reassure me, but I took his comment to be condescending considering I was the clinician and he was the researcher.

"Yes, Bill," I said, defending my specialty and level of expertise. "I understand this is normal. That doesn't make it any easier to go through."

"Sorry," he said. "I didn't mean to suggest you didn't know that."

"I just can't get him out of my mind. And his shoes; they were on the floor, but neat, left next to right, placed there with care. Why did he take his shoes off? Not just that. That's just one part. The whole thing doesn't make any sense. Why did he do it?"

"I don't know, buddy," Bill said as he began to sip on his black coffee. "Depressed people do unexpected things. You can't blame yourself for it."

This time I ignored what I considered to be a condescending remark. "He seemed to be doing fine. He wasn't suicidal as far as I could tell."

"Maybe that's your problem," he said, holding the large coffee mug between his palms, warming them on the hot summer day.

"What do you mean?"

"Maybe you're actually disappointed with yourself that you didn't see this coming. Maybe you're asking yourself what kind of psychologist are you to let something like this slip by."

"Well, that couldn't be more obvious. Thank you, Doctor." I responded defensively and sarcastically to a well-intended suggestion that was fully accurate. It had not occurred to me until that moment that there was a reason behind my emotions. The concept had simply not been in my thoughts. All I knew was that I was feeling something. The why had not been explored.

I continued to talk about Courtland. "This kid was scared of death, like any normal person; not terrified, just scared. He didn't want to die. He thought about it as much as anyone does, but he didn't ruminate over it. There were no signs of being suicidal at all."

"Maybe he did think about it," Bill offered. "But, he just didn't tell you, for some reason."

"And maybe he wanted to create the illusion of control by choosing when and how death came," I said sarcastically. "We could go back and forth and back and forth with cliché diagnostic criteria all day. Let me guess, your next question is about control issues?"

Bill was silent for a moment. "I suppose we begin to become a little predicable, don't we?" he asked rhetorically.

The two of us said nothing for a while as I drank my beer and he sipped on his hot coffee.

I broke the silence, quoting Courtland to Bill. " 'Why am I fighting to live, if I'm just living to fight? Why am I trying to see, when there ain't nothing in sight? Why am I trying to give, when no one gives me a try? Why am I dying to live, if I'm just living to die?' " (Well, actually I was quoting Courtland quoting Edgar Winter's "Dying to Live" from *Edgar Winter's White Trash* album. But still it was poignant.)

For a moment, Bill was unsure how to respond. His confused thought process rippled along his taut then loose then taut then loose face, furrowing his brow, pursing his lips, wrinkling his nose, and pulling his mouth's corners, all in random combinations.

Finally, I explained. "It was something that Courtland said to me in session once. He told me it came from a song. I listened to it over and over, trying to understand after I found him there on the floor. Retrospectively, there is an obvious meaning, but it didn't satisfy; I wanted a real explanation. I listened to every recording I could find, every cover by other singers, every song that sampled or referenced it."

"Sometimes song lyrics are just song lyrics," Bill offered.

I said nothing for a while before adding, "I'm glad I'm not dying slowly…"

"What's that?" Bill asked.

"Courtland had mentioned that to me one day in session. He said that he had met a middle-aged man who had been diagnosed with some kind of stage four cancer. Courtland volunteered at a hospital upstate when he was younger. He said it 'mutually mitigated loneliness.'

"The doctors, they only gave the man a couple months. Courtland told me that the guy had a smile on his face all the way up until the end; not just happy but elated. 'I'm blessed to be dying slowly,' the man told Courtland." At that I laughed to myself; the thought of a couple months as *dying slowly*.

"The man told him, everybody from friends to family to neighbors and acquaintances had a chance to come to him and tell him how much he's meant to them, to show him how much he's meant to them.

"Courtland told me he hoped to never to be in that situation; to never be *dying slowly;* because he didn't think anyone would tell him how much he'd meant to them. He said he 'just wanted to die quickly and be done with it all.' "

"That's nothing," Bill responded. "Don't let that make you second-guess yourself. You didn't do anything wrong. No one could have seen this coming. You couldn't have been in his head. You couldn't have known all his thoughts."

Whether Bill was or was not correct, I could only mentally acknowledge that, if anyone should have seen it coming, it was me. *I hardly knew him,* I thought. But, aloud, I said nothing, allowing silence in.

The sound of the door opening caught my attention, so I turned to see a blind man and a blind woman make their way through the opening. The man held a walking stick while the woman held on to his arm.

No dog, I thought, amazed as I always was when I saw a blind person magnificently navigate their life without sight, the one sense that I would not have the strength to survive without.

He called out, "May we have a seat please?"

I looked at Bill but he was oblivious to what was happening. The bartender glanced at me, looking for confirmation on the obvious appropriate course of action, then she made her way toward the door.

"Yes, Sir. This way." She took his arm and led him leading the woman to a table.

The man hit Bill in the back with his walking stick as he passed. Bill, still submerged in his thoughts, turned around and gave the blind man an angry look.

I pushed Bill's left shoulder with my open left hand, scolding him for his inappropriately directed anger. I put my hands over my eyes and mimicked a blind person running into a wall, then closed my eyes and pointed at the blind man.

Bill realized the misunderstanding immediately, but unfortunately my little show had been witnessed by a larger audience than I had anticipated.

The bartender, the presumed stripper, and the woman Bill had harassed were visibly appalled. They gave me disgusted angry looks even though I meant no harm. I only wanted to inform Bill of the situation in a manner which was silent and thus invisible to the blind man and blind woman.

I put my palms up and shrugged my shoulders while mouthing "I'm sorry" to those who doubted me. Then I realized that I had indeed done no harm. I was mimicking a blind person with gestures.

I turned back toward the brick wall behind the bar and thought about how the previous event was analogous to making fun of the Amish on television. *They will never see it, so they will never be offended by it. However, it does promote hate toward a group of people, and at some point it will get back to them in a negative manner. There is no reason to make fun of these people anyway. They should be praised due to their ability to basically be super human with the absence of what others would consider to be absolutely necessary for living life. That's blind people, not the Amish. They're just backward.*

I chuckled at my humorous thought process.

"Well, I need to get back to work," Bill told me.

"As a lazy tailor would say, *suit yourself...*" I responded.

Bill stood up from his stool, unintentionally exposing his socks before they were hidden by his pants legs. They were bright green despite his brown suit.

"Nice socks!" I exclaimed, pointing downward.

He looked down before lifting up his pants legs slightly and taking a look for himself.

"Yes! I'm wearing my festive green socks," he said rather mockingly. "Happy St. Patrick's Day!"

"St. Patrick's day was about four months ago," I said, calling his bluff.

"I change my socks every six," he quipped.

I suddenly was reminded of what a fool Bill made of himself earlier. "I'm sure that fact didn't help with the ladies today, eh? Oh and don't forget to pay," I said.

"Oh, I'm a little shy," Bill said.

I laughed. "I'm sure there is not one woman in this bar that would agree with that statement!"

Bill shook his head and said, "I'm a little short."

"You're not that short," I said, jokingly assuming Bill was trying to give me reasons why he struck out earlier.

"I was referring to my monetary situation," he informed me. "Can you pay today? I'll get the rest of the week."

I laughed again. "Sure. Have a good one, Bill."

As he rose he explained his socks further. "You know, I'm forced to wear a suit and tie and buttoned shirt and a lab coat all day. There are very few opportunities to express myself, my individuality…" He trailed off, face turned toward the door as he made his way in that direction and waved his good-byes behind his head.

"Oh," I said, realizing I had not asked Bill about himself. "How are things going for you?"

He took several small slow steps back toward me answering as he approached and lowering his voice with each step. "You know; same old same old. I ask for better cases and to be the Principal Investigator on projects and publications and I get nothing."

"That's a shame. Sorry. Anything you can do about it?" I asked.

"Nope. I just keep on complaining…"

"Well, keep on complaining then," I instructed. "It's the squeaky wheel that gets the grease."

He laughed and said, "I'll never get what I want. You remember what Einstein said, don't you?"

I thought for a moment then asked, "About what?"

"You know… The only two things that are infinite in the world…" he began, jogging my memory and prompting my response.

"Oh yes; 'Only two things are infinite, the universe and human stupidity, and I'm not sure about the former.' "

"You've got it," Bill responded.

"How about this," I added. "You have colleagues who study artificial intelligence. You study natural stupidity."

Bill smiled at that. "Amos Tversky?" he questioned a moment later after turning and walking toward the door again.

I nodded before saying, "I'll see you tomorrow then."

"Tomorrow is merely a future yesterday," he called out while exiting. With that, I was left in the restaurant with only the other patrons and the server.

Bill's words echoed in my head, their significance becoming more and more clear and apparent. The same thing that occurred yesterday will surely happen tomorrow. It was the same thing over and over. Never ending cycle. Tomorrow is merely a future yesterday. Lather, rinse, and repeat.

I rotated my stool to face the restaurant previously behind me to use the open room as my own personal stage, hopeful for amusement.

The first woman Bill had harassed in the restaurant approached the woman he harassed later. A silver credit card stuck slightly out of the small black plastic bill folder which was handed from one to the other. The server began to walk toward me to run the card through the machine behind the bar.

I smiled at her. She smiled back and looked around me.

"Did your *friend* leave or is he still here?" she asked politely with a strange emphasis on the word "friend."

"Oh, he left. Had to get back to work. Sorry about his behavior. We were just messing around."

"Oh, no harm done," she responded. "You *two* seem like good *guys*." Again, her emphasis was odd, but I ignored it.

"Well, thank you," I replied smiling.

"Will that be all for you today?"

I looked down at my mug, considered another round, then answered. "Yes, Carly. Just the check. Thank you."

She opened the black bill folder and looked at it for a moment before going to the machine to print out a legible bill with the appropriate taxes.

As she worked, I swung around to continue observing the restaurant patrons. The same man who showed such trouble in decorum while eating the previous day squeezed through the door followed by a beautiful woman half his age and a quarter his size.

He walked straight to what he had decided would be his table for the inevitable feast he was about to ingest. He dropped his hat on the table and lowered himself indelicately onto the squeaking chair which, by some miracle, did not collapse under his immense weight. His hat was of a pattern of flannel that was different than and thus clashed with the flannel pattern of his short-sleeved shirt. As I smiled to myself, I thought about how it was the first time in my life that I had seen a short-sleeved flannel patterned shirt.

His lady friend placed her small blue leather purse on the table as she walked straight to the back of the restaurant to search for, I assumed, the bathroom.

The man watched her disappear from sight then leaned forward with a great deal of strain and grabbed her purse before leaning back in his stressed chair. He searched through it for a moment, then strained himself once more to get the purse back to its original place on the table, looking back to ensure she had not witnessed the invasion of her privacy.

I shook my head in his direction in an attempt to indicate that I was not a supporter of this mistrust and blatant disregard for personal property and privacy. In every aspect, this man epitomized the delicate and refined art of tastelessness.

I had to look away so I then directed my eyes to the far corner of the restaurant. The woman Bill had harassed second was gone. Five feet closer, seated at the next closest table and replacing the stripper who was also gone, was a woman with what appeared to be her young son.

Beautiful, they both had the same dirty-blond hair and sharp blue eyes with bushy dark eyebrows perched half an inch above. Both were dressed very well. She in a light blue dress; simple, flowing, and elegant; and he in khaki shorts with suspenders over a tucked-in short-sleeved collared white shirt. His hair was parted on the left side while his mother's was in a loose hair bun. The crayons in both of his hands were mashed and scraped against the children's menu/ place mat designed brilliantly to keep children quiet and unobtrusive in restaurants. His mother was on her cell phone speaking quietly as her son was happily inebriated with his own contained immaturity.

After staring blankly for five or ten minutes, maybe longer, I regained my ocular focus and shook myself back into reality. The screen on my phone showed that it was time to pay the bill and make my way to work. 1:14 p.m.

I walked out with a significantly lighter wallet; their prices had been going up slowly for years, but this was the way of things. I accepted the increases and paid them with as little care as the rest of the city dwellers. *It's just money,* I thought, trying not to focus on the injustice.

The air, humid and thick, slapped me in the face as the door of the restaurant opened under the power of my right arm. My nose attempted to inhale as little as possible of the dirty stench of summer in New York City and, despite feeling extremely lightheaded, I stuck to my oxygen depleted ways throughout my time in the great outdoors.

Traveling from the doorway of the restaurant to the doorway of the park-side building that held my office was a quick blur of greens and browns and the loud fast bright yellow of the city cabs. I felt as though I had closed my eyes, then was immediately where I needed to be. My phone, however, suggested a different story. 2:01 p.m. The trip from the restaurant to my office had taken significantly longer than it did on an average afternoon. I questioned if my breathless pace was slower than when I breathed more freely. Or maybe I had passed out. Both theories made sense to my oxygen-starved brain.

Chapter 22

Tuesday at the Office

The office door was locked which I responded to in an unexpectedly stoic manner; I ignored it. All the mounting anxiety over its ambiguous status should have culminated in relief when I finally learned it had been secure all along, but there was no feeling of remission for my aching conscience. I checked the back of my pants with my left hand. Still a sticky gum spot.

The wooden closet door creaked loudly as it quickly opened under the force of my left hand. The extra pair of pants I kept in the office was for emergencies only and thus was a pair I would never be caught wearing under normal circumstances due to their aesthetic deplorability.

I took them off the hanger and examined their color, fading from dark brown to light brown with a tinge of blue and green somehow prevalent underneath. A Christmas gift from Julie for our first Christmas as a married couple. Throwing them away was forbidden, despite the fact that their appearance had been destroyed by a novice launderer, so they found their way into the closet of my office. For emergencies only, and yet I had never found myself in the unfortunate position of needing these putrid pants until I unexpectedly picked up a precariously misplaced ball of gum.

After a depressing examination, I considered the alternative; sitting on a sheet of paper or a plastic bag, maybe even wearing no pants but staying seated behind the desk throughout the sessions like a TV news anchor.

I brought the pants to the chair opposite the couch and, after untying each shoe, left before right, I slipped them off simultaneously with the hand closest to each one. Midway through the pants swapping process, there was a light tapping at the door which I ignored, assuming it to be just a draft or the sound of me moving in the chair.

A moment passed before the tapping returned, this time louder and in a slower, less urgent tempo.

Chapter 23

Kristin

"Hey, Dr. Thesiger. It's Kristin," came through muffled.

Still changing I called to the other side, "Yes, Kristin." And before I had a chance to say "Hold on a moment," the door began to open. "Wait! Wait!" I shouted frantically.

"Oh, I'm so sorry!" Kristin said before pulling the door to a slam.

"Just hold on a moment," I said, questioning in my mind how she could open it without the key. Maybe I had not closed the door fully after I had entered.

After a few seconds, I made my way to the door, opening it and smiling, extending my hand to shake hers. Kristin looked down at my right hand before filling it with her left hip as she hugged me tightly. For a moment, I stood there motionless, uncertain of the level of inappropriateness. Then, ignoring it, I hugged her back, tightly, securely. After several seconds, I slid my hands from her back and lightly pushed her away by her shoulders. Her hands remained around my waist as she spoke.

"And how are we doing?" she asked playfully, with a whisper of juvenility.

I took a step back, forcing her hands to slide away, before closing the door as she walked to the couch.

"I'm doing pretty well," I said as I grabbed the box of tissues, carelessly left out from the previous day, then placed it in the top drawer of my desk. "I was just changing my pants. I sat on some gum."

"Sorry to have barged in," she said, appearing to be fully relaxed, absolutely no stress in her entire body. The mere sight of her made all the stress in my own body fade away.

I sat beside her, to her left, on the couch, looking in her direction for a silent moment of mutual comfort. She stared back with a smile peaking the left side of her mouth slightly more than the right. She wore a thin red hooded long-sleeved sweatshirt, neckline a loose fringed cut that swooped down five inches below her rounded chin. I tried to determine if she had done the modification herself or if it was manufactured. I failed to come to a conclusive determination.

Her skirt was short, above her perfectly oval knees, and pleated to flare out, creating an almost springy bouncing quality, dancing beautifully when she moved. My mind wandered to Little Red Riding Hood skipping through the forest before being bombarded by the big bad wolf. I looked away and fought for the image to flee my mind. I wanted to stitch a big "A" on her thin red hooded long-sleeved sweatshirt to remind myself of the possible consequence.

"So what's on your mind, Kristin?"

"You," she responded quickly.

I smiled and laughed. "Me, you say?"

"Well, I'm sitting here in front of you in your office alone with you. Hard to think of anything else."

"Hard to disagree with that," I responded, placing my right arm upon the back of the couch and twisting to position myself more comfortably facing her, right leg bent at the knee and horizontal, resting on the couch. She too adjusted her position to better connect with me. We looked at one another for a while smiling and communicating silently.

An in-office patient for four years, Kristin was a sophomore in college on her summer break; she sent e-mails in addition to our video sessions while she was away during the school months.

Her father was in the military so, as a consequence, she had moved around a great deal during her younger years. He and his wife, *an inadequate replacement* for Kristin's late mother, presumed that this lifestyle had the potential to hurt her emotionally and psychologically so, when they finally settled in New York, she became one of my favorite patients.

It took no longer than a short conversation with her to learn that she was not merely psychologically unharmed by her scattered, rootless youth, but that she was among the strongest, most intelligent, talented, and most self-aware people I had ever come across.

Before meeting her, I assumed what I read in the textbooks and journal articles to be true; that, without years of wisdom to make sense of their observations, young people had a very shallow understanding of their experiences. Kristin made me rethink much of what I had learned. The researchers mislabeled what impeded deeper processing in children. It was not wisdom obtained solely from the passing of time and resulting maturation of the brain, it was actually variety of experience that was the key to understanding their world.

In our first session, she put it more eloquently than I ever could. "I am a child of many countries and proud to be the product of so many conflicting ideologies, philosophies, and cultures. It is what makes me uniquely me and taking away any bit of that would result in a completely different person, mentally, physically, and socially."

Her straight dark brown hair, almost black, matched her eyes, set perfectly on her beautiful face which was perfectly rounded until it came to a slightly squared point at her chin. Kristin was years more mature than her age indicated.

We sat there, next to one another smiling and gazing into the other's eyes, thinking, imagining. I questioned my emotions silently, what I felt during sessions. I was going through something in my own life or maybe I was just finding an outlet for the problems in my marriage. Whatever it was, the hour each week with Kristin was the most invigorating hour spent with any patient, with any friend, with any person. And yet we hardly spoke.

I knew it was wrong, both my feelings and hers, so I constantly tried to get her to think about and consider her previous relationships, hoping that she would stumble upon a pattern that would put her feelings for me into a more realistic context, so she could see the flaws in her desire; getting involved with controlling older men who were already in relationships with someone else, who could never truly be hers.

"How was your week? Anything happen of note?" I asked, unable to wipe the genuine smile off my face.

"I had a dream…" she responded before I cut her off.

"Oh, please tell me about it." I realized that I was coming off as overly eager; I was overly eager.

"I was killing him. Stabbing with a big knife, over and over and over and over. But, he was enjoying it; smiling and laughing. And he just wouldn't die, but I knew I was killing him. What does that mean?" It was always full disclosure with her. She never held anything back from me. She was completely honest, one of her many admirable characteristics.

"It probably means you're angry with him still, not that dreams really can be said to mean much of anything," I responded.

"Oh, that's right. I always ask you about my dreams… I guess it was more of a fantasy than a dream. As if I wasn't sleeping, just kind of imagining it, almost consciously."

I smirked. "You're fantasizing about killing your ex-boyfriend?"

"Well, I suppose. Is that strange? What do you fantasize about?" she asked, slight smile on her face as she looked to me for the answer.

"Well, certainly not about killing people with whom I am angry." I spoke a lie, a blatant lie. I immediately felt a lump in my throat. I hated lying to the one person in my world who was consistently honest and open with me.

"I don't fantasize at all," I continued. "I just make the most of my situation so I don't have anything to fantasize about. My fantasy is my real life or at least my unrealistic skewed perception of it."

"You're lying to me…" She laughed softly, smiling flirtatiously on the left side of her mouth.

"Yes… I am, you're right."

"So what do you fantasize about then?" She adjusted how she was sitting again, facing me directly on the couch with each leg folded under the opposite. Her footwear, sandals, were left empty on the floor displaying her beautiful naked feet. She placed her elbows on her thighs and allowed her hands to fall limp, appropriately adjusting her skirt. It always took very little time for her posture and mannerisms to regress toward behaving in a manner that fit a child much younger than she, forcing me to go in the opposite direction, taking on the role of a father, parent, guardian, authority figure.

I thought about her questions for a moment. I did not want to continue the lie. I hated my life and she knew it. Of course I fantasized about other things. She could sense my emotions and I could hers. How she felt about me; probably just emotions about authority figures projected onto me; transference. And my emotions in response; just my mind and body reacting to her behavior toward me; reverse transference. This is what I kept telling myself over and over and over.

I decided to ignore the question and change the subject the best I could. "Would you like to try something?"

"Anything you would like me to do. You're the boss, Dr. Thesiger."

I wondered what would have happened if we had met in a bar somewhere. I was not married. She was not my patient. What would happen? Could it work? I always considered the possibilities about countless intriguing women, but none more than she. I tried to mentally ignore the fact that she was not even old enough to be in the bar of my fantasy.

"Maybe you could relive your dream. Tell me about it, but in present tense, first person point of view. Tell me what you're doing, not what you did. Bring it to the here and now. Close your eyes and start at the beginning."

"No, I don't want to do that," she responded honestly. It was hard to ignore her feisty personality, refusing to perform the exercise. She had, for the previous handful of sessions, been taking control, changing the tone from therapy to a flirtatious conversation. It was difficult to fight.

"How about you pretend he is here?" I offered. "You can tell him what you don't like about him." I pointed to the empty chair across from the couch, the couch upon which we sat increasingly closer to one another. "Maybe pretend he's sitting right there? I can put a stuffed animal there if it helps."

She shut her eyes tight, crossed her arms, and shook her head in the most adorably childish way imaginable. Then she opened her right eye, peering at me inquisitively, and said "You have stuffed animals?"

"Yes, sure," I responded, laughing the lie to her, but one that was clearly a mutually understood joke.

"Oh really? What kind?"

"A wolf," I said without thinking at all.

"A wolf?" she questioned. Her dark eyebrows went up at the ends, reshaping themselves to angle toward her nose, her little nose coming to a round scrunched-up point.

I did not respond as I admired her beauty. Again there was a long silent period of facial and ocular communication, this time broken by her pouty red lips.

"I'm not as happy as I feel," she said unexpectedly.

"What? Are you crazy?" I spoke, again without thinking.

She looked at me with a shocked face, a silent exclamation representing a self-inquiry of *Did my psychologist just ask me if I am crazy?* I decided then to reintroduce my verbal filter into the session.

"No, no, that's not what I mean," I said. "We both know you're crazy." I tried making a joke out of what a psychologist should never say to a patient. She smiled again in her own flirtatious way.

I continued. "What I mean is that you *are* as happy as you feel. Happiness or joy is an emotion. Emotions are defined by how you feel; that is the emotion. If you feel happy, you are happy."

"No, I'm just not as happy as I feel," she stubbornly insisted against my logic.

"But do you see how that doesn't really make any sense? How about this, I can explain it very well," I said.

"Okay, let's hear your argument," she challenged, ready, as always, for anything.

I got up and walked to my desk and retrieved from the top drawer a piece of paper and a pencil and brought it back to the couch. "Here," I said. "Draw a picture of yourself."

"Seriously?"

"Yes."

"Okay," she said slowly.

She turned herself 90 degrees, placed her feet flat on the floor with her sandals in between, and then sat up straight at the edge of the couch in front of the coffee table. Her arms and hands slowly moved up in front of her body past her chest, face, and ears, then through her hair, bringing it up with both hands, elevating its weight as the tips followed their roots back toward her shoulders. She was merely moving her loose hair from her face, but she did it in the most beautiful way imaginable.

I watched her closely for the fifteen minutes that she spent creating a magnificent pencil representation of herself. She used her fingers, nails painted with a muted deep rich red, to pull and smudge the markings to create shadow and depth. She looked up at me several times as she worked, smiling and looking for confirmation.

When the masterpiece was completed, she stood up and walked barefoot into the bathroom, leaving the door open as she washed her hands. When she returned, she plopped herself onto the couch, resting in the position she had adopted before she had begun to create; legs folded and directly facing me. She held up the assignment, clenched at the top with her small right fist.

"How does it look?" she asked, knowing very well that it was magnificent.

I had been utterly unaware that she was so artistic, creative, talented. What other hidden abilities did she possess? Would I ever discover them? At that moment, I wanted nothing more than to know more about her; to know everything about her.

"It's... it's beautiful," I managed.

"So why did I do this?"

I had lost focus as I normally did in session with Kristin. She had asked me a direct question, so I had little time to regain my composure and give her an answer. The appropriate amount of time to answer her query went by quickly. I hoped she would venture her own answer so I would be released from the duty, but she did nothing but raise her eyebrows as if to say, *Well...*

Suddenly, it came back to me. "Oh yes," I said, again without thinking about what words I should and should not say aloud. "What emotion do you think that person is feeling?"

"The person in the picture?"

"Yes."

"So, you mean me?" she asked.

"Yes."

"Well, happy. She feels happy."

"Alright, so would you say that she is happy?" I asked.

"I suppose I would."

"There you go then. You're happy," I said, smiling.

Kristin thought for a moment. She looked herself in the face for a while before she decided, "I still feel happy, but I know I'm not actually happy. And did I really just spend fifteen minutes drawing a picture of myself for that?" She laughed her charming infectious laugh.

Laughing myself, I said "But, if you feel happy, then you are happy, Kristin." I came close to calling her "dear" or "darling" or some other term of endearment inevitably inappropriate for our situation.

"No," she said. "I'm not happy though. I just know it. Deep down inside, I am just not happy. I'm sad. I'm empty. I'm lonely. I desire, long for something that I don't have; something that's right in front of me that I just want to take hold of, but I can't. That's the feeling I get. That's the feeling I have. I'm not happy. "

I was startled and uncomfortable that she may have been referring to me. My heart began to beat noticeably harder and I could feel myself blushing, luckily unnoticeably.

"Do those negative feelings affect you?" I said, trying to pretend to be anything but aflutter inside.

"No, not really."

"So then how can you have these conflicting feelings of joy and sadness?" Again, I was speaking without thinking. I had just asked a stupid question that seemed more argumentative than logical.

"I don't know," she said slowly with an upward inflection at the end.

Answering my own question, I said, "It's because you are happy. The sadness and emptiness are just emotions you think you should be feeling because you still think you're unhappy."

She put her left elbow on her left thigh and leaned her head on her left hand, taking some time to comprehend my words. "No. That can't be it," she said. "It's like being sick. I can take medicine that gets rid of the symptoms of being sick, but I will still be sick. The virus will still be in my system. My autoimmune system will still be fighting it off. I feel healthy, but I'm still sick."

Her analogy was good and proved her point. I loved that she challenged me, backing me into a logic corner and forcing me to reason my way out. She was sweet and caring about this kind of back and forth. It felt playful and fun. I found it impossible to converse with Julie on that level. She would just get angry at me, assuming that I was talking down to her, but, of course, I was not my wife's psychologist.

I looked Kristin straight in the eye and thought without blinking for a stretched moment. My thoughts kept drifting from a response toward how beautifully smart she was.

After some loosely relevant ideas were compiled, I responded. "You, Kristin, are a smart and knowledgeable young lady, but you appear to be letting your preconceived ideas about depression control your perception of your current state of emotions.

"Your analogy is good, but feeling sick and being sick are different from feeling happy and being happy. The former are not mutually exclusive, while the latter are. With emotions, the way you feel is the way you are. That is the definition of emotions. With health, the way you feel is not necessarily the way you are. For clarification and to correct your analogy, acting happy and being happy are like feeling sick and being sick. You can act happy and not be happy the same as you can feel healthy and not be healthy."

Kristin looked as though she was going to respond immediately after I finished; she opened her mouth and inhaled, lifting her shoulders and leaning back slightly. Then she closed her mouth and put her recently formed loose left fist in front of her mouth and turned her head, looking away from me, thinking.

After some time, she turned back to me, eyes before head, and asked, "How does that make you feel, Dr. Thesiger?" This time she wiggled her little nose at me. I was incapable of holding back my smile.

"What, no comeback?" I responded.

She laughed aloud, throwing her head back and forcing her hair to follow; straight up then back. She ran her fingers through her hair again, this time holding it tight, out of her face and off her shoulders. "Tell me a story, Dr. Thesiger," she commanded.

"About what, Miss Kristin?" She loved to hear me talk. She respected what I had to say, knowing well that there was always something to learn and she loved to learn.

"How about you?" she said.

"What? A story about me?"

"It will be fun. Come on. I'm always telling you stories about me. Tell me a story about you." She bent her head forward and looked up at me with her puppy dog eyes. It was difficult to say no.

"You always tell me stories about you because I'm your psychologist, Kristin, but I will comply. This one happened to me during my first year at college. A place to which you'll soon return."

"Eh. Don't remind me," she complained.

"Still not too enthusiastic about going back?" I asked.

"No, I don't want to go back. Whatever. I don't want to talk about it. Go on with your story."

The mention of returning to college began to change her mood and I wanted nothing more than to keep her smiling. When she was happy, I was happy and the same was true for any other emotion she experienced in session so I continued with my story despite the fact that I probably should have explored her reasons for not wanting to return to college.

"It was my first semester at college. This was back in the days when the Ivy League was actually challenging." I laughed while her expression remained the same. Her stepmother was forcing her to attend the only Ivy League school to which she gained admission, even though she wanted nothing more than to stay in the city.

"It was the day of my Physiological Psychology final; Psych 26, if I remember correctly." I stopped and thought for a moment for dramatic effect. I knew immediately and without question that I had labeled the class correctly. I even remembered the professor. A modest genius of a woman who never glanced at her notes when lecturing and who always had the time for students' questions before, during, and after class.

"I hadn't slept the previous night because I was studying with my roommates who, like myself, had done none of the readings and paid little attention in class the few times we actually decided to show up. We were a rowdy crew of misfits."

Kristin laughed at my choice of words. She enjoyed when I showed my age through outdated semantics equally as much as she loved when I tried to use more contemporary phrases.

"On that test day morning, the dozens of hours without sleep were draining, but further frustrating me was the fact that I had a paper due in the same class the next day, so there was the hovering knowledge that I wouldn't be sleeping for dozens more hours.

"Like the good student I obviously was, I wanted to be sure I knew all of the material so I conducted a one man last minute cramming session. Somehow I had lost track of time and the cramming session ran a bit late. And I had in the back of my mind the knowledge that showing up late would have been just as bad as not showing up at all; the professor was generous with grades and lenient on many levels, but there was no tolerance for tardiness."

"What kind of day was it?" Kristin asked, yearning for a more vivid picture.

"It was actually a beautiful spring day. A nice cool breeze, sunny, birds, buds, leaves."

"Oh, that sounds nice. I like that."

"Well, there was one bad thing about spring in New Hampshire," I informed her.

"And what's that?"

"It snows a lot during the winter, then come spring all the snow turns to water. The water ends up going into the ground and creating vast stretches of deep thick mud."

"Eww! That sounds disgusting! How did people get around?"

"Boots are a must until mid to late June when the sun bakes all the mud to dust and the grass covers it all up."

"I guess that's not so bad," she said.

"Eh, we got by. We were all so happy for the temperature to be above zero that we hardly cared about the mud."

"Really? Zero? It gets that cold there?" she questioned.

"Yes, yes. During the winter terms, there was always a one month stretch when the temperature wouldn't go above zero. It was pretty brutal. Involuntarily inhaling after sneezing, yawning, any kind of quick deep breath would give you an ice-cream headache or a brain freeze."

"Wow… I can't imagine that. I don't want to imagine that," she said laughing.

I laughed along. "I can't imagine who would want to, but you do what you have to do when you're there and it can actually be quite magical."

"Magical? How? Freezing to death isn't magical," she said, again laughing.

"No, no. It was cold, but below zero or so everything feels pretty much the same. What really gets you is the wind. Some days it would be so windy, people would be blown right over; right to the ground."

"That must have been funny!" she exclaimed, almost clapping at the thought.

"Oh it was, but everyone fell; there was ice everywhere. The salt spread on the ground to help melt the ice would get frozen into the ice, it was so cold. Everyone would slip and slide and fall. It was all in good fun."

"But what was so magical about all that?" she asked.

"Oh well, at night, the temperature would go down to negative twenty or negative thirty, some nights colder, but it felt like it was eighty or ninety degrees warmer," I responded to her disbelief.

"How? Hypothermia?"

"No, no. There was rarely any wind at night so, if you stood still, the heat that your body creates and radiates would stay there right next to your skin, surrounding you and keeping you warm."

"No way! Does that actually work?" she shouted.

"Yes, yes. It's really rather amazing. And, because it was winter, nobody would be outside at night so it was completely silent; no sound whatsoever. No hum of the symphony of trillions of bugs and birds and beetles squeaking and chirping and buzzing. On cloudy nights, if you stood at the edge of campus, facing away from the lights, there was nothing for your mind to process or filter out from the external world; no sound to hear, no objects to see, nothing to feel. It was as if everyone and everything just wasn't there, just didn't exist."

"That sounds amazing," Kristin responded, trying to imagine the feeling.

"It was," I agreed. "I used to go out on calm nights and just stand for a while, completely clearing my mind of all my stresses and issues. I could be alone and feel like I was without anything, like I left everything including myself back in the dorm. I could just stop being aware of everything. It all seemed so clear and simple on those nights. There were no bothers, no worries. Everything was just… perfect."

Kristin was looking into my eyes as I spoke, but I was looking off, reliving my college winter nights of solitude. I said nothing for a while as she watched me.

"Oh, continue your story. I almost forgot about it," she said finally.

"Oh yes. That's right. So I was trying to get to the testing room as fast as possible. I kept checking my watch."

She laughed. "Was it one of those old-fashioned wristwatches that only tells time?"

"This was a long time ago," I said, rather embarrassed that I was forced to keep highlighting the fact that I was many years her senior.

I continued. "So I finally made it to the building, all the way across campus, then I spent two minutes looking through my pockets and my wallet for my ID card. Even though the security guard saw me enter every day multiple times, he needed to see the ID to let me through."

"Oh no! Did you leave it in your dorm?" Kristin asked.

"That's right!" I responded, commending her intuition.

"Oh no! What did you do?"

"Well, I begged with the security guard and he finally let me through after I gave him fifty bucks."

"Sounds like a nice guy…"

"Oh, he was. He actually saved my life that day."

"How?"

"Well, if he hadn't let me through, I would've returned to my dorm, missed the test, and failed. Also, there was a terrible fire in my dorm."

"Oh no…" she said, sounding worried.

"Yup, I would have made it back to the dorm and decided to take a depressed nap knowing that I had just failed a very important class for my major and I probably would have been burned to death because I was so tired from not sleeping the previous night."

"Fifty bucks, huh? I guess that was worth it."

"More worth it than imaginable," I agreed.

She nodded before saying, "Go on, go on."

"Okay, so finally he let me through after I paid him off with all the money in my pockets and jacket."

"You were wearing a jacket?" she questioned, interrupting. "I thought it was spring."

"Yes, it was a *spring* jacket. Remember, 'cool breeze.' "

"Oh yeah. Good point. Go on," she allowed.

"So the stairs were closed for some reason; being cleaned or repairs or something; so I had to wait for the elevator. When it finally came I packed myself in with eight or nine other people, also elevator bound by the 'out of order' sign at the bottom of the stairs.

"Most were leisurely holding and reading newspapers or their mail. Teachers, grad students…"

"Wait, wait, hold on a second!" Kristin interrupted again. "Newspapers and mail?"

"Yes… this was a long time ago."

She laughed for a while then allowed me to continue.

"So, I was mentally going over every bit of information that I had processed the previous day as the elevator ascended."

"Makes sense," she said.

"Then, I felt something poking me in the back."

"What? Poking you in the back?" Kristin asked.

"Yup. At first I assumed it was someone shifting around so it would stop in a second or two, but it persisted. I became more and more and more annoyed. I was frustrated and tired and probably late and then this inconsiderate person behind me was poking me in the back for no reason at all. I was planning on letting it go, forgetting about it, not letting it get to me, but the unusually long ride allowed for me to be pushed beyond my breaking point."

"Oh no! What did you do?" she asked.

"Seconds before the elevator reached my floor, I swung around ready to physically and verbally confront this inconsiderate jerk."

"What did you do?" she asked again.

"I found myself face-to-face with a blind man. It was his cane that was poking me in the back."

"Oh no!" she exclaimed, so engrossed in the story that it could have been her who almost assaulted a blind man in an elevator.

Then I asked her, "You know how I felt and what I did then? How would you feel, what would you do?"

"Well, I suppose I would feel like a pretty horrible person for assuming a blind guy was intentionally trying to bother me," she responded.

"Okay. And what would you do?" I asked.

"I would turn back around and get off the elevator at my floor. Why, what did you do?" she asked.

"That's just what I did," I responded.

"Okay, good. For a moment there, I thought that you beat him up or something."

"No, no, of course not! It was actually a pretty amazing experience. After I saw that it was a visually impaired gentleman who was poking me, completely inadvertently, I immediately stopped stressing about the test. I stopped going over facts. I just relaxed and laughed about it. All the anxiety, fear, fatigue, anger, and everything just melted away."

"Really? Why?"

"Well, I realized that I was getting myself all worked up and for what? For nothing. When you're all agitated about something out of your control, you try to find things that are within your control to take your anger out on, to control. You contribute all that anger to whatever is controllable and, for me on that day, it was the poking in my back. I was going to tell the inconsiderate person off which would have made me feel like I had some kind of control over the situation, all situations, and then I would have hoped to have control also over my test performance. It's silly, but it's how we think.

"The funny thing is that I probably would have done worse on my test if I hadn't been as relaxed from this (to me) funny encounter. It showed me that I was far too stressed, stressed enough to come shockingly close to beating up an innocent blind man in an elevator. He showed me that there is nothing worth getting myself all worked up for. It's no way to react to adversity. It's no way to live life."

"That's a beautiful concept," she said.

I nodded and smiled.

"So," she said, "the moral of the story is not to let the little things… to not let anything stress you out to the point where you can't function properly?"

"Right on the money, honey!" I said, immediately regretting calling her "honey," then, when she laughed at me, regretting rhyming "money" with "honey" back-to-back.

When she stopped laughing, I, embarrassed, tried to bring the conversation back to a more appropriate level. "So, how can this story and the underlying moral relate to your own life?"

"That's obvious," she began. "I shouldn't let my ex-boyfriend get to me, but I really don't like him… That's pretty much it." She responded quickly, obviously not wanting to think or talk about it.

"Let's try something that might help us get further into it, okay?" I suggested.

"Okay."

"I'm going to have you exaggerate the emotion until it feels real. Alright?"

"Actually, that doesn't make any sense," she responded after a bit of thought.

"What do you mean?" I asked. "Of course it makes sense. I want you to think about the emotion you said you feel toward him, the 'hate,' and I want you to exaggerate it and exaggerate it and exaggerate it until it feels real."

Then she questioned, "How can exaggerating something make it more real? By definition, exaggerating makes something less real."

She was right. My mind quickly dissected this method of emotional exploration and how I never realized its contradiction time and time again, this fundamental flaw in logic at its core.

All I could conclude was, "You are absolutely right, Kristin. That makes no sense. I guess this method is supposed to make you feel the hate so you can maybe remember exactly why the hate was there; maybe there was more behind it than you can remember; but exaggerating an emotion past the level that you feel it doesn't sound like it would help it become more real. This method helps some people sometimes, but, if you don't want to do it, we don't have to."

She smiled triumphantly and I allowed it before adding, "I do want you to think about it though; why is the anger there and, if it is sourced in an external source, why did you endure that external source for so long."

"I feel like you're getting at something," she said wisely.

"I'll cut to it," I responded quickly. "I think he was treating you badly the same way that all of your ex-boyfriends have and you endure it and seek out guys who will treat you badly because you tend to seek out the kind of relationships that you think you deserve."

She looked at me for a moment and then looked away. Her bouncy demeanor was gone and she seemed put off, almost angry with me. "I don't want to talk about that," she said. "Tell me another story."

I wanted to stay on topic, but I wanted the room not to lose its joviality. "How about you tell me a story this time," I suggested. "But we will come back to that at some point, okay?"

"Okay," she responded. "What kind of story should I tell? A story about what?"

"How about a story about you? I just told you one about me so that seems fair."

"Okay."

She adjusted herself and, naked feet still on the couch, stiffened her posture and sat up straight, facing me. She put her palms together, left hand on top facing down and right hand on the bottom facing up, with fingers hooked and elbows about twelve inches from her torso; the position an opera singer takes while performing.

"'T'was a dark and stormy night," She then paused before adding, "And all through the house." Again, a pause. "Not a creature was stirring, not even a mouse." Her eyes moved quickly side to side to side, searching for a next line in her head before she lost her composure and posture and burst into laughter. I laughed with her.

"Seriously," I said. "A true story about yourself. A real one."

"Yours wasn't true or real," she replied.

"You don't know that," I said without directly denying her true statement. I shot her a competitive smile to see if she would back down or step up to the plate.

After a short staring contest, she yawned with her entire body; mouth open wide displaying her beautiful healthy white teeth as she stretched out and lifted up her legs and arms and leaned her head back onto the small pillow behind her. She then laid down on the couch; her beautiful bare feet resting gently on my right thigh, and her head horizontal as she stared at the white ceiling above the couch.

She was, as I saw her, fragile and very likely incapable of accepting a rejection of seemingly innocent physical contact, so I stayed there, frozen, not moving an inch, tense and rigid as a statue.

"I don't think I'll be able to handle going back to college," she said, still staring straight up.

"Oh," I said with a shaky uncomfortably preoccupied voice. "Why do you say that?"

Her feet started moving side to side in sync with one another. I watched them for a moment then allowed my eyes to follow her legs, up her torso, then to her head, thankfully still staring straight up.

Her mouth began to move, but I was paying far less attention to her words than I was to the dancing of her feet that was beginning to make its way up to the rest of her body, her fingers and hands moving in sync with her feet.

Suddenly she jumped up from the couch into a fit of dancing. I was unable to determine if her dancing was wild and psychotic or if it was the standard for girls her age.

"Dance with me, Dr. Thesiger," she insisted.

"Oh no, no. I couldn't do that."

"Come on," she sang as she spun around. "I want to dance! And you said you were voted best dancer in high school."

"Well, yes. That and best looking, most athletic, and best smile." I smiled at her to prove two of the four.

"Are you going to get up?" she asked with a guilt inducing tone. "What was it that Hemingway said… 'When you stop doing things for fun you might as well be dead.'"

Never had Hemingway's words been more applicable. I might as well have been dead.

"No, Kristin…" I responded, angry at myself for doing the right thing or, more accurately, not doing the wrong thing.

Suddenly she stopped her movement and threw herself onto the couch, arms folded tightly as she faced the chair opposite the couch with her lower lip extended far further from her face than her upper lip.

I hated to see her like that, pouting to make me feel guilty, but there was little I could do.

"Kristin…" I said slowly.

"Yes, Dr. Thesiger," she responded with the tone of a child whose favorite toy had just been taken away.

"I have another story for you."

"You do?" she exclaimed.

"Yes. Would you like me to tell it to you?"

"Please, Dr. Thesiger!" she shouted.

I went on to tell her the story about my aunt and uncle's Dalmatian, just as filled with fantasticfully fictitious facts as it was when the tale had been created the day before.

Kristin did not interrupt or ask any leading questions, but her facial expressions followed the emotions of the story closely. Bright and ready to listen at the beginning. Worried and scared with a distinct fear for the dog in her eyes in the middle. And, by the end, happy and smiling and ready to make the most of her life or at least the rest of the day.

"That's a great story. Thank you, Dr. Thesiger!" she exclaimed as she slid her feet into her sandals before standing.

I stood with her and accompanied her to the door, walking behind her, close enough to recognize and identify the brand of shampoo she used that morning to be the same as Julie's. She stopped short just before putting her hand on the doorknob and swung around, throwing her arms around me and squeezing tight.

I froze as I usually did when she touched me, then I gave in to the exchange of physical emotion. There we stood for an uncertain duration, holding one another lovingly, the same as we had done at the beginning of the session. I lost myself in her embrace, forgetting who I was, where I was, when it was, and what my purpose was. My whole world was crashing to nothing, but, for that moment, I felt that she was the thing that could help me fix it, help me regain myself. She was the key to everything.

I pushed her away gently when I realized what I was considering. "You should go," I whispered to her forehead, her arms still holding my torso. My hands then directed her forearms away from my body before opening the door and saying loudly, "Good session today, Kristin. I will see you next week?"

Every emotion imaginable was going through her mind and body. I could sense it. Despair, anger, and sadness were the predominant three shown on her beautiful face. She wiped away the few tears that began to trickle from her beautifully dark eyes.

Then her demeanor changed in a split second. Her face was smiling, happy, gleeful and her voice was back to its normal upbeat tone and volume. "See you next week, Dr. Thesiger!"

She bounced off out the door and down the hall. I watched her rather shocked, but also not shocked at all. Happy that she was okay, but hurt that she was able to turn her feelings around in an instant, I shook my head and smiled.

"You have a good week, Kristin," I shouted down the hall as she entered the elevator.

Her small hand popped out of the elevator with a delightful wave before I lost her to the lower levels of the building and, beyond that, the vast cityscape. It amazed me that she was able to make me feel simultaneously both empty and full inside, but that was the power she had over me. That was Kristin.

———

After pulling my head back into the office, I found myself on the couch with the bottoms of my palms over my closed eyes applying immense pressure, trying to push out the mix of emotions within. At that moment, the words of a former patient, Ashley, bounced around in my head. I had paid little attention to her at the time because I saw no logical meaning in much of what she spouted; her silly little adolescent life just bored me endlessly; but these words still stuck with me.

" 'My brain told me to follow my heart and my heart told me to follow my brain,' " I said aloud, quoting Ashley's words.

This cyclical, never ending, yet dead-end, headache of the autonomic feedback loop eerily accurately depicted Kristin's position in my life. It could never happen. It just could not, yet it was there, living within me, no place else. But it was not real to begin with, more of a game played within us over which we had no control. Every person has felt emotionally irrational or irrationally emotional at some point and I was no different.

And the whole thing was completely irrational, just our emotions toying with the other's without either of our control. Through the path of the psychologist-patient relationship and the inevitable emotional forces that come up in sessions and their need to attach to something, we were both caught up in something far more complicated and dangerous than could easily be ignored. But ultimately, ignoring would help neither her nor me. These emotions, these transferences and countertransferences of emotion had to be discussed and explored for her therapy. Hopefully, in an upcoming session, she would allow me to broach the topic. Hopefully, I would allow it.

I released the tight muffling of my eyes and turned my head toward the coffee table to see Kristin's beautiful pencil drawing. I picked it up with my right hand, then held it up above my head with my left, grasping from the top just as she had. I smiled at her smiling at me, but I knew she had to, just had to go away until the following week.

I pulled myself to the desk then she slid comfortably atop the framed photo of Courtland which was, itself, atop my wedding photo. I tried not to think about any of those as I addressed Kristin. "Until next week," I whispered.

Chapter 24

Courtland

Lying on the couch, just as she had, I found myself thinking not of her, and not of my wedding, but of Courtland. As vigorously as I tried, as steadily as I concentrated, he was near impossible to push away.

I had scattered doubts about if he was still there, possibly following me. Over these recent days during which he was gone yet still present, I would notice him and turn to get a better look but he would hide, out of sight yet still in mind. Strangers who resembled him in no way resembled him. Even familiar faces pulled my mind in his aesthetic direction. Even my reflection would summon his impression, an image of an illusion in my mind's mirage.

I saw him, I knew I saw him, but I knew with similar certainty that he was not there. It was difficult to reconcile the dichotomy, this unresolved cognitive dissonance. The feeling had been inside me from the hours following his parents' loss, my loss.

My phone, computer screen, clock, none were needed to tell the exact time, none were needed to inform me of which time slot was now vacant after years of occupancy. 3:10 p.m. Always, I called it a "time slot;" a degradingly simple set of words to describe the hour each week during which I had met with, worked with, laughed with, learned with, and cried with Courtland. Now I just cried for him.

I stood from the couch and walked to the door. It opened by the sheer force of hope; hope that he would be there, behind the door, standing, leaning against the opening, smiling; it was always a fake smile, utilizing only the bottom half of his face, hiding something else, something deep inside that he would never let free. Had he been standing there when the door became ajar, the time that passed between his death and the present would have been but a dream, a nightmare; something I could and would forget entirely.

But empty. No one stood there filling up the space filled with nothing. I closed the door, slammed it. Then opened it again and slammed it harder. I shouted a guttural deep roar out of the anger that overtook me. What was he thinking? Why would he do that to himself? To his family? To me.

I returned to the couch, throwing myself helplessly into its grasp, same as Kristin. I felt disrupted inside, as though things were not right. I wanted to cry, but I knew I had lost that ability, and yet I could feel tears ready to well up my eyes. I swallowed them back as I stared at the ceiling, going over the events of that day in my head. Unconsciously I began to rub my still sore shoulder, remembering. The uneasy feeling that something was very wrong when my e-mails and phone calls went unanswered. Going to his apartment the day after his missed appointment.

I arrived first, before his mother who had the extra key. I knocked for a duration, shouting through the door, then stopping for some time, and starting again and stopping until she finally arrived a half hour later. The key she had, the extra key, did not work, so I went to work on the door, my left shoulder to it two dozen times before it allowed us entry. Seeing him there lifeless. Giving my statement to the police. The viewing. The funeral. The sleepless nights that followed...

Ironically, as I laid there on the couch, I found myself asleep, dreaming of our last session which took place exactly one week—to the day, hour, minute, second—before.

The dream was surreal and was, as many dreams are, from the perspective of an onlooker incapable of making any kind of change or reaching out, incapable of telling him not to do it, unable to stop him.

It was experienced more as a bombardment of emotions than as a chronologically linear dream with a storyline that could be easily explained. Still, I must try.

—

(Dream)

It began with us both already there, in the office sitting where we sat; I, in the chair, and he, on the couch leaning back with his arms down; relaxed, but not fully comfortable, never fully comfortable. There was no entering, no knock at the door, no coming in. He was just there.

I must have been somewhat aware that I was dreaming because my mind questioned the absence of an entrance. Suddenly Courtland was entering, smile on his face that looked out of place, reminiscent of the smile stitched onto the face of the corpse at an open casket funeral or even the sly intriguing smirk on the Mona Lisa. She knew something I did not. He knew something I did not.

We were sitting again, immediately. The action of sitting never occurred, just the end result of being on the couch and the chair. He peered at me with his dark brown eyes, understated, but sharp and focused.

Courtland told me that someone made a joke about them. The joke was never repeated to me, but the punch line had something to do with the assertion that his eyes were as old as he was, twenty-seven. His humorless response was that his eyes were a satisfying blue when he was born, and then green for the first several years of life, but their pigment had darkened over the years.

I never questioned him. He had no reason to lie, to make up a story like that. I once described him in my notes as having an extremely introverted honest soul. When I looked back over that description after he was gone, I questioned what possessed me to describe him in that way. I remembered only that it was the raw truth and that it should be written. Nothing more.

His eyelashes were long, almost artificially long, almost comically long. He looked like he might fly away if he blinked too quickly; a joke he only smirked at when I posed it. He normally wore glasses to hide his attention grabbing lashes, but they rested in their case on his nightstand; contacts were taking their role, doing a better job of it. I was unsure how I knew the whereabouts of his usual eyewear, but the dream was unaffected by the inquiry.

His black short curly hair showed signs of a man much older than he; hairline swooping back on the top corners of his squared face forming the letter M when he bent to tie his left sneaker.

He only dressed in dark clothes, blacks and grays, never anything with a hint of color. When he stood in the doorway, with the white wall behind him and the dark carpet under his feet, he appeared as though he were on a black and white postcard, a postcard one would have sent years ago to inform their loved ones that something tragic had occurred. It would have been stamped with DECEASED in red block letters.

Speaking with him uncovered his dulled affect, dulling all the colors around him. Color was absent in his life and had been for years. His depression was constant, but not severe. He was capable of getting through his days and his life without being noticeably impeded by it, but he would never reach his full potential physically, emotionally, mentally, or by any other measure.

He moved slowly, spoke slowly; I would presume he was being cold to me had I not known him, had I never listened to his words. There was a suggestion of monotone that his voice failed to escape. He set no goals for himself in life because he would immediately dismiss them as fairy-tale wishes that would never come to fruition. He told me that, years before, in college, he majored in Psychology in hopes of one day becoming a psychologist, but he gave up on that path shortly thereafter; just another dream lost to depression.

Storyboards were his job. The preliminary physical sketch of an idea for an advertisement for clients of the advertising agency at which he worked were what Courtland created. He was more on the illustrating side than the creative side so he normally worked alone, no brainstorming with the group.

The complete absence of aspirations or dreams was something the two of us could relate on; he, because his depression did not allow him to dream, and I, because I had realized that my dreams were impossible to attain.

We both had given up on life and were floating through, going through the motions without much actual thought. Lather,

Rinse, Repeat… I saw far too much of myself in him and he did not see enough of himself in me. I wanted him to make the connection, to see that he would end up like me if he kept on his path, but the dots never came together. Or, maybe they did. Maybe that was why he gave up.

Dysthymic Disorder was the long-standing diagnosis, which he knew quite well. He had been slightly depressed for the entirety of his adult life. His parents assumed it was just a slump during high school. Even when it persisted throughout his college years, they insisted it was just homesickness, but their perception changed over time. Maybe they were ignoring an obvious problem or maybe they were just accepting the situation in their own way, but they settled on thinking of this, his situation, as what their son was; a depressed person without hope.

He was easily expendable within the advertising agency. If only one of his "creative" bosses took the time to learn how to express their "creativity" in the form of a storyboard, Courtland would be let go. And he would not fight it. He would not bother anyone or even ask any questions. He would merely put his few belonging in a small box and make his way to the subway and back to his cramped studio apartment. But, luckily for him, the inefficiency of the company and the absence of any kind of artistic talent in his bosses kept his job safe.

And despite his status as easily expendable, it was those with whom he worked who were concerned enough to suggest therapy. He seemed indifferent to the entire thing. He believed what his parents believed; that this was just the way he was, his destiny for the remainder of his time, never to change, never to get better. I disagreed with him energetically on his first day, but he was unfazed by my assertion that he could be a happier person, that his life could be a joyful one. I tried in several ways to help him show some emotion, good or bad, happy or sad, positive or negative, but to no avail. Finding real emotion was an unavoidable step of the therapeutic process but it never found its way into him.

"Do you think about death?" I asked him in the dream. It was the question that was required when treating a depressed patient. I had asked it years before, but it was the first interaction in the dream. It echoed over and over again fading quieter and quieter until it was inaudible.

"Well," he answered, "I know I'll die at some point in my life, I suppose." He paused for a moment and thought. "I'm supposed to be fully honest here with you, right? Say anything, no judgment?"

"Yes, of course," I responded.

"Well, I think about death. It's the end of things. I don't want to get there, but it's something that's on my mind sometimes, like when I'm not concentrating on what I'm doing. I mean, death is easy, peaceful. Life is the hard part."

It was the answer that I was looking for when taken in the simplest of terms, yes or no. "Yes" suggested that he was a safe patient; he was not planning on hurting himself or anyone else. It almost did not matter what his words were, as long as he admitted to thinking about it and he did.

"Everyone thinks about death sometimes," I said to him. "You don't need to be worried about that. It's just that no one really talks about it because they think everyone else will think they're suicidal or something."

I had followed the rules so closely that I missed what I should have seen. I had focused on this mistake, obsessed over it, agonized over it the moment I saw him in his apartment, facedown; I was so focused on the answer that I completely missed its meaning, his cry for help.

—

Just as an old bandage is torn from a partially healed wound, I was ripped viciously from my deep slumber, quickly and with a sharp moment of intense pain. My neck was sore and my eyes felt dry. The computer was chiming loudly, piercingly. I stood up to realize that the rest of my body was as sore as my neck. I rubbed my left shoulder and frowned.

Chapter 25

Melinda

After falling down into the large leather chair behind the desk, my eyes adjusted to see the screen on the right flashing "Melinda J." She was attempting to initiate our video session. The corner of the screen read 4:17 p.m. I quickly positioned myself then turned on the camera, checking my appearance before answering the video call.

"Melinda!" I exclaimed, powerfully hoarse voice cracking in the process.

"Good afternoon, Dr. Thesiger."

I cleared my throat then asked, "How are you doing? You look great!"

Her hair was down and straightened from its usual up and curly configuration and she was smiling. It also appeared that she was wearing lipstick and makeup; a rarity for her. The wall behind her had a light tan hue with diagonal wide lines of bright yellow. She had decorated her off-campus dorm room based on something she had seen on a television program; she had mentioned it weeks earlier.

"Thanks, Dr. Thesiger," she responded confidently. "You're not looking too bad yourself."

"Oh, this old thing," I said, pointing at my face with both pointer fingers. "I got it years ago."

She laughed at my immodest joke.

"So," I continued, "what have you been up to? How are things going?"

"Dr. Thesiger, not great."

"How do you mean?"

"You know I want to be a doctor..."

"Okay," I replied.

"And I completely feel like I've failed."

"Why do you feel that way?" I asked. "You're at a fantastic college and you're on your pre-med track. You volunteer in the hospital and you did that trip to a developing country to teach children English. I mean, sorry to trivialize all you've been doing by listing your accomplishments in five seconds without specifics; I'm just trying to convey that you've made all the right moves. I feel like you're well on your way."

"Well, yeah, all that, whatever. But, I got my grades for last semester..."

"Yes, go on."

"Well, I'm a little ashamed to tell you, but I got a B."

"And..." I said, elongating the word to encourage an explanation of the relevance of this reluctantly divulged information.

"That's it, Dr. Thesiger. I got a B in one of my pre-med classes. Now I'll never get into med school."

I sat still for a moment and blinked several times. "A *B*? A B is not a bad grade despite the fact that both are B-words," I quipped, then shook my head at myself for that terrible pun.

"No, Dr. Thesiger!" she exclaimed. "It is a bad grade! Everyone else who'll be applying to med school will have all A's. Now I'm not getting in." Melinda's voice sank and deteriorated into a sad mangling of sounds.

"So, now what?" I asked her. "You sound fully defeated, ready to give up."

"I guess I could be a dentist?" she offered.

Again, I sat still for a moment and blinked several times. "First of all, Melinda, dentist is an extremely respectable profession and, contrary to idiotic popular belief, dentists are not people who couldn't get into medical school. They are extremely intelligent well-trained people who made the decision to pursue dentistry on a professional level. Maybe they were interested in teeth or maybe they were enticed by the prospect of owning their own business and working for themselves, making their own schedules and being in control of their lives. Having the ability to have and spend time with their families once in a while..."

"Oh, sorry, Dr. Thesiger," Melinda responded. "Is your wife a dentist or something?"

"No!" I shouted, which I could see startled her; she jumped slightly in her chair. "Sorry," I said to her shocked expression. "I merely understand and can relate to the lack of respect that dentists receive and the unfair treatment they endure, especially when compared to medical doctors."

"Sorry, Dr. Thesiger," she said.

"Second," I continued numerically, "I was trying to find out if you are serious about giving up on your dream."

There was silence for a moment. "Do you want me to respond to that?" she asked.

"Of course," I said loudly, just below a shout.

"Well, I don't want to give up, but I don't know what to do now. I mean, I got a B. That's going to ruin me with applications and stuff. I'll have to explain it in interviews. I don't know what to say…"

As she spoke, I thought about what route I should take with her. I decided that being a bit harsh was what would suit her best. I chuckled to myself as she spoke and thought, *Some tough love is just what the doctor ordered.*

"You know why you failed, Melinda?" I did not give her a chance to respond to the rhetorical question. "You failed because you had the wrong dream. There is no sense in telling you what you should have done because that's all in the past. All you can do is move on from here and adjust your dream so you can succeed."

Caught off guard, she stammered, "H-how do you mean?"

"Your dream was to become a doctor, but now you've decided that you can't make it all the way, so you have to adjust your dream so you can actually attain it. You had the wrong dream, now you need the right one."

Melinda's face was becoming sadder and sadder, looking as though she was about to cry. She was not responding with the fight that I knew was in her, that I had seen so many times before. I knew that she just needed to realize how much she wanted it so she would chase it no matter where it led her.

A minute of silence later and with tears running down her face, she argued, "But I still want to be a doctor."

"No!" I shouted, again startling her. "That's the wrong dream! You need to find another dream!"

"But that's the dream I want. That's my dream. I want to be a doctor," she said, the tears multiplying.

I decided my harsh demeanor had served its purpose so I softened it to help guide her. "Melinda, it sounds like you really want to be a doctor and you're not willing to give it up. Am I right?"

"Yes," she said smiling through the tears making their way down her face, her left sleeve wiping them from her left cheek and then her right, smearing her makeup, before she pulled her face taut with a stern expression.

"Then you have to go after it and not let yourself believe silly things like one little B is going to keep you from your dream. You need to find a way to get there regardless of what is thrown in your path. You're stronger than that. You're stronger than anything."

She smiled again and laughed, still with tears running from her eyes, but they were immediately wiped away. "I do want this, more than anything," she said.

"Well then, you need to keep going after it. You'll make it, don't worry about that. Just be realistic about how powerful your setbacks actually are. You don't want to get yourself all worked up about one little grade in one little class."

"I guess you're right, Dr. Thesiger."

"Can I tell you a little story, Melinda?"

"Sure, Dr. Thesiger."

I adjusted in my large leather chair and searched my mind for the appropriate words. My head throbbed slightly from my abrupt awakening so I decided to let my mouth ramble while my brain relaxed.

"When I was a year younger than you are and I first arrived at college, one of the speakers at the convocation ceremony said to the freshmen class that '95 percent of us were in the top 5 percent of our classes in high school.' Then she paused before adding, 'Now 95 percent of you are not in the top 5 percent.'

"The two sentences were so simple, but they carried with them such a weight of failure for us all, or at least 95 percent of us. I looked at these brilliant people around me and thought, 'How many of them will really start to think of themselves as average for these four years of college?' Statistically they are, but they'll all ignore the realities and continue to believe the 'you're the bests' they've been hearing their entire lives.

"As the speakers came up, spoke, sat down, I continued thinking about those two sentences and their effect, or lack thereof, on the audience. Since the entire class was going to continue to believe that each one of them was better than the next, those who performed average or slightly below average were going to feel that they were huge failures because they wouldn't take into account that they are among the best and brightest in the world.

"I remember reading a study at some point that said the vast majority of Americans believe that they have above average intelligence. Very few believe themselves to have average or below average intelligence.

"Now, Melinda, I am not suggesting that you're average. Even at your school, you're smarter than most. But you're expecting far too much from yourself. Expect a lot, yes, but, if you fall short one time, in one class, don't suddenly give up on yourself. Just be sure to do better the next time. Acknowledge the misstep and learn from it. And don't ever forget that you are competing with a group of the smartest people your age in the world."

Melinda sat back after I ended my unedited stream of consciousness speech. She thought for a moment, nodding slightly during her short silence, before informing me, "Dr. Thesiger, you are a smart man."

"Smarter than you," I said joking, but not joking at all.

She laughed again at my immodesty.

"I've got to go, Dr. Thesiger. I just wanted a quick pick-me-up and you delivered as always."

"Yeah?" I questioned. "Well, I'm glad to help. It was nice talking to you. As you know, you can contact me anytime. E-mail me and I can fit you in for a session or just send me a video call invitation; I'll probably be around like I was today."

"Thanks, Dr. Thesiger. Oh, I almost forgot. I heard a joke the other day I thought you would enjoy."

"Let's hear it."

"Well, it's not really a joke, just a one-liner. 'Freud's theories were the greatest *phallusy* of their day.' "

I laughed aloud. "Good pun! I like it!" I exclaimed.

"I thought you would. Have a good day, Dr. Thesiger."

"Be well, Melinda."

And with that, the session was over. The video stream went black. I smiled at my small picture on the screen smiling back at me.

"Phallusy... Fallacy," I chuckled to myself.

———

The inbox had three unread messages. Having no desire whatsoever to read or respond, I leaned back in my large leather chair and spun myself around. The chair, well balanced on its slick ball bearings, completed three and one quarter rotations before slowing to a stop, facing me toward the closet door and the bathroom door but separated by what New York City studio dwellers call a "kitchenette": a small refrigerator, two cabinets, and a double-burner electric cooktop built into the counter.

I sped the pace of the continuation of rotation with my feet another two and one quarter turns to rest facing the trees and grass and ponds and lakes of Central Park. The sun was beaming in directly through the windows forcing me to squint to avoid ocular damage and additional aggravation of my persistent headache.

My strained eyes drifted ever so slowly from the upper end of the trees to the far lower end. The remainder of the day could have easily been spent in that position; calm, relaxed, serene; but my sight would have been lost before the sun disappeared from view. After another minute of squinting, my right hand came to rest snuggly against my brow, saluting the outdoors and blocking the sun from my eyes.

Following were several minutes lost in solitude, but the beautiful absence of thought was soon replaced with the agony of anxiety created by the unread messages in the inbox. Reluctantly I turned away from the outside world to face those who needed me.

Chapter 26

Winston

"Winston" the subject of the first message read, redundant given that his clearly displayed school e-mail address was his first name followed by his middle initial followed by his last name and ending in his projected year of graduation. He was a freshman in college, just starting his orientation week, and a relatively new patient, seeking counsel without discussing it with anyone.

Three weeks before, we had had our first scheduled session, a video session. His answers to my questions had appeared to be rather rehearsed; as though he had spent hours writing down everything I could possibly ask him then memorized an answer he appraised as appropriate. He denied my assumption, but I still doubted his authenticity.

I also noticed that he repetitively touched the corners of his desk when I asked a question for which he appeared ill-prepared. His answers for unexpected questions were brief and vague.

I sent him numerous assessment tests and questionnaires and requested that he complete as many as he comfortably could in the coming month. The next afternoon, every assessment test and questionnaire was completed and waiting in my inbox; an attachment to an e-mail marked "Tests." To have completed them all, he likely did them one after the other all night and through the morning. I did not need to score them to know that obsessive-compulsive disorder would be the diagnosis.

—

(E-Mail from Winston)

Dr. Thesiger,

What brings me to seek the aid of a psychologist, you asked, but I did not answer fully then so here I will.

As interesting as all the information taught during my classes is and the information I read in the textbooks is (and I'm not being sarcastic), the thing that resonated with me most of everything people said about college was that I was going to learn a great deal about myself as school progressed.

Well, school has taught me nothing about myself so sessions with you are my big chance to learn about myself or at least give what I already know a label. This is what brings me to you.

In high school, a teacher once said to a group of students that we were likely to have obsessive-compulsive personality disorder. He explained that, to be admitted to such a prestigious college-preparatory school, we had to be quite obsessed with perfection and probably spend an oddly large amount of time making sure things are perfect.

He was right, from what I could tell. We spent all our time on each assignment making sure it is A+ work.

That's what I have so far; obsessive-compulsive personality disorder. That's the diagnosis that I am giving myself. It might not be accurate, but it's my own educated assumption and my education is still at the preliminary stages.

Maybe more will unravel during our sessions together. Please let me know what you think and what you're thinking about me. I don't think I'm bonkers (to use a clinical term), but there is certainly more for me to learn about myself.

-Winston

—

I debated for a while about how I should respond to Winston's e-mail. I quickly decided blatant educational honestly was the best and quickest route.

—

(*E-Mail to Winston*)

Sir Winston!

From our first two video sessions and your five previous e-mails from the past three weeks of our time together, I feel as though I have gathered an above average amount of information about you and your personality.

I am impressed with your insight, but I must make some small suggestions. Allow me to preface them with the caveat that I rarely discuss specific diagnoses with patients, but I feel as though you are mature and intelligent enough to not get caught up in the specific definitions and the labels of my preliminary assumptions for diagnosis.

Also, another caution, try not to play into my preliminary assumptions. This is the main reason that diagnoses are rarely spoken of this early in sessions. Your subconscious desire to be consistent with the diagnosis may guide you toward behaving in a manner that you assume is what is expected from an individual worthy of the diagnosis. In addition, it is common for patients who know their diagnosis to fall back on it and use it as an excuse for specific behaviors or as a crutch through life.

First of all, someone with obsessive-compulsive personality disorder pays particular attention to detail and feels as though things, such as academic papers or memorized facts, should be done to their best possible extent. These are the people who study for three hours longer than the study group to make sure they know everything backward and forward.

By contrast, obsessive-compulsive disorder is a debilitating condition that is marked by intrusive, repetitive thoughts that lead an individual to perform compulsive behaviors that the individual feels he has to execute in a systematic way and according to a specific set of rules. Deviating from these rules results in the need to repeat the rituals over and over again. These rituals alleviate stress, but the rituals rarely decrease because the obsessions about intrusive thoughts continue.

An example would be if you kept checking the door of your dorm room every time you left to make sure it was locked. Even when you got to the end of the hall after checking twice you would have to walk back and check again. The same would be true for when you reached the street. You would have to go back and check again. Then again when you reached the classroom. Then again ten minutes through class. If you didn't go back and check, your anxiety would increase and you would attempt to decrease it by performing rituals such as touching everything blue in the classroom or maybe repetitively touching the corners of a table. These rituals would calm you down. Fighting the urge to perform these rituals would be nearly impossible.

Now, does this sound like you at all? Do you have any stories about your life that sound somewhat similar to this? How about those assessment tests that I sent you? It appears that you completed them fairly quickly. Most patients take days or weeks. You took hours. I might assume that you obsess over things that need to be done to the point where you can do nothing but get them done. That or perform some kinds of rituals to alleviate the anxiety of not doing what needs to be done.

Let me know what you think about my preliminary assumptions. And don't play into them!

—Dr. Thesiger

—

After a quick proofread and spellcheck, the message was sent. I pictured Winston in his dorm room receiving the e-mail and opening it immediately. The thought saddened me.

So that I would forget about Winston, I quickly moved on to the next message. I knew there was work to be done and I had no intention of losing my focus because of useless personal emotions. I did the opposite of what I encourage my patients to do; I completely and fully ignored my mood and made no attempt to think about it in any kind of relevant context.

Chapter 27

Arthur

"T-u-e-s-d-a-y" filled the subject line of the next e-mail.

"Correct," I said aloud, mostly to keep myself going.

Moving uncharacteristically slowly, the computer attempted to open the message. I took this stretched out time period to blow my nose with a tissue from the desk which found its way to the garbage.

"Attachment" read the line above the blank e-mail. The computer's video player took over the screen.

Arthur, a college senior at a university in Colorado and one of my more dramatic patients, was very proud of the fact that he was capable of sending video messages as opposed to standard e-mails. It was a form of messaging that I tolerated, but did not encourage because it was uselessly complicated and, most times, ended up with a patient sitting in front of the camera with nothing to say so they would just speak complete nonsense for the duration because they felt that they needed to fill each second with sound.

The awkward stream-of-consciousness regurgitation that ensued was merely a period of time during which they responded to and talked to themselves. Typing words as opposed to speaking them is slow enough to allow for some reflection and appropriate word choice and, shortly thereafter, editing.

Video sessions are far superior to all other methods, not counting in-office sessions. Making one's own video consists of blurting out random unstructured thoughts whereas video sessions adds the responses of the therapist to help put the untamed thought process into the appropriate context and aid the direction of the following sentences with questions and comments, encouraging the patient to think about what they are saying before they say it.

Arthur, however, was slightly different. He greatly enjoyed performing and watching himself perform. It appeared that he would write a message, memorize it, tape his performance of the message, watched his performance, critique it, then repeat the process again and again until he was pleased with the product. The resulting videos were always an obviously well-rehearsed show executed with perfect timing, pauses, and diction. He even varied the setting, ranging from a backdrop of the mountains to the bathroom to the classroom during class to the food hall to Arthur's own dorm room.

I looked at the timer on the bottom of the video box. The video was short, less than five minutes long. I pressed "play."

—

(Video from Arthur)

He appeared to be in a library. There were shelves with very large and very wide books and maps on the dark wood paneled wall. He sat at what appeared to be a wooden desk which supported a brass colored study lamp with a long green tinted glass top and his oddly large laptop. The camera was set high, two feet above Arthur's head level, so it had the appearance of the viewer standing, looking down at him. All of Arthur's words were spoken with drama, as though his audience had paid to see him perform his one-man show.

"It feels amazing to get things done or…" He paused and he looked off toward what I could only assume to be nothing, then continued. "…even really just to get things started."

He quickly turned his head and looked straight into the camera and bugged out his eyes, "Doc, one problem I have is I'm too ambitious, as you have so astutely pointed out."

As he spoke he used his hands to articulate emphasis, but in an oddly unnatural way, and his pronunciation of each syllable was overemphasized, like that of only the worst of stage actors.

"I sit down and I plan out absolutely everything I have to do on a sheet of paper and in no specific order."

He put his right hand on his chin and looked up, as if to be deep in thought for the three seconds he held this pose.

"It's a problem because I look at the list and I try doing things on it. Picking up a package from the mailroom and going to the financial office to straighten out financial aid are not big things. I can get them done without any problem, cross them off without pain. But, the problems lie within the bigger harder items. For example, studying for the GMAT or taking a practice test. Or even creating a video to send blissfully to my psychologist two thousand miles away in New York City!" He sang the last three words of the sentence in a Broadway kind of way.

I rolled my eyes.

"These are the kinds of things that are important and have a specific deadline so why do I put them off and put them off and put them off and put them off and put them off?" The volume of his voice decreased, simulating a kind of echo, but a terrible simulation.

I questioned his intention as he continued.

"During that time, the time that they are put off..." He paused before shouting and emphasizing the word "I." "*I* am putting them off, *I* grow sad and depressed; *I* get mad; mad at only myself, none other than *I*."

The back of his left hand was quickly and gently pressed to his forehead as he turned his head to the left and up, reminiscent of damsels in old westerns sighing or fainting.

"I'm in a constant state of kicking myself which leads me to being even more unproductive. Why does this happen? Oh why oh why oh why does this happen to me, Doctor?"

I rolled my eyes again, knowing the question asked over and over again was fully rhetorical.

"All that can be done is to just jump in, jump right in, and do those things. Sitting around and writing them down may be suggested as the first step, and it was, but all that does is waste time and make me think I'm doing something when I'm not, oh I'm not! Maybe some planning needs to be done. Oh yes, I can see that argument, but essentially this is wasted time, if you ask me."

"Well, I didn't ask you," I said, rather enjoying being able to respond aloud truthfully to a patient without the obvious harm that would normally cause.

"People need to just jump in and start on some level. The easiest level is to just start small. If you have to apply to business school, and I do according to my father, then, gosh darn it, go to the website and research what you need to do and then start filling out the application or writing down your accomplishments for your personal statement." He was shooting glances side to side and he spoke as though he had an audience sitting on either side of the camera, but not right in front of him where the only real audience actually was.

"I'm right here," I shouted.

He then began to speak faster and faster as his words added to each other and his breath came closer and closer to running out. "Another important thing is to pace one's self and take time to do these things. Start one day and then continue the next. If you're trying to do it all in one day, it'll be put off more because you just don't want to dedicate that much time to it. You'll also make excuses like you don't have the time or you had other things to do or your favorite show is on tonight so you can't do it at any point today because the whole process is too long."

When his voice no longer had the wind to continue, he breathed in a huge and intentionally loud and obtrusive breath before saying, in a quiet and slow moving voice, "Small steps, spread out, just jump in. It needs to be done and the feeling afterward is... absolutely amazing!" He sang the last two words, smiling wildly.

Arthur then pressed a button on the very large laptop to his left, prompting the camera to zoom out slightly. He stood up, head just in frame, and put his open right palm, fingers together, in front of his face, completely hiding his face from the camera. Slowly he moved his hand, palm to his face, down. The expression of angry bliss was effectively wiped away to expose a serious expression.

His head turned slightly upward as he slowly shut his eyes before he declared, in a directorial voice, "Scene." He then reached down and, with a tap on his laptop's keyboard, stopped the recording.

—

I sat in my large leather chair staring at the black empty video box questioning what I had just witnessed. Did he mistakenly send me his audition tape for a dramatic play or was he simply that eccentric? Why did he basically just repeat all of what I had said to him in the previous session? And how was I to respond to something that esoteric? I questioned if I should respond in a fashion that assumed there was no mix up or if I should question his outward ridiculousness. His videos had been getting odder and odder over the weeks, but this one was by far the oddest.

I decided that I would play both sides of the coin and keep my response as short and eloquent as possible.

I turned on my camera, checking my appearance on the screen before pressing "record."

—

(*Video to Arthur*)

"Thomas La Mance once said that life is what happens while you are making other plans. Be well, Arthur."

—

I then pressed end and sent my ten second video as an attachment in a response e-mail to Arthur.

In an attempt to continue my semi-productive momentum, I took no break or time to reflect, and instead scrolled down to the next e-mail.

Chapter 28

Suzanne

"Hello, Dr. Thesiger" read the subject line. The message was from Suzanne. She referred to herself as a native New Yorker to friends, but was always laughed at when she specified "Upstate." Nevertheless, she adjusted well to college in the city. She was squarely in the middle of her college experience; the summer between her sophomore and junior year; and was going through a kind of mid-college crisis.

She had decided to stay in the city through the summer, volunteering in one of her professors' research labs in her school's physics department. Our previous three sessions focused mostly on her dissatisfaction with her decision. She expected the summer to be filled with parties and friends, but most of them had gone home or abroad for the summer.

—

(E-Mail from Suzanne)

Hello, Dr. Thesiger,

I am so lonely right now. Staying here this summer was such a bad idea. It's not worth the resume building like we decided it would be. Before I wrote this email, I was fighting with myself trying to figure out if I was going to request an in-office session because I have gone such a long time without talking to anyone; that is, someone who didn't just hand me a cup of coffee and prompt me for payment for said coffee or someone who didn't just ask me to crunch some numbers or complete their data input in the lab.

I know what you're going to say: "You're always more than welcome to come in." Well, thanks, Dr. Thesiger, but I have no intention of a pity in-office session. Thanks, but no thanks.

Sorry, I don't really mean that. It's just hard here. It's wearing on me. I don't have anyone here right now; no friends, family, nothing. And they're all so close. Less than an hour and a half north. But, I never get to see them or really even talk to them.

You know how I spend my free time? Just sitting in my room, lonely, looking out onto the bricks making up the side of the adjacent building, probably less than ten feet from the bed, napping, maybe watching old episodes of old cartoons.

When I leave my little nest and look around, all I see is thousands of people, all with friends. Having fun, good times, not even knowing I exist, but why should they? I'm no one to them. We've never met. Nice to meet you, I'm Suzanne.

I never realized how much I dislike the city until just now. My exposure, other than this summer, has been through school. Now I'm here for something more and I'm receiving something less.

Everybody in this small four floor walk-up is friends too. That makes it even harder. Why did I decide to sublet a studio in the one building in New York City in which everyone knows each other and are friends?

And it's somebody's birthday so they're all having a party for him. They're all there on the third floor with their doors open, walking from room to room being loud and having a merry old time. From the lobby to the top floor, everyone is there enjoying themselves and I'm here just, well, not. Just me, alone here in my little space watching old cartoons and eating pretzel sticks, drinking from my juice box.

In your last e-mail, you said that you could relate to my depression because you were once a bit depressed because you were lonely in the city. Then you said you became less depressed because of your motivation or something. I didn't quite understand that. What is your motivation? What drives you?

Maybe knowledge of how you got through could help me...

-Suzanne M.

—

Without a moment of thought, I pressed the "reply" button to respond and complete my e-mail sessions for the day, eager to lie on the couch and lose myself.

—

(E-Mail to Suzanne)

Suzanne,

It's great to hear from you. You sound a bit sad and a smidge perturbed at the tenants in the building where you're staying, also at your school; really at the world in general. Things will get better. It's hard to survive without people to talk to. I understand that. I understand it too well.

It's hard to feel lonely. What makes people lonely? Some people are always lonely no matter how many friends and outlets they have. They just feel alone all the time because they feel like they don't have any real connection to anyone or anything.

When I was in college, an art major friend was drawing caricatures of all the guys I lived with, my roommates. When she came to me as a subject, she didn't know what characteristics of mine to emphasize. She told me that there was just nothing about me that stood out. Some of my friends had sports memorabilia. Some dressed in unique clothes. Some were active in their fraternities or were very religious. And so on.

I had nothing because I just wasn't distinct enough. I had no connection with anything. I had no outstanding interests that made me different, that made me unique.

"Maybe that's what makes me unique?" That's what I thought for a moment, but no. That was a pathetic conclusion to rest on. I spent quite a while thinking about this, my absence of an identifying trait. Maybe this was the reason I felt so lonely.

So I decided to try to find something that I loved and that I wanted to make my own. And, hey, if I couldn't find that one special unique thing, then that's my thing. The endless search. A new thing every week. The search. It's the means to the end. It's the path. It's how you attempt to reach your goal, not if you make it or not.

What you're doing now is basically what I was doing. You're on that path to find out what makes you you. You're going through life moving toward a goal. It's not always going to be easy. In fact, it's going to be very hard at some points. Now, this moment in time, is one of those low points. But, you can get through; just don't get too caught up in the fact that this is a down time. Things will pick back up when people start returning to the city when school starts up again. Stay focused on your goal and try your best to enjoy the path you take to get there while acknowledging the low moments as low moments that won't last for long. They'll pass.

And maybe talk to some people in your building? Maybe reconnect with some friends via the phone or e-mail, video calls? Anything to remind yourself that you have a support system. And I expect you in the office next week at the latest. E-mail me times when you're free and we'll work something out. The only excuse I'll take is that you're spending some time with a friend, old or new.

Be well, Suzanne.

—Dr. Thesiger

—

After a spellcheck and a quick skim, I questioned for a moment the merits of sending this particular fabrication. Why would I spend my college days searching for something about myself so some random person could draw a picture of me? And then be content with "the search"? How would someone draw a caricature of that?

———

I looked at the time on the computer, 5:27 p.m., and realized I only had time for a short nap before my next client would walk through the door. Disregarding my second thoughts, I sent the message and stood up quickly only to hunch over in agony.

I had not realized how long I had been sitting in that chair. The sun was almost down below the tops of the buildings across the park. My muscles were sore from the absence of movement and the prevalence of a post-sickness induced fatigue.

I hobbled over to the couch and collapsed, then pulled my legs up. My eyes stared at the ceiling as a feeling of satisfaction began spreading from my head down. They began to blink, right just before left, remaining closed for a duration lengthened in darkness from blink to blink.

I grabbed my head with both hands as my shoulders and stomach tightened painfully; the ringing was far louder in my head than what was coming from my cell phone. I had forgotten that it was programmed to vibrate only for the first few seconds of an incoming call before blaring out an audible ring if not answered. My much needed nap had ended and would never return.

Placing my right hand on the couch to stabilize myself, I rotated my legs off the couch and feet onto the ground before pulling my body up and hobbling toward the ringing.

Once I reached my gummed pants behind the desk, I slid the phone from its front pocket. "JULIE" flashed on the screen over and over and over. My head ached vigorously, undulating between an increasing intensity then decreasing then increasing then decreasing.

"Julie," I said in a raspy angry voice.

"Nick! I didn't think I'd get you." She sounded unnecessarily energetic.

"What?" I insisted.

"What's *your* problem?" she snapped back.

"I was napping."

"Is that what you do all day?"

"Yes," I said. "Why did you wake me?"

"I just wanted to remind you that we're having dinner with the Lowerys at eight tonight."

"I know!" I shouted angrily at the phone before pressing "end" and throwing it violently against the couch. The throw was controlled, taking care to direct the bounce onto a comfortable horizontal couch cushion; no floor involved. I was taking out my anger, but I was cognizant enough to protect my phone. Destroying it would only anger me further; something I knew because I had made that mistake several times before.

Dinner with the Lowerys had been blissfully out of my mind all day and would not have re-entered without Julie's incessant assistance. I wished she had not called; that she had trusted me to remember. I wished my phone had died or the ringer was on silent. The thought of dining with the Lowerys would ruin the rest of the day.

I found my way back to the large leather chair behind the desk and closed the e-mail program, inbox empty. The lesser used screen to the left reminded me at a glance that Harry would be showing up in only a few minutes.

I wanted nothing more than to relax, but my headache would not allow it, so I leaned back in my large leather chair, rotated to face the park, and stared at the dark treetops broken by glimmers of light from scattered streetlamps littering the edges of walkways below. For six minutes I stared forward through my slight reflection, through myself, and onto what was behind it, what was beyond: nothing.

Chapter 29

Harry

A loose palm knock, resembling soft banging more than knocking, turned me in its direction. The computer screen to my left informed me that Harry's appointment was not for another handful of minutes. 5:51 p.m. He was never early, usually late actually; always taking a different route to get to the office then doubling back for perceived safety reasons.

I quietly tiptoed to the door. First attempting to peer through the peephole to see nothing but darkness, then removing the black electrical tape to give it another try.

Harry stood hunched over slightly, leaning to the left on his wooden walking stick and rocking smoothly. I watched him for several seconds for no reason at all.

He wore brown corduroy pants and an olive colored shirt with thin brown vertical stripes tucked in and with the top two buttons unbuttoned to display the white T-shirt beneath. Atop that he wore a thin gray jacket against the summer heat.

His sneakers were worn, slightly more so than the previous week. My mind paid close attention to them every time it had a chance. After he had retired thirty years before, according to his stories, his only form of footwear had been those blue sneakers with faded off-white soles, holes many times repaired with patching material or duct tape.

His hair was thin and unkempt and, despite his name, there was not very much of it, occupying mostly the space directly above his ears and connecting on the bottom half of the back of his head. This irony always gave me a chuckle when it passed through my mind.

Harry's wristwatch, a relic from a different era, was a knockoff of a luxury brand. Its gaudy gold color commanded attention in the least flattering of ways. He was, despite the story his watch told, not a man of façades. I suspected he was misled by a salesman on a corner in Chinatown. Harry was honest and humble, polite and soft spoken. I always assumed that, had he any friends, they would describe him as "having a good soul."

"The things of dreams and the devils of deliciousness," he shouted through the door. "Do you digress or deliver to me the door through the door?" His voice sounded as it normally did; a bit scratchy with an arrhythmic broken uneven waver. It was this inconsistent timbre that always made me recall an experimental science course I audited during graduate school. The latest algorithmic technology for computers of the day allowed doctors to determine if an individual had or would develop Parkinson's disease based on the sound of their voice. Those who tested positive, they had the same timbre in their voices as Harry. I often dreaded the day when he would develop more noticeable symptoms and when he would receive the diagnosis.

I opened the door quickly. "No, no, come right in."

Harry walked in slowly and looked around the room; even walking into the bathroom and opening the closet door to inspect. This was his routine; check the room before sitting. Once he sat down on the large couch, his wooden walking stick leaned against the coffee table, I closed the door and made my way to the chair opposite.

"You're early," I told him before I looked down to his mismatched socks; one blue and one gray; exposed by his slightly lifted pants. "You're usually a couple minutes late."

"I am like the satiated bird, no?" he insisted.

I thought for a moment then agreed with a slight smile and nod. I assumed he was referring to the adage, "the early bird gets the worm."

"Nevermore!" he cackled in a witch-like voice.

We laughed aloud together at his joke, equating his satiated bird to the raven. It was much less amusing than we gave it credit for.

"Appearance of a sloth?" he asked.

"Oh yes. I was napping a bit earlier," I replied.

"You are a dead cat, no?" he asked.

I spent a bit of time thinking about what he was suggesting, then gave up and asked. "Harry, I don't know what you're trying to convey with this one…"

"You know," he said. "The cat who dies. He is dead."

I thought for a while in silence and came up with only "curiosity killed the cat," but, not satisfied, I continued to try to decipher his words.

He added, "Or maybe it obtained an appendage aiding in deglutition?"

I assumed he was asking if the "cat got my tongue" because of my silence, the absence of a response. "Just deciphering slower than usual, Harry," I explained. "I take it that they are here now?"

Harry's face remained without expression while he said in a monotone, "The undulating tides of the east crash violence onto the west, all the while aiding the tides to come in and out, in and out, in and out by the power of the moon."

"I see, I see," I responded assuming he meant that "they come and go."

Harry looked deep into my eyes and I into his. I saw that he was scared, but he hid it magnificently. Fifteen years of practice hiding the fear that drove his life made him appear calm. The only indication of his battle was his eyes, his fearful eyes. That and his odd speech pattern.

Fifteen years before, Harry and his lovely wife, whom I had never met, had been traveling from Manhattan to a small cottage they rented in Montauk at the far end of Long Island each summer. She initially insisted on driving because the deterioration of Harry's eyesight had accelerated after the age of seventy-five. By then they only drove once each year, to travel to the rented cottage for the week, second week in July. Living in the city rendered their car useless the remainder of the year.

Harry's bravado defeated his wife's better judgment and he took the wheel which ultimately led to her demise, upside down in a ditch on the side of a dark winding road only two miles away from their summer destination. Harry was physically fine, minor scratches and bruises, but he was emotionally broken.

The funeral was attended by only three people, the pastor from their church in the city and Harry. The third was sadly Harry's wife.

When explaining it to me, Harry said, "She was always late for things, everything. I would always be waiting for her, wondering where she was, only to have her burst in as though she had just run The Marathon. Have you ever noticed that people who are late are always happier than those who are on time? It wasn't until she was my late wife that she finally showed up on time for something…"

He told me, "At that moment, walking up to her in the casket, the first time she arrived somewhere first, I realized that it was the last time I would see her, but the first time I didn't have to wait to do so."

The funeral was held in the cemetery nearest to the cottage. Harry always said that for the entire year she looked forward to their week in Montauk. It was her favorite place in the world. Despite the fact that they had never discussed funeral arrangements, Harry knew that she would want to be there indefinitely.

Devastated, Harry made his way back to the city on the train. It was unclear to him what he was going to do with the remainder of his life. They had no children, had retired long before, and outlived all of their friends; she was truly all he had in life. Lost and confused, he sat in his apartment trying to determine what to do until they reunited.

Three weeks to the day, hour, minute, and second, Harry believed, after the accident, he began to see things he had never before noticed were there.

Harry claimed that it began in a nightmare. He believed that they were the spirits of the ancestors of his late wife; they appeared to share her features or resemble her aura somehow.

The "spirits," he called them, began to be with him always, standing, never sitting, and staring at him. After weeks of this, the tacit standing, staring spirits began to approach Harry then disappear before they reached him. Then, after weeks of this, they began to scream at him, not words but shrill screeching sounds that sent shivers down his spine.

Harry began to have trouble determining who was real and who was a spirit, but, after some time he learned to live with them, live with their presence, but he was in constant fear of the day when they would gain the ability to physically attack him or the ability to take over his body. He was resigned that it would happen, but not knowing when was what scared him.

Over the years, he discovered that the spirits only followed him if they knew where he was going. If he showed no direction or plans; verbally, written, or otherwise, the spirits then almost never found him.

Using backward metaphorical coded speech patterns to express himself was his way of communicating without the spirits understanding him. He had a knack for mixing metaphors and confusing real life listeners.

Whenever the spirits were present, he disguised his speech patterns in an attempt to confuse them. This convoluted form of communication emerged frequently in the presence of others and walking around the city spouting seemingly nonsensical phrases ended up getting him admitted to the psych ward at one of the city hospitals where he was diagnosed with Schizophrenia.

Harry refused the medication that was strongly suggested for his condition and this is what brought him into my office. He was against the idea of "being drugged up" and he knew in his mind that the spirits were real, but he was willing to try therapy and consider the possibility that these spirits following him around and harassing him were in fact hallucinations, a vivid figment of his imagination.

I had no reason to doubt him other than the fact that his situation was in stark contrast to the scientific belief that spirits do not exist, but that is not really a proven theory, just a hypothesis. This *theory* is, as many other *theories* in science are, only capable of truly being disproved by the presence of a spirit. But, the absence of an observable spirit does not prove their nonexistence so the hypothesis of spirits existing is just as valid a hypothesis of spirits not existing.

I considered for a moment, as I stared into Harry's eyes, so we might communicate silently in the presence of the menacing spirits, that maybe Harry was making it all up. Maybe the old man was just so lonely that this was the only way he felt he could have a conversation with someone on a regular basis.

It was a fleeting thought that I realized was fully irrelevant. He and I both benefited from our sessions; he, with a vocal companion, and I, with challenging verbal puzzles and monetary compensation for the successful completion of those puzzles.

Harry broke the silence. "The emperor has no clothes?" he asked.

I assumed he was referring to my inquiry as to whether or not the spirits were with us. Inquiring if the spirits were there was akin to being uninformed about Harry's situation; and I, as his psychologist, should obviously be well informed.

"True. A silly question to ask," I said. "When will it be just us?"

"We are, for the moment, without the company of the commander in chief," Harry replied.

There's no precedent, I thought. Then 'an unprecedented question,' replaced it in my mind. I settled on the assumption that he did not know the answer.

"Is there anything I can do to help?" I asked.

"Your bottom," he said with a sad look on his face. "There must be pain, pain, pain from my direction."

I interpreted his words to be an apology for his inability to communicate properly, referring to what he believed my perception of him to be: a pain in the butt.

"No, no," I said. "We can wait it out."

"The bottom of the rat," he responded quickly.

Sometimes I wished I possessed the Rosetta Stone so I could understand everything he said rather than attempting to put words in his mouth.

"They're gone, friend," he said with a smile on his face.

"Fine," I said happily with a nod. "And how are you doing today, Harry? How was your week? And the young lady you have been spending time with?"

"Oh, Nicholas," he began. "Things have been going so well with Sienna! We've seen each other twice already this week. I think things are moving in a good direction."

"So what are you looking for with this girl? She is how many years your junior?"

"Sixty-five years!" he exclaimed. "But, I only desire a companion for daytime chatter and company at the museum and in the park. We saw a show just yesterday!" He seemed extremely happy that he had found a companion.

"So what do you and Sienna talk about? What does she do?" I asked.

"I do most of the talking actually. She listens a lot. She's very good at that. I've been wondering though, what she sees in an old man like myself."

"You're old?" I asked with dramatic surprise. "I wouldn't have assumed you to be a day over thirty-five!"

"Oh, Nicholas!" he said with a big smile. He laughed for a moment before continuing. "At nearly a century old, I've seen a lot and I know people and I couldn't for the life of me understand why this beautiful girl was spending so much of her time with an old guy like myself."

"Maybe she is into older men?" I offered.

Harry laughed again. "Possibly," he said. "Possibly, but I believe it to be something altogether more sinister. I think she may be after my money."

"You have a lot of money?" I asked without thinking. Then I quickly added, "I mean, how would she know anything about your monetary situation?"

"Oh, Nicholas, Nicholas, Nicholas. So young and naïve." He laughed at the prospect of paying each week to see a naïve psychologist. "You see, I have no more money than enough to survive and maybe donate a bit to charity posthumously."

Harry froze suddenly, his eyes widened quickly.

"Harry?" I asked. "Everything okay?"

"Rain," he stammered quietly. "Rain... sunny day... mattress... clock..." He looked down at his golden watch then back up into my eyes.

I thought about our conversation and where it was going and tried to put the few words he was stammering into some kind of context. *Saving for a rainy day,* I thought, but did not say aloud.

We sat staring at one another for a moment, then Harry's face relaxed and his smile returned.

"Nicholas, she probably assumes that I'm a rich older man because I live in the city and I'm old."

I thought for a moment. "True. The only older people who can afford to live in the city are very wealthy. Generally retired older people move to a warmer climate and to an area with a lower cost of living, not to one of the most expensive cities in the world."

"Precisely," he responded.

"Why is it that you choose to stay in the city? I'm just curious."

"Oh, Nicholas... Look at me! I stay here because if I were anywhere else in the world, my mind would have gone to mush by now. Here I can take care of myself; live alone in my rent-stabilized apartment, run my errands, go to restaurants, there are laundry services, everything within walking distance. Anywhere else, I would need a car, but someone my age; no one would let me drive. Here, I can keep my mind sharp." He pointed at his right temple. "Anywhere else, I would be in an 'assisted living home,' that's what they call them. I would be mush if I were anywhere else."

"Good point," I responded.

"So, about Sienna, we're in agreement? She is just spending time with me for the prospect of being penciled into the old will."

I thought for a few seconds before responding. "I can't make any presumptions about her, but it's hard to suggest you have no reason to be concerned, Harry. Certainly don't discount the fact that you are an enjoyable guy to spend time with, but, tell me, why spend time with her if you think her intentions are less than honorable?"

He sat back and thought for a moment, arms crossed, then leaned forward and said, "There's just something... something about getting old and being alone..."

"I can understand that," I told him. "But have you ever thought about it this way? They never seem to bother you when she is around..." For many weeks I had pondered when it would be the right time to bring this up with Harry. I was curious to see his reaction or lack thereof.

"I had a dream last night, Nicholas. It had my father in it. I haven't dreamt about him in some forty years. He died at sixty-seven. That's twenty-seven years younger than I am right now."

"Is that so?" I said somewhat reluctantly, unhappy that I was going to allow the subject to fall away, hopefully to reemerge at a later date.

"It's funny because that's exactly how I remember him. I remember him as a man in his sixties because that's what he was when I saw him last. And, in the dream, I was older than he was, quite a bit older. I was older than my father. You never think something like that is going to happen. Never could imagine that I would ever have an experience like that." He leaned back on the couch and looked away, thinking.

"How did that dream make you feel?" I asked.

"Felt strange, you know? Made me think about death; how long I still have left. The dream continues, that's not all."

"Oh, please continue," I insisted.

"In the dream I was sleeping and I was aware of it. Then I woke up, but I didn't actually wake up; I was still in the dream. I could see around me. I saw the ceiling and the room I was in. It was just me in the room thankfully so I was calm, but I couldn't move. Then the paramedics burst into the room pushing a stretcher and an oxygen tank; one of those big metal tanks with the plastic mask that covers your mouth and nose. They had one of those old defibrillator machines too.

"They examined my seemingly lifeless body and tried to resuscitate me, but failed. And all the while, I was there, conscious of what was happening, feeling everything. Then they put me on the stretcher and put a white sheet over me and tucked it under my sides before strapping my body down.

"But even though the sheet was over me, tucked in and such, I could still see. I saw straight up. My neck and head couldn't move. My whole body couldn't move. I was paralyzed. I was dead. Couldn't even move my eyes. I watched the ceiling of the apartment, then the ceiling of the hall and the elevator, then the sky. There were some trees. It was overcast, a little cloudy, those thin clouds. What do they call them? Cirrus? After that, I saw the inside of the ambulance, the ceiling only, of course. Then suddenly, it was all dark. I was in a casket, underground. Dead."

Harry stopped talking.

"Harry?" I asked assuming the spirits were the source of his silence.

"That was it," he responded. "It was over. That's when I actually woke up. It bothered me, the dream. It all seemed so real."

"Well," I began, "maybe I can help you see how unrealistic it all was. It might help you."

"Please, Nicholas!" he responded, gesturing with his flat hand for me to continue.

"Well, let's assume that they are investigating your disappearance, because that would be the only reason anyone would go into your apartment like that, and, if so, the police, not the paramedics, would probably be the first ones there.

"And, even if the paramedics were the first on the scene to investigate your disappearance, it is very unlikely that they would be pushing a stretcher with an oxygen tank and defibrillator. The proper protocol is to enter, assess the situation, then retrieve what is needed. And, once the paramedics are aware of a dead body, they are not hurrying. The person is already dead."

Harry laughed aloud. "That is true, very true."

I continued. "That's why you usually see paramedics with stretchers walking into 'assisted living homes,' as you put it, at a somewhat cavalier and lackadaisical pace. They assume the person is dead. What is the probability that they would be alive? If they're pushing the stretcher into the assisted living home, chances are they'll be moving slowly because they'll be leaving with an already lifeless body strapped on there. It just makes sense. What's the hurry?"

Harry continued to laugh through my material and for a while thereafter. I chuckled along with him. Then I encouraged him to talk about Sienna again. I wanted to discuss her in more depth in relation to the spirits never bothering Harry when he was around her.

"Tell me a little more about Sienna."

"She has a son," he told me.

"I don't recall you mentioning that. How old?" I asked.

"In third or fourth grade. I can't remember. He's a very shy one. Hard to get him to talk. She told me his teachers told her he

277

hides his lunch during lunchtime. I told her I would ask you about that. Does that suggest some kind of psychological problem?"

"Well, probably not. But, I can't really say for sure unless I had him in sessions, spoke with the child. It could really be a number of things or it could be nothing."

"Oh, of course. I thought I would just ask. See what you said."

After a moment of thought, I said, "Well, if you want to scare her, you could tell her that he is probably embarrassed by what she packs for him so he hides it. He'll probably grow up to have some kind of serious eating disorder."

"Oh, that doesn't sound good!"

"True. You probably shouldn't say all that to her."

"Good idea," he agreed. "I just wish I could talk to him somehow; maybe help him out with whatever he might be going through."

"Maybe do something with him. Take him to a movie or something. Bond with him."

"Bond?" he inquired. Then he confirmed, "James Bond."

Caught off guard, I laughed aloud. "That was funny," I said. "That was funny."

Then Harry again got silent. He smiled, but it was clearly not genuine. He stood up and hobbled toward the far wall with the kitchenette and stared at the bathroom door.

"Do you need to use the restroom, Harry?" I asked, but no response.

He picked up two mugs that were next to the never-used coffeemaker and made his way slowly over to my large mahogany desk. He placed the mugs atop, closest to the window and said, "One in the wine is worth two in the bush."

I thought for a moment, then decided that his sentence was too hard to understand. "I'm sorry, Harry, I don't follow."

He then put his hand at the level of his head and said, "Don't make me ball this." Clinching his fist, he knocked on the desk three times while saying, "Touch wood."

I assumed this to mean, "knock on wood," but I could not determine how it was relevant or in what context it would be.

Then, with a somewhat demonic look on his face, he moved toward me, stopped, looked me straight in the face, and said, "I'm killing these birds one stone at a time."

"Harry. I am having trouble following."

He looked around the room frantically, spinning and tripping as though he was being knocked around. "Endoderm, mesoderm, ectoderm, endoderm, mesoderm, ectoderm, endoderm, mesoderm…" He continued to repeat the labels for the three layers of skin as he slowly moved toward the door.

I picked up his wooden walking stick from the coffee table and handed it to him as he opened the door. With his hand clenching the nob tightly, he slid through then filled the passageway with the door.

I stood for several seconds trying to determine what had just transpired. Unsuccessful, I sat back down in the chair and went over everything that was said prior to Harry's strange exit. I determined that the repetition of the words referring to the three layers of skin was to inform me that he was "thick skinned."

I had significantly more trouble coming up with a hypothesis about the coffee mugs. After much thought, I could only assume that he may have been suggesting that, when fruit is on the vine, it ripens much quicker than when it is in a bush because, when fruit is in a bush, it is shaded from the sun. The other main factor in ripening fruit is the nutrient-giving connection of the vine. When the nutrient-giving mechanism is taken out of the equation, the fruit ripens about twice as fast as when connected to the plant. The Wine Master had talked about this, but I had not realized that I had been listening until this moment.

I presumed this was why Harry placed the two mugs on the desk. They would receive the most sun in that position and, if they were capable of doing so, would ripen twice as fast as they would if they were not in the sun and attached to a nutrient-giving vine.

After several minutes were spent trying to connect the mugs with fruit and vines and wine, the word he used, and bushes and shade and the sun, I gave up. I billed Harry on the computer then turned it off before straightening up the chairs and pillows. I then took the carafe from the coffee table and poured the filtered water out into the sink before refilling it with newly filtered water and placing it inside the refrigerator. I grabbed my gummed pants from behind the mahogany desk and swung them over my sore left shoulder before shutting off the light and locking the door behind me.

Chapter 30

En Route to the
Apartment

The elevator was lonely and dark. I informed the doorman of the blown light as I exited. He apologized profusely and assured me it would be taken care of immediately. I had no strong feelings about it one way or the other. As I turned to walk down Fifth Avenue, I questioned why I had informed him at all.

The night carried with it a humid breeze, neither refreshing nor welcome. Few people littered the sidewalks. Few cabs battered the roads. Each step separating me from the office, farther and farther, was an increasingly powerful detoxifying process allowing me to separate myself from my patients, further and further. As I turned from Fifth onto our street, my attention was drawn to the street lamps' circles of illumination on the ground as their edges faded into darkness.

A police car sped past, no flashing lights, as I made my way up the steps in front of our Brownstone. A loud buzzing filled the immediate vicinity when I pressed the button for our apartment. My intention was to have Julie come down so we could take a cab to dinner. The gum-tainted pants would be fine in the lobby until we returned. But Julie seemed to be stubbornly disregarding my attempts at efficiency. I considered the possibility that she was dressing or in the bathroom with the water running and thus unable to hear the buzzing, but I grew weary of the excuses.

My head began to hurt, maybe from the buzzing sound created by my repeated pressing, or maybe fasting through the day was catching up with me. Or possibly it was the lingering sickness by which I had previously been afflicted. But it was more likely that I was emotionally projecting forward in time to the inevitable disaster of a dinner that lay ahead. As little as I wanted to see the Lowerys, I wanted to eat. I needed to eat.

I waited for several minutes, taking a small break to alleviate the piercing pain, gummed pants between my clean ones and the damp dirty concrete. An elderly couple walked by holding hands, both wearing hats and thick coats as though the absence of the sun automatically sucked all the humidity and heat from the air. Their appearance made me uncomfortably warm.

After mentally labeling the wait as *many minutes of uselessness,* again the buzzing filled my head, but again to no avail. Annoyed I fumbled with my keys and unlocked the door, then made my way up the winding staircase, experiencing the uninviting yet uniquely distinct aromas of each separate floor on the way.

Rounding the corner to ours, I was struck with the brilliant idea of calling Julie's cell phone. I stood waiting in front of our apartment door as the phone rang in my ear.

"Nick!" she shouted into the phone. "Where have you been, I've been trying to reach you for an hour."

"I'm at the front door. Open it so I can come in."

"I'm at the restaurant with Isabella and Michael. I waited as long as I could. I didn't want to be late. I tried calling you fifty times."

My angry silence gained me the upper hand in the conversation.

Julie continued, "I left the address of the restaurant on the table with a note. I can send it to your phone, okay? You'll leave soon?"

"Julie, I don't want to go. I was only going because you wanted me to, 'needed me to,' if I recall. If you're already there, I won't bother."

"Come on, Nick, I'll see you in fifteen minutes, okay?"

"Julie, I am not coming!" I said angrily, hoping she would allow me to stay in and avoid uncomfortably interacting with her foolish friend and her friend's equally foolish husband.

"Hold on a second, dear," she said into the phone before I heard her say she would "be right back" to her company.

I assumed she was excusing herself to leave the table.

"Nick, I would *really* like you to be here tonight. It would mean a lot to me."

By that time, I had unlocked the door to the apartment.

"Aaahhhh," I groaned as I sat on the couch, throwing my gummed pants to the floor. "I'm really not interested in showing up, Julie. You shouldn't have left without me."

Her voice became stern and almost condescending. "You were late, Nick. I didn't want to be late for this. Can you please be here soon?"

I did not respond for several silent seconds as I pulled the phone from my face to check the time. 8:07 p.m. I questioned where I had lost an hour between Harry's session and the walk back to the Brownstone. I almost forgot that I was on the phone with Julie.

"Nick," Julie said, breaking the silence. "Please do this for me."

Her voice was breaking, tearing. I did not want to deal with it then or the inevitably lengthy duration she would hold it against me. And maybe I felt a touch guilty about walking out on her at the wine tasting.

"Fine," I told her reluctantly.

"Thank you! And put on the jacket that goes with your pants. I saw it in the bedroom this morning," were the last words I heard before she ended the call; no chance to inform her of the midday pants swap.

Getting up from the couch proved harder and more painful than I had anticipated. I changed into a charcoal suit, deciding strongly against a tie. The address to the restaurant was scribbled on a torn off piece of yellow paper on the small wooden table with a short paragraph explaining the situation. I ignored it having received Julie's "address message" on my phone.

I knew that Michael would drive his most expensive, most ostentatious automobile to the restaurant just so he could watch me ignore it jealously. My only defense was a good offense; the backdrop of my own ostentation; so I decided driving myself was a better choice than allowing a cab driver the great honor.

The garage in which our cars spent more than 99 percent of their time was only a few blocks from the apartment. I walked slowly, allowing as much time as possible for the dinner to progress before I arrived.

Two stories down, Julie's car and mine were parked adjacent to one another. Hers, a mint green, *environmentally friendly* hybrid electric, had the license plate SUPEREGO, referring to Freud's label of the part of personality that acts in a socially acceptable manner and that controls the sense of right, wrong, and guilt; encompassing morals. Julie chose the car while I chose the license plate. It was an inside joke as she had never been completely aware of its meaning.

My license plate read merely ID, referring to Freud's label of the part of personality that contains the basic primitive drives and that acts on the pleasure principal, seeking immediate gratification. Tastefully bright, yet subdued in deep dark metallic paint, emphasizing the curves and arches and edges and corners and bulges of the beautiful custom molded hand-built body. When I was a boy, I heard an older man, a wiser man, say that geniuses favored the color green. This fallacy had influenced many of my decisions ever since.

The windows, tinted dark for privacy, protection from the sun, and aesthetics, swooped around the upper half of the vehicle. The wheels, larger than many would consider necessary, had a simple elegance about them; five spokes of unreflective, lightweight yet extremely rigid, carbon-fiber polymer.

This car was perfection itself but Julie never forgave me for its purchase. She had a clear picture of what our life was to be: children, a home in the suburbs, grass and a driveway, a fence and mailbox, a garage and an attic. We had even saved enough for a down payment on the life she had planned, but I was scared, not ready for the commitment, not capable of the change.

While she searched for just the right home, I panicked and used the money for a down payment on this substitution for courage. She cried and screamed and told me to take it back. "You didn't even ask me. How could you spend all our money on a car when we were saving for a home?"

Julie moved out for a week before talking to me again, but by then it was too late. I was unable to take it back or even sell it for the exorbitant amount I had paid for it to be made, special order, custom. I was trapped within the terrible terms of the car loan for years and years to come.

So there it sat, in the garage, used on the few occasions that a car is needed in the city or the even fewer occasions when I needed to exit the city. Satisfying to gaze upon, but a constant reminder of my fear of moving forward and my impulsive method of compensating; there it sat. The license plate truly and clearly said it all. In this car, I felt as though I had arrived even before I had departed for my destination, but it was also what ended our new life together even before it had begun.

"Superfluous" was the word Julie often used when referring to it in anger. But, in a cowardly rebuttal, I would encourage her to surrender to Voltaire's words. "The superfluous, a very necessary thing." Yet this only made her hate me, it, and Voltaire.

As I approached, my thumb depressed a button on the key remote. The lights flashed and the driver's door opened upward, outward, then inward above the roof. I slid myself down into the perfectly sculpted dark seat, easing the impact by supporting my weight, left hand on the roof. I inspected the interior made up of only the highest grade hand-stitched leather, suede, carbon fiber, and aluminum. The door descended with a pneumatic thud at the slight movement of my left arm. My phone left my pocket to find its place in its custom setting in the dashboard. The magnificent engine came to life, revving above idle for a moment before coming to a rest at a low hum. Then we floated off, engine remaining near to resting speed.

I drove slowly through the city, deliberately and purposefully, avoiding potholes and pedestrians. The navigation system calculated the allegedly quickest route to reach my destination, taking me through the park then down Broadway which made absolutely no sense whatsoever. More scenic and more soothing, it was, thankfully, a more time consuming path.

As Broadway took me downtown, I thought about the idiocy of its existence; cutting through the grid diagonally, confusing all motorists and pedestrians, creating traffic and congestion and complicating light schedules. Why the city just did not turn all of Broadway into a park was beyond my comprehension. It would do nothing but good.

I circled the West Village, a somewhat unfamiliar neighborhood, searching for an appropriate parking garage with which to entrust my greatest of all prizes, my most valuable and cherished asset.

I hoped for one as close to the restaurant as possible, not because of my concern for walking at night through the neighborhood, but because I fully intended to leave slightly before the rest of the table and retrieve my vehicle so I could parade it in front of Michael to rub his face in my apparent success.

As I circled, feeling fatigued and famished, my mood found its way into my thought process. It became increasingly apparent that my reason for driving across town was rather pathetic. I had sank to a level so low that I would greatly inconvenience myself just so I could pathetically parade my car in front of my wife's successful friends to save face in some immeasurable way. The car was not even half paid for, not even a quarter paid for. I would likely go bankrupt before it was fully mine.

With my declining patient base, the rent for the apartment, the exorbitant rent for the office, and the loan payments, I could not figure out how Julie was balancing everything and still showing up in a new dress at gallery openings and the opera, but I tried to push the thought from my mind.

I considered turning around, returning the car to its comfortable parking space in the garage near the Brownstone, then taking a cab back to the restaurant. It would all take too long. I wanted to be late, but not that late. I was already too late.

My last resort was the one I feared the most, but somehow I ignored my prejudice as I pulled up slowly to the front of the restaurant sidewalk cordoned off with orange cones that bore the title of the feared ones. "Valet" they proclaimed; the word sending a tremor down my spine.

They, these children, take pride in destroying the pricey prices that people work their whole lives to attain. I opened the door to a boy who could not have had his license for longer than a month, if he even had a license, wearing a bright red vest and a huge smile.

"What is this thing?" he inquired in a squeaky prepubescent voice.

"A car," I said slowly, condescendingly. As I unplugged my phone from the dashboard, I realized talking down to the person to whom I was about to hand over my prized automobile was probably not the most well thought through of plans.

Quickly I reached into my pocket and took out some bills in hopes the grease would awaken the boy's conscience before he destroyed my car, transforming my rear tires into scattering rubber and smoke.

He looked down at his fist and smiled the money away as he handed me my valet ticket and slipped himself down into the seat. I walked quickly away so I would not witness his reckless manner of *parking* my car.

Chapter 31

Dinner with the Lowerys

Entering the restaurant was like entering any other upscale building in the city. Never did any part of me touch the door because the extremely tall man standing at the entrance was employed to open it for me. I thought about how many doors, other than my own, that I had touched in my life and how so few of those were during the second half.

For a Manhattan restaurant, the dimensions were on the larger side, and tables were spaced generously. Despite the distance from one to the next, it seemed vibrant, pulsating with the bounce of dozens of different conversations, but all probably quite similar.

Luckily though, the sounds were much more muted than I had anticipated.

Thank God I'm still sick, I thought, trapped inside my head by the stuffy hazy mellowing of my sense of hearing.

I walked past the beautiful auburn-headed long-legged hostess, catching a cloud of her fragrance; to me a muffled bouquet of assorted flowers; and allowed my eyes a walk around. I spotted them long before they found me. My pace slowed considerably on approach as I considered turning around.

I still have time; they haven't seen me yet, I thought.

There they sat, laughing and talking loudly. Joining a dinner conversation already in progress is difficult and painful; joining one with excruciating guests is exponentially more difficult and painful. I did not have the strength or, more importantly, the desire.

Michael Lowery was his name, a partner at one of the premier law firms in the city, which was to say, one of the premier firms in the world. Had he felt any motto prestigious enough to attach to himself, he would likely choose, "Can't win in life? Sue someone who can." Truthfully, I felt this way about most lawyers, but Michael Lowery typified my justification.

I was always envious of his name. Michael Lowery. Mike Lowery. Based on the way he encouraged people to pronounce it, it was spelled with no *o*, but two *a*'s three *u*'s and about six *w*'s. Michael Laauuuwwwwwwery. Mike Laauuuwwwwwwery. The way it flowed together, the way he said it, it was slow, smooth, almost sweet sounding.

When we first met, I had anticipated a quick conversation. Julie had dragged me to one of her gallery openings, so I planned to spend maybe ten minutes walking around, talking to no one, pretending to be the silent artistic type, averting my eyes whenever anyone made a passing attempt at connection. But Julie forced me to meet Michael, the husband of the gallery owner with whom Julie worked.

What should have been a two or three minute perfunctory introduction of obligatory flattery and excessive name-dropping turned into an hour and a half of Mike shouting about how much his wife's "little hobby" was costing him, but also how "it was okay" because he "brought in so much money otherwise."

She, a slender stoic looking little thing, had no concept of money. She had opened her gallery because one summer she "grew bored of East Hampton, the South of France, Newport..." She had continued listing the cliché locations of summer play for the wealthy, but, at the time, I had acquired the ability to effectively tune her out.

Julie, on strict orders from her controlling and disapproving parents and, despite our own unfortunate financial situation, was only granted permission to associate herself with society-level jobs such as head of an art gallery; "a position befitting her name." "It shows education, culture, class..." her father would suggest when describing her.

Her name, Julie's friend, Michael's wife, was equally as smooth sounding as her husband's pronunciation of his own but far more intellectually provocative; a treat to the mouth and mind. Isabella Rosenblum. When first her name grazed my ears, I was enchanted by its beauty yet perplexed by the secret of what made it so sweet. Isabella Rosenblum. Why so beautiful? Why so perfect? The obvious iambic pentameter did not fully satisfy my intrigue. Isabella Rosenblum. I once asked her if she had been named by Shakespeare; the significance of the inquiry was lost on her.

Isabella Rosenblum. Hundreds of times I wrote her name down during one particularly boring session, but I was unable to break the code. Isabella Rosenblum. Then, one night lying in bed, it struck me; I had discovered the hidden meaning that I was previously incapable of seeing, the message that was right there in front of me. "Is a bell a rose in bloom?" Finally, the secret revealed itself; I could sleep, stop obsessing. Isabella Rosenblum. She was, of course, unaware of the structural and semantic beauty of her own name, but, for some reason, that irony just felt right.

My pace slowed to a stop as I watched them laughing, talking. I would only disrupt the group dynamic if I joined. Why was Julie forcing my presence? She had a horrible time with me; our lunchtime rendezvous had been a disaster. And why them? I disdain them more than any other of her friends. Why was she doing this to me? Internally, I became violently angry at Julie. *She is doing this to me intentionally,* I thought. *She is trying to get back at me for something.*

Before I could leave in disgust, Michael noticed me standing there angry, bitter, resentful. He stood up and extended his right hand to shake mine on my inevitable arrival to the table.

"My friend!" he addressed me, despite the fact that he and I were not, in any definition of the word, friends.

"Ahh…" My eyes moved around wildly. "Yes, hello, Mike. I am glad to be here." I was lying.

Isabella stood up, hugged me extremely lightly, then kissed the air six inches from either side of my face, left before right. I stood stationary with a blank expression as she performed her pompous greeting ritual.

Michael pointed at me with both hands in the shape of firing guns, stupid grin on his face. "New York, New York, eh? A city so great they named it twice," he said, trying to be clever.

"Yes," I responded dryly. "Manhattan is the other name."

"Oh," Isabella said before pausing then letting out a controlled bout of laughter. Her face moved very little, less so than normal. I quickly realized that the excess of work she had her cosmetic surgeon perform on her face probably did not allow it to show any real emotion anymore.

I sat down in the empty seat between Isabella and a still seated and yet-to-make-eye contact-with-me Julie.

I then looked over at Isabella and gave her a big smile, egging her on to mirror me, attempt to do the same. She was, of course, incapable, but that did not stop her from struggling to flex her face, to my great entertainment.

Isabella was always changing her appearance with clothes or accessories and often with surgery. The only moments of pleasure I found when around her was the time spent attempting to determine what she had changed since our last encounter, much like a *Sesame Street* game. I laughed a bit to myself after singing the song in my head.

—

One of these things is not like the others,
One of these things just doesn't belong,
Can you tell which thing is not like the others
By the time I finish my song?
(Words and music by Joe Raposo and Jon Stone)

—

Michael's appearance never changed much, which was suspicious. His hairline was strong, he had no wrinkles on his face, and he appeared to be in fantastic shape. "Arch nemesis" would be a fair description if I were a superhero. I suspected that he and his wife did not share the same cosmetic surgeon. His practiced much more restraint.

After Julie first introduced him to me, she had asked my opinion. My response: confident far past arrogance, but just shy of narcissistic personality disorder. And their three children, obnoxious little brats, took after their father with his cunning calculating thought process and favored their mother with her flattened affect. I feared they would grow up to be serial killers.

"Nicholas," Julie said, finally addressing my presence. "While we were waiting for you, Isabella mentioned that she saw you in the park early last week pointing and laughing at a homeless man who had tripped and fallen."

I looked at Isabella and was unable to determine if she was smiling or frowning.

"Okay. That may have happened," I said, slight laugh in my voice as I mentally recalled the hilarious incident.

Julie, of course, then found it necessary to publically chastise me. "I can't have you walking around laughing at homeless people, Nick. It makes us look bad." She paused, then added, "And it's bad for the homeless people too."

Julie's anger toward me likely had little to do with the homeless problem in the city, but may have had something to do with my tardy arrival. My performance at the wine tasting earlier in the day may also have negatively affected her mood.

"I like the homeless as much as anyone," I responded, then added, "well, I like them as much as anyone *should*. And I was actually being nice to that guy. In fact, after his unfortunate fall, I tried cheering him up with a funny *knock knock* joke. He didn't seem to get it though."

Julie, always quick to know when I am making a bad joke or making fun of someone, shook her head in disgust. This only encouraged me further.

"And I saw him eating grapes later on. I said to him, 'Buddy, you need to *wait...*'"

The process of fermentation was apparently lost on not only the homeless man, but also my dining partners as evidenced by the awkward silence during which it became apparent that we were joined by dozens of other people in the restaurant. My attention went toward interpreting the scattered sounds and bits of conversation coming from the tables closest to ours. Julie held her wineglass to her lips and sipped slowly. Isabella and Michael did the same.

Julie interrupted my attempt at eavesdropping, breaking the silence. "I always walk by here but I've never actually been inside. Always thought about it."

"Really?" Isabella started. "We actually came here once, when we were still living in the city, but by accident. We had reservations at another place, just down the avenue, but they wouldn't seat us for an hour so we just came here. That was before it became the popular cliché it is now. I'm almost embarrassed to be seen here." She looked around the restaurant as though everyone in it was watching her, then sipped from her wineglass again. Julie and Michael did the same.

A waiter appeared at my side, mildly startling me. "Good evening, Sir. My name is Troy. I'll be your waiter tonight. May I pour you a glass?" He pointed to a bottle of wine in a freestanding elevated chrome wine-bottle-chilling container filled with ice sitting at the corner of the table between Michael and Julie.

"No, thank you," I said, putting my hand over the wineglass at my place setting. "I'm a recovering alcoholic. Sober for four years this Sunday. I'll be fine with the water."

Troy was awkwardly unsure how to react, stunned motionless until Michael laughed loudly. Isabella attempted to laugh while Julie stared at me angrily because I was clearly referencing the wine tasting earlier in the day about which she was undoubtedly still unhappy.

Troy allowed himself a small smile before waiting for Michael's laughter to die down. "The full party is here?" he then inquired quite declaratively. And he had good reason to declare his question given that all four chairs at our table were occupied. "May I take your orders please, ladies, gentlemen?"

Julie looked up at Troy. "Oh, he hasn't had a chance to look over the menu. Can you give us a couple more minutes?"

"No, no," I interrupted fearing mandatory additional time with the present company. "I can decide while everyone orders." I picked up the menu lying across my bread plate and browsed as rapidly as possible.

Julie ordered quickly. She knew exactly what she wanted and had obviously been waiting quite a while to order it; orders are always spoken faster when the orderer is hungry. Isabella then began to order before being interrupted by Michael.

"I'll have the Organic Black Angus Beef Tenderloin and she'll have the Lobster Tamarind Salad." Michael was ethnically Italian despite his last name, but one would never know unless they witnessed him order food. His voice shifted to a clearly fraudulent and badly executed Italian accent as he put the fingers of his left hand together at the tips and shook his loose fist.

I looked up from the menu to see the expression on Isabella's face, to see her reaction to being interrupted by her overbearing husband. I hoped for anger, but there was nothing. I had momentarily forgotten about her taut face. Disappointed about the absence of visible facial emotion, I buried my eyes in the menu again to locate an appetizing meal.

"And you, Sir?" Troy said, turning in my direction. I was clearly not ready to order having expected the ordering process to take much longer.

"Uhhh…" I verbally stalled. "I'll have the…" I spoke very slowly, my eyes racing through the menu. "Duck," I noticed aloud. "I'll have the duck."

"Which duck dish would you like, Sir? I believe there are three on tonight's menu."

For the first time in our conversation, I looked up at Troy. He was average height and college-aged with perfect fashionably styled dark brown hair and a broad muscular stance, oddly perfect skin and sharp hazel eyes, prominent eyelashes and perfect eyebrows. His chiseled features were astonishing and rather breathtaking. I lost myself in the discovery of the unexpectedly handsome young man.

"Uhhh…" I said again.

"Which one would you like, Nick?" Julie reminded me.

"Oh," I said. "Which one do you recommend?"

Troy smiled, displaying his perfect teeth, and said "The duck l'orange, Sir. Poached before being lightly sautéed in our special house orange sauce. It's the special sauce that gives us our panache, Sir."

I spent a moment silently questioning his use of the word "panache" before responding, "Yes, that sounds fine, thank you," as I handed him the menu.

Despite the absence of change in her facial expression, it seemed Isabella was, after all, uncomfortable that her husband had publicly demoted her from partner to peon.

"Michael knows me better than I know myself…" she said, pretending to support his machismo. "We do everything together."

"Oh?" I said. "It sounds as though your identity is very well tied to your husband. Do you do anything on your own? Do you have any life of your own, any identity, any self?"

"Nick!" Julie shouted, chastising my line of questioning as she punched my arm.

"I'm just kidding around, Julie! You know; psychologists ask silly questions. It's funny. She's knows I'm kidding. There's no problem here."

The rest of the table said nothing as the awkward tension built, between and within spouse couplings. This could only be alleviated by drinking from wineglasses, raised practically in sync.

"How are your children?" Julie asked in an attempt to change the subject.

They began to speak, Michael interrupting Isabella and finishing her thoughts and sentences, smothering her life. I shut out the sound of their voices and concentrated on being anywhere but in their company.

Unable to get off topic, my mind drifted to the appropriate name for their son instead of Michael Junior. Bastardo maybe? Bastardo Lowery. Bastardo Laauuuwwwwwery. Laauuuwwwwwery. Laauuuwwwwwery. I lost myself in their surname and how Michael's pronunciation of it rolled off the tongue. I may have said it aloud without thinking.

After talking endlessly about their children, Michael drifted into a lengthy non sequitur story about his day on the golf course. The game was apparently quite close. He blamed his loss on his partner's inability to get a good chip shot off, always pulling back and decelerating the swing before impact, resulting in an inaccurate short sloppy shot every time. And apparently, on every teeing box, his partner set up on his heels then swung on his toes, resulting in miss-hits. "A mockery" was what Michael suggested was made of the course.

Michael then went on to talk about his new set of clubs, describing them and their manufacturing process, in great depth. The materials he listed seemed only mildly plausible as existing in the world; I was sure he made some of them up on the spot. Fused fullerene titanium something and chemically milled hyperbolic ultra-thin something else. Aerodynamic double-tungsten something and high-strength maraging stainless steel something else. My total disinterest led me to drift away mentally.

"Don't you agree?" Michael asked, ripping me from a blank daydream.

"Pardon me?" I inquired, hoping he would repeat what I was clearly not paying attention to.

"Friends," Michael said. "They are the best people to compete with. Like I was saying, my buddy brought some random guy for our fourth and he ruined the game. There was no chemistry, just didn't work good together."

"Yes, friends do work *good* together," I said with a condescending tone, pointing out his incorrect choice of the word "good" over "well."

Apparently, he took offense to my tacit grammatical correction. "Right," he said slowly. "But, what would you really know about how people actually work together? You psychologists just ask your patients about their childhoods then charge them an arm and a leg to tell them they hate their fathers."

Julie pulled back in her chair in surprise that Michael had just attacked me and my profession. I could see her quietly praying that something would happen to prevent me from retaliating in an inappropriate manner.

I decided to stay silent after his rude outburst, which prompted him to continue after drinking from his wineglass. Isabella and Julie drank as well. "You don't know anything about people; dealing with them and their problems," Michael said. "Lawyers; we know how to fix problems. You psychologists just talk about feelings and emotions. We lawyers fix things in the real world, we don't play around in Emotionland."

Again he drank from his wineglass. I glanced at Julie to see a frightened look on her face, one that was begging me to *just let it go*. Then she drank from her glass. I looked to Isabella. Her expression had not changed all night. She drank from her glass as well.

To the surprise of everyone sitting at that table, I responded in a soft, almost apologetic voice. "I can assure you that there is a lot more to psychology than the common understanding of Freudian psychoanalysis." I could feel myself becoming increasingly angry inside. First at Michael for challenging me, then at Julie for forcing me to be there, then at Isabella for her expressionless face, then at myself for allowing Mike Lowery the upper hand.

"Oh, is that right?" Michael responded arrogantly. "Well then, Professor, why don't you tell us what makes psychology so superior to law?"

It seemed neither Julie nor Isabella was willing to step in and end this idiotic line of questioning.

"Well, Mike, psychology really isn't that different from law."

"Oh, I'd love to hear this," Michael said with a sarcastic tone.

"Sometimes, in session, the psychologist has to manipulate the patient into coming to the appropriate conclusion to fix their particular issue as opposed to allowing them to think in an unhealthy manner. I'm told that lawyers frequently have to massage information to make it fit with their argument."

"What are you getting at, Nick?" he asked tersely.

"Nothing at all," I said. "Just trying to explain that you and I, we're not so different." I realized shortly after comparing Michael and myself that a comparison is automatically a competition in the mind of a man such as he.

"You saying you could do my job? You wouldn't last a day in our firm. You couldn't manipulate your way out of a paper bag!" he exclaimed.

I did not have to think before responding, so I didn't. "I think that I could pretty much make anyone do pretty much anything at pretty much any time."

Knowing I was setting myself up for a competition, I shifted my weight in my seat so I could lean forward aggressively in an attempt to intimidate Michael away from pushing me any further.

But instead he merely attempted to shift my wrath onto an innocent bystander. "Okay," he said quickly. "You're on."

"What do you mean, 'I'm on'?" I asked.

"Let's take the waiter. Make him do something."

"Okay," I said. "What do you want him to do?"

"Humiliate himself," Michael responded quickly.

Julie finally gathered up enough courage to attempt to end our idiotic conversation and interjected, "Come on, you two, this is getting a bit out of hand, isn't it?"

I paused for a while, hoping that Michael would give in and retract his challenge or that Isabella would say something to calm her husband's competitive drive, but there was only the silence of Michael's stare, no blinking.

"How?" I asked confidently.

Julie tried once more to end the escalating conversation. "Come on, you two. Stop this."

"You see how he is so well made up?" Michael said. "Gelled hair and pressed little waiter outfit and I think he may even be wearing makeup!"

"Fascinating that you noticed so effortlessly, but continue," I said mockingly and unfortunately provoked him further.

He continued. "I happen to know that this restaurant requires their waiters to look impeccable; their appearance has to be flawless. Without touching him, I want you to make him change his appearance so that he no longer looks so presentable."

"That's dumb, Mike," I responded. "All I need to do is make him feel uncomfortable about his appearance and he'll change it. This is stupid."

"Fine then. Here's a rule: you can't directly mention his appearance to him," Michael responded quickly.

"How am I supposed to make him change it if I don't point it out?" I asked.

Michael then shot back, "Oh well, you're the great manipulating psychologist. You tell me, Big Shot."

I thought quickly of many different ways I could get myself out of this without actually backing down and appearing to be the weaker, the loser of us. I decided quickly to request a prize I believed he would never risk.

"If I succeed, you have to give me your new clubs." I was sure that with that I had ended the competition so I leaned back in my chair, savoring my victory without the need of battle.

"Done," he said without a thought. I felt as though I could have requested his wife and he would have agreed to it. I tried again to end it.

"Mike, I don't want to make this poor guy humiliate himself."

"Don't want to or can't?" he said aggressively.

Again I wracked my brain for a way out. I remembered from a friend's textbook I had skimmed at college one boring afternoon that Gandhi's Satyagraha Theory suggests something to the effect of, "The first thing you have to do in a conflict is give your opponent a face-saving way out."

"Your clubs must be worth more than this kid makes in a year. He's not worth it," I said.

"He," Michael replied, "has nothing to do with this bet. Your ability, or inability, is on trial here. Come on, Nick, let's see if you're as good as you think you are."

Julie again tried to end it, this time by encouraging just me to back down knowing that addressing Michael was a waste of time. "Forget about it, Nick. This is really silly."

"Calm down," Michael said to Julie. "This is just a little wager between two good friends. Nothing to be scared of here, right, Nick? Best to compete with friends?"

"Fine," I muttered quietly.

"Sorry, what did you say?" he asked obnoxiously.

"Fine," I said louder.

He then extended his right hand. "Okay then, it's cast in stone."

Begrudgingly, I shook his right hand with mine, ignoring the fact that items are *cast* in *concrete* and *etched* in *stone*, but not *cast* in *stone*.

Chapter 32

Troy

An awkward silence had fallen over the table for some time following the solidification of our wager. As always, Julie was the catalyst to a new conversation.

"So how is life outside of the city?" she asked.

"Yes!" Isabella exclaimed. "We're in a huge home now. Largest on the block in our gated community. We didn't want to raise the children in anything too small. Let us know when you two are ready to move out of the city. I'll give you the name of our Realtor. We got a terrible deal, but what do you expect? Right? They knew we have money so they took advantage. No matter though; we love the house."

"That sounds wonderful!" Julie exclaimed.

That doesn't sound wonderful at all, I thought, not bothering to feign interest.

"And the kids got a dog," Michael said. "They found this mangy mutt barking around their school so they brought the thing home. Isabella told them they could keep it."

Isabella continued. "You know animals are always able to draw themselves to the best room in the house. The most comfortable one with the best light, the best vibe. It's amazing. He spends all his time in the living room sleeping in the sun."

"Nice life," I said.

"Yeah," Michael agreed. "Freeloading mutt."

"When we first moved in, we had Ribbons, our cat," Isabella said.

"Oh yes!" Julie exclaimed, probably not remembering their ferocious little cat.

Isabella continued. "It was impossible to get the little guy ready for the move so we left him for last. We instructed the movers to take all the boxes and furniture and everything to the new house. Then the last trip was to pick up the cat and some things from the kitchen.

"Ribbons took one look at the cage and ran off into our sprawling empty apartment. You would think it would be easy to find him with nothing to hide behind, but we couldn't. He just didn't want to leave."

"What did you do?" I asked, actually a bit interested in where the story was going.

"Nothing," she said. "We couldn't do anything but leave some cat food and a dish of water. We went back every day, calling his name and shaking his toys, trying to lure him out of his secret hiding spot, but he just wouldn't budge."

"How did you know he was still there?" I asked.

Michael responded, "Because the little bastard was eating the food, drinking the water."

I laughed at Michael's disgust for the resourceful cat.

Isabella continued. "Finally we got a call from the new owners. Their painters had found a cat. We heard Ribbons meowing in the background."

"So you got him back?" I asked.

"Yes," she said.

"How is he doing now?" Julie asked.

"And how does he get along with the new dog?" I added.

"Just fine," Michael said. "The cat's dead."

"Oh, I'm so sorry," Julie responded, sounding genuinely sorry for their loss.

I laughed at the unexpected ending of their story, then Julie gave me an angry look. I then sat back in my chair and frowned as Julie, Michael, and Isabella drank generously from their wineglasses.

Emptying his glass first, Michael placed it down just before his female competitors finished their own, Julie second and Isabella third.

Michael said, "You get a lot of those schizos coming into your office? That's not safe, you know. It's dangerous. They'll kill you without a thought."

"No, no, you've got it all wrong. Schizophrenics are mostly not dangerous at all. The vast majority are completely harmless. In fact—" I was then interrupted by Michael.

"Immaterial," he practically shouted at me before proclaiming loudly, "I need more wine." It seemed the volume of his declaration was meant to attract the attention of our waiter so he would pour another glass for Michael from the wine bottle not two feet from his own shoulder.

"A psychologist listens and a lawyer interrupts," I mumbled quietly, luckily only Julie heard me.

Our aesthetically perfect waiter, Troy, materialized by Michael's side instantly. "I'm sorry, Sir," he said as he poured wine into Michael's glass. The last drops were wiped away and the bottle was turned sharply clockwise to avoid a spill. "Another bottle, Sir?"

"Yes," Michael answered without consulting the rest of the table.

Then, as if by magic, another waiter immediately placed an identical wine bottle in the chrome wine-bottle-chilling container filled with ice. "Is that all, Sirs, Ladies?"

The ladies and I nodded before Troy smiled, bowed.

"Garçon," Michael said. "Pop the bottle, let's check it out before we settle on it, eh?"

Troy removed the cork with the bottle opener that he had already pulled from his pocket. Another waiter brought over a clean glass for Michael's personal tasting. He swirled the wine in the glass for an inordinately lengthy duration before it founds its way into his mouth. He then swished it around for an equally lengthy duration before looking upward and thinking for a measure of time equivalent to the two previous steps combined.

"Fine," he declared quietly.

"It is acceptable?" Troy asked.

"Yes!" Michael shouted, not appreciating being asked to repeat himself.

"Oh, I am quite sorry, Sir. I've been having trouble with my ear. My apologies."

"You've been having trouble with your left ear?" I asked, sounding concerned.

The perfect looking waiter then broke protocol and openly discussed his hearing issue. "Yes. I woke up this morning and I was having trouble hearing out of it. We were at the beach last weekend, so I figure it's just water or something."

"Does it feel like pressure building up?" I asked.

"Yes," he responded, looking rather relieved to have found someone who may hold the cure.

"In the inner ear or does the whole ear feel pressure?"

"Inner ear, I suppose. Not the whole ear," he said, somewhat unsure.

"Does it hurt or is it just pressure?" I asked.

"Not that much pain really, but everything sounds muffled."

"Come here," I instructed with my words and my hands.

Troy approached then looked around to make sure no one was watching before following the direction of my encouraging hands and leaning down so I could examine his ear.

"Does this hurt?" I asked as I slowly twisted, prodded, and poked his ear.

"No. Not more than it normally would," he responded.

"It's probably pressure in the inner cochlea cavity caused by the change in barometric pressure triggered by this genus *Cirrocumulus stratiformis* and exacerbated by the altitude differential between here and sea level," I said, having no idea what I was talking about, but sounding confident enough.

"What can I do?" he asked intently, assuming that I was some kind of doctor or meteorologist or some mythical combination of the two.

"You should submerge your ear in water then yawn five or so times. It will stretch the cavity while putting it under the right amount of pressure to then release the excess pressure and build up."

"Really? Thank you very much, Sir."

As he turned to walk into the kitchen to try my outlandish advice, I said loudly, "Submerge both ears at the same time. It won't work unless you submerge both at the same time."

He waved and stuck up his right thumb to which I smiled and nodded. Julie and Isabella were happy to see that I was going out of my way to help the waiter instead of trying to make him humiliate himself, but Michael saw right through the advice.

"You tricky bastard," he said.

"I'm sure I don't know what it is that you are talking about, Mike," I said with a straight face, smile underneath.

Neither his wife nor mine thought twice about the advice and Michael had decided to allow my plan to unravel without trying to derail it, so we drank on and waited to see what would happen.

After smiling and nodding sinisterly for some seconds, Michael then started on a story of his experience skydiving the previous weekend. "It was amazing! I went with a couple of buddies from work. They were scared to death. The guy let us all jump at the same time because I told him we had done it before. Those guys were screaming on the way down how they hated me, how we were going to die, how they couldn't believe I talked them into it! They were cursing and screaming! It was great!"

As Michael told his story, I questioned if Isabella knew that he was lying or if she was as clueless as Julie clearly was. No skydiving association would blindly let a handful of people jump out of a plane without first checking their certification. And when someone jumps out of a plane, they can hear nothing except the deafening wind rushing by their body. Anyone who had actually jumped out of a plane would know that. Michael Lowery had never jumped from a plane. Lowery. Laauuuwwwwwwery.

I decided that pointing out his lie was not worth the inevitable argument.

Michael ended his story abruptly when Troy came by the table. "Thank you. My ear feels great now!" he said quietly. "Your food will be right out."

Poor Troy appeared to be melting, makeup running and his hair a complete mess. He had obviously followed my horrible advice, then attempted to towel off quickly, completely forgetting that he had been wearing black eyeliner. He looked like a hooker who had been crying black tears all night. Julie and Isabella caught on immediately.

"I can't believe he did it… and it worked," I said in astonishment.

"I can't believe you did that to him," Julie said.

"I can't believe he bought it," Michael said.

Isabella just stared blankly.

We all sat in silence, a bit stunned, until the food arrived, brought by two waiters, neither of whom was the puppet whose strings I had been pulling. They had no knowledge of which dinner belonged to which patron. This scared me.

"Where is our waiter?" I asked, concerned.

"My name is Marko. I will be your waiter for the rest of the evening."

Shocked, no one said a word. We all knew what had become of Troy. After Marko left, an unexpected guest visited our table.

"Hello, Ladies, Gentlemen. I am the owner of this restaurant. I just wanted to apologize for your previous waiter. I can assure you that he has been let go and will never work here or any other restaurant in the city again. There is no place for behavior like that and I apologize profusely for it. Your dinner tonight, it is on the house."

Michael immediately chimed in. "Well, it was disturbing, but we appreciate your apology."

Julie, Isabella, and I were too shocked to say anything.

After the owner nodded and left us, Michael exclaimed, "Free dinner! Nicely done, Nick! Nicely done!"

I looked down, a bit ashamed of what had just transpired. The plate in front of me held one square inch of thinly sliced duck surrounded by an amalgamation of garnish. I laughed at its pathetic appearance. Julie looked at me angrily, assuming that I was laughing at the firing of the waiter.

Making things worse, Michael laughed too, only louder and more obnoxiously.

"You'll all have to excuse me," Julie said. "I am going to powder my nose." She took her napkin off her lap and placed it onto the table next to her steaming plate.

"I'll join you," Isabella said.

"Women," Michael began. "They don't understand a good competition between men."

I agreed with a nod and a half smile before Michael went on to tell me about how he got drunk with his buddies at a bar on the Lower East Side after skydiving. I ignored it as I thought about the poor waiter who I had just gotten fired until my thoughts were interrupted by the wives' return.

"Oh, Daddy loves to sail!" Julie exclaimed, responding to whatever Michael was saying.

Julie continued as she seated herself. "He taught me to sail when I was a little girl."

"Oh, that's great!" Michael said enthusiastically. "What about you, Nick? You got your sea legs?"

"No, I like my feet planted on good old terra firma."

"Scared are ya?" he inquired.

"Yes," I said blankly, in an attempt to forcefully excuse myself from the conversation and any future competition he was concocting.

Julie elaborated. "Daddy tried to get Nick interested, but it just didn't stick."

Suddenly infuriated, I felt obligated to tell my side of the story. "I hated sailing with that controlling dictator. Julie dragged me onto his boat after he specifically told her that I was not welcome there. Then, on the boat, he was yelling orders at me; telling me to pull this rope and tie another to some obscure part of something else using some obscure kind of knot only a knot connoisseur would recognize, then push a sail one way, then another. And he couldn't just say the one to my left or my right or maybe aid me by pointing. Everything had to be conveyed in sailing code words.

"How was I supposed to understand what he was talking about? I expected a leisurely boat ride, maybe sit on the deck and relax in the sun, but no. It was running side to side, pulling ropes, praying they were the correct ones, and concentrating vigorously on not getting knocked overboard by the quickly moving sails.

"I find sailors to be anal obsessive-compulsive perfectionists which makes sense because you would have to be that way to have positioned all the ropes to display the taut sails precisely at the right time to catch the wind to push the vessel along at a painful sluggish, but proclaimed to be 'brisk,' 6 knots."

"That's what I thought," Michael responded after I ran out of breath. "You just couldn't handle it." He then laughed at his assessment.

I ignored him and turned my attention to my minimalist meal which looked about the right size for the amount of money we were going to pay for it.

"My spoon is too big," I said with a smile, but it went unacknowledged.

The conversation moved around unbeknownst to me. I tuned it out and concentrated instead on how magnificent my slumber would be in only an hour or two. I pictured myself lying comfortably in bed with a large smile on my face.

My dining experience consisted of little more than pushing aside the garnish, skewering the minuscule portion of duck with my fork, placing it in my mouth and, only ten chews later, fending off starvation with an effortless swallow. Afterward I placed my fork and knife together on the plate devoid of real food with the utensil handles facing my heart and rotated it ninety degrees counter-clockwise.

I tuned back in to the conversation to hear Isabella complain about her spontaneous bout of the hiccups. Again I offered fictitious medical advice. "If you pull on your tongue, and I mean pull on it hard, your hiccups will go away."

"Really?" she asked skeptically.

"Yes," Julie said. "I heard that before."

Baffled at where Julie could have heard such ridiculous advice, I nodded along.

Isabella then went to work tugging at her tongue with her right hand, white cloth napkin in between to maintain some semblance of decorum. As she continued to hiccup for several minutes while tugging, I recalled laughing inside at Julie after I had suggested the same thing to her two summers before. I smiled and again tuned out until the question of dessert was raised by our new waiter.

"Oh no, thank you. I'm stuffed," I said quickly, pointing at my plate. Then I looked to the other members of the party. "That is, of course, unless you all would be interested?" I turned to Julie and Isabella knowing that their femininity would never allow them to admit a desire for dessert after a male turned it down.

"No, no," they chorused.

"Just the check then," I said, trying to get us out of there but forgetting that the meal was to be "on the house."

"Your dining experience tonight is compliments of the owner, Sirs, Ladies." The new waiter smiled and bowed. "May I offer you some tea or coffee?"

"No, thank you," I answered quickly before anyone else had a chance. "We'll be on our way."

After the waiter backed away in a bowing stance, Julie asked, "Should we leave a tip?"

"Yeah," Michael replied. "Twenty percent of nothing!"

I laughed aloud and stuck out my right hand to shake his. I had to respect his humor. "I couldn't have expressed it better myself!"

I was first to rise from the table, followed by Michael, then the wives shortly thereafter. Behaving without class, I stretched and yawned dramatically.

"Getting old!" I announced.

"Yup," Michael agreed behaving in the same classless manner.

"You know what Orson Welles said?" I began.

"What?" Michael asked.

" 'Old age. It's the only disease that you don't look forward to being cured of.' "

Michael let out a roar of laughter as we walked toward the restaurant door. I moved slowly in an attempt to get the blood flowing in my legs before trying a normal pace. It did not take long for the achy bones, joints, and muscles to rush back all at once as my eyes began to water and my nose began to run.

Still sick, I thought.

I handed the yellow ticket to the valet and Michael did the same. One uniformed youth scurried around the corner while another sat idle, oblivious to the world with earphones plugging his head.

"You drivin' that sweet little sports car of yours, Nick?" Michael inquired.

"You know it, buddy," I said, knowing well that Michael was not my buddy, but, at the same time, acknowledging that I was warming up to him.

"What are you in these days? Has the burden of children made its way into the garage?" I asked.

"Only for the primary vehicles!" he exclaimed. "I have to keep a couple toys to play with."

It was the tone of his voice that suddenly made me fear what was about to turn the corner. I was paralyzed by the possibility that it would be better than mine, faster than mine, prettier than mine, more expensive than mine. If it turned more heads, my pride would be rubbed into the concrete. I looked at Julie, who was avoiding eye contact with me. I looked at Isabella, who was eloquently staring into nothingness as if pausing before her soliloquy in her own personal Shakespeare performance. Isabella Rosenblum.

"There she is," he said.

A large bright silver, pristine, stylistically boxy and large Sport Utility Vehicle lumbered its way inelegantly toward us before attempting a U-turn, failing, backing up, and completing the 180 by turning a U into a K; three points.

"The boys and I take her camping in the woods up north during the summer months," Michael said. "You wouldn't believe what she cost me."

Not at all interested because I knew it was but a fifth of what I paid for mine, I let out the breath I had been holding and smiled.

"I probably *wouldn't* believe you," I said, knowing he would fictitiously inflate the figure, rounding up liberally. "You could liberate a hippo from the zoo then drive it to its natural habitat with that thing…" I added.

"And that hippo would be comfortable too," he said, proudly smiling.

My car slithered its way in front of Michael, the driver side door rotating up then above. A small crowd gathered as the valet exited. I fought back a smile and pretended to be oblivious to the celebrity status to which I had suddenly been catapulted.

"Awesome car," the long haired valet exclaimed.

"Thank you, young man," I said, hoping he would leave me.

"Who makes it?" he asked.

My head was no longer facing in his direction, but there he stood in front of the driver side door. I knew what he wanted, but the smirk on his face suggested he was undeserving. I reluctantly pulled some dollar bills out of my pocket and handed them to him. Then I reached into the car and pressed the trunk release before turning back to smile expectantly at Michael.

"Oh," he said reluctantly. "Let me get those clubs for you."

"Nick," Julie said, "don't take his clubs. Mike, the whole thing was just a joke. Nick doesn't want your clubs."

"No, no," Michael said. "A bet is a bet. And I'm a man of my word. This is what real men do." He went to the back of his behemoth of an automobile, opened the trunk, and pulled out his pristine, prestigious, perfect, and extremely expensive set of clubs in his personalized designer golf bag.

He handed the strap of the bag to me. "Take good care of them, Nick. You've earned 'em."

For a moment, I almost felt bad taking the strap and all that was attached to it. I don't even like golf. I gently placed the bag into my trunk before closing it. The bag was engraved with MCL. Michael Caruso Lowery. Laauuuuwwwwwwery. Laauuuuwwwwwwery. I smiled at the silly sounding name.

Julie huffed loudly, slid into the car, and pulled the door down to a harmful slam.

"Pleasure doing business with you, Mike," I said as I stuck my left hand out to shake his.

He shook it firmly and patted my left shoulder with his right hand. I winced a bit, shoulder still just a touch sore.

"Good man," he said. "You'll have to give me a chance to win them back?"

"Anytime," I agreed as we parted ways, walking in opposite directions.

He then turned and said, "Your car, too small. No safety in there. Mine is big. I've got a lot around me. That's safe. I could drive into a brick wall and walk away fine."

"Why would you drive into a brick wall?" I asked, but he ignored the question.

I waved to Isabella, already in the passenger seat of their truck, before lowering myself down into my seat and pulling the door to a close. I expected Julie to chastise me before I even had the chance to accelerate, but she surprised me and remained silent.

I watched Michael drive forward then make a K-turn to face the opposite direction, as I placed my phone in its place in the dashboard. He opened his window and I opened mine.

"Those valet guys ruined my car," he said. "It can only make left turns now. You?"

"Same," I said smiling. "Remember, three lefts make a right!"

Michael laughed and pulled away, engine booming in a deep beastly broken burble. In the side view mirror, I was able to make out his license plate; BIGRTHNU.

"Bigger than you," I could not help but saying aloud. "Right…"

Chapter 33

Back to the Apartment

I accelerated to the end of the street and thought, *Three lefts make a right and apparently so do two wrongs,* before turning right to head uptown.

"Oh, another lie," Julie said. "Apparently you can make right turns."

"We were just kidding around," I said of the nonexistent damage to our cars, knowing Julie wanted to shout at me regarding something else entirely.

She said nothing for less than a minute; I watched my phone in the dashboard and it did not change from 10:12 p.m.

"I cannot believe you did that to that poor waiter."

"I didn't know he would actually stick his head in a bucket of water in the middle of his shift," I said defensively, ready for her attack. "That waiter should've had more sense than to listen to a stranger. He had no idea who I was. He assumed I was a doctor—I suppose because who else would give medical advice—but he didn't even ask."

Furious that I was placing blame on the waiter, Julie snapped back, "If he had asked, would you have told him you weren't?"

I thought for a moment, even though I knew the answer immediately. "I suppose I would have informed him that I *am* a doctor."

"You're not a doctor, Nick! Real doctors save lives. You destroy them. You happen to have a PhD. That's all." She stopped shouting for a moment, her frustration twisting her in her seat angrily. "He could have drowned by sticking his head in a bucket and yawning like that. You could have killed him. You could have killed that poor waiter."

"I wonder if our meal would have been free if he had drowned to death," I thought aloud.

"Why is everything a joke to you? Everything and everyone are just objects to manipulate for your own enjoyment." She was shouting again.

As I thought about an appropriate response, I began to consider the extreme degree to which Julie was reacting, or rather overreacting. Was it the wine tasting or my tardy arrival or Troy's premature dismissal from the restaurant, or Mike's golf clubs? Could she really be this angry at me about one or all of these or was she actually mad about something altogether different?

She knew well that I disdained the Lowerys yet still she planned this dinner then forced me to go. I was beginning to think that it may have been meant as punishment; she was attempting to hurt me for an unknown reason. Her attempts at manipulating the situation and me, however, failed because, despite the inane company, dinner turned out to be a bit of a triumph for me.

Julie was not angry with me; she was angry at herself for her failure to win, to beat me. This realization first made me smile, and then I was overcome with disgust at her failed attempt to manipulate and mistreat me. My jovial yet unapologetic mood began to degrade toward hostile as I suddenly understood we were at war. Had been for years.

"Julie, if he was dumb enough to die in a bucket of water, he really shouldn't be passing on his genes. It's called natural selection; survival of the fittest…"

"Why did you even do it?" she asked.

"Julie, I had to show him I was superior…"

"Superior?" she interrupted. "You aren't superior to him or me or anyone! You were lucky that our waiter was gullible and desperate to fix his ear."

" 'I know he's a brilliant general, but is he lucky?' " I said, my tone moving swiftly toward condescending.

"Excuse me?"

"Do you know what Napoleon always wanted to know about generals that were suggested as formidable leaders for his armies?" I asked her.

"No, Nick. What?" she asked in a disgusted voice, knowing that I was about to lecture her about Napoleon Bonaparte.

"He would ask if they were lucky. If we can learn anything from Napoleon, it is that one's luck is the characteristic that, in the end, matters more than any other."

Deep inside I was ashamed of the arrogance that I felt forced to exude, but I had no choice in the matter. I felt threatened and attacked by the true reasoning behind the planned ambush of this dinner and I had to retaliate appropriately.

Not a word was uttered on the rest of the ride through the streets of the city, in the parking garage, on the walk to the Brownstone, up the stairs, and into the apartment. For those dozens of minutes, I felt victorious.

With a mixture of confidence and fatigue from the day, I closed the door and turned the locks before unbuttoning several buttons of my collared shirt, and taking off my jacket. I placed the golf bag by the small wooden kitchen table while Julie went straight into the bedroom.

As I readied myself for bed, my stomach began to feel as though it was imploding, pulling along with it all the surrounding muscle and soft tissue. I decided that I would eat a large breakfast in the morning, but I knew my morning mind would disregard those plans in favor of additional sleep. Always I craved more sleep.

Even before opening the bedroom door, I knew she would be under the sheets pretending to sleep. She would always do that when she was not speaking to me; get into bed before I did then cover herself completely, not even her forehead was visible.

How can she breathe? I wondered as always.

Without a word, I walked around the bed and slipped in on the other side.

Then, from beneath the sheets, I heard her say, "You know, Nick, I look up to you because you let me down."

"Eloquently dramatic" were the words that came to my mind first, but I buried them away, deciding that this was merely her attempt to capture a bit of my triumph, to stand closer to the winner's circle by pulling me down, manipulating me into sinking closer to her level.

After my silent response, she said, "The best thing to do with mistakes is to not make them."

This time I had to comment. "Are you reading from a self-help book of marital clichés under there?"

She ignored my question then told me, "I have been praying every night for a long time now."

Feeling as though all I could do next was to ask the obvious question, I decided to play along and asked it. "What do you pray for?"

"I ask for strength and courage; what I actually get is hardship and problems, but, by getting through it, I gain resilience."

Unsure how one should respond to something so contrived, I told her, "Praying and being overly dramatic won't get you anywhere. You might as well just lie there in your emotional vomit until you pass out."

Although I had expected to feel satisfied with my clever retort, surprisingly, instead I immediately felt sick to my stomach after this particular attack. She didn't deserve this, what was I doing? I needed to stop myself before my abhorrent behavior crossed the line into unforgivable.

Those words I spoke, I felt that they had come from a place of which I was unaware, some hidden and malicious part of me. The only way I could fight it was to separate myself from the situation. Abruptly, I got up, jumped up out of the bed and left the bedroom, practically running. I threw the door shut behind me and winced when it banged shut. My intention was never to shut it in such a manner. It had just happened; had I done it on purpose? I was losing control.

I moved in the dark toward the other room, bumping into the hallway wall during the short trip. Everything was coming back to me, filling my head, all of the anger and frustration and sadness and despair. It seemed that all I was successful at was failing. I truly wanted to change, to make things better, to improve our marriage, our lives, but something always got in the way and this time it was Julie herself. Why was she trying to hurt me?

Retaining only a minute quantity of self-control, I sat on one of the small wooden chairs by the half table against the brick wall and bent down, head in hands and elbows on knees. I kicked over the golf clubs and roared out in pain and frustration. Then I silently blamed everyone and everything in a continuous fury of mental hatred; but it was myself whom I blamed the most.

When did I fix this? I suddenly thought in a burst of emotional focusing, directing it all at the chair upon which I was mentally melting down. *You never fixed it, but it's fixed,* a little voice inside me whispered. And the thoughts kept coming, clearer and clearer. I quickly became convinced that they were not coming from me, not coming from within, but that these actions and thoughts and ideas had an origin elsewhere; they seemed more logical and truer and clearer than anything I had in my own mind at the time.

It was Julie, I thought, all the pieces suddenly clicking into place. *She told me I fixed it, but I didn't fix it. Why did she tell me that? Why would she lie to me? Is she trying to get into my head, play these mind games? What is she trying to accomplish? And why did she force me to that dinner? She's trying to anger me, confuse me, trying to get me in a haze so she can do something, but what? What is she planning?*

I could feel myself becoming more and more paranoid while simultaneously becoming angrier and angrier at the situation, at the world, at Julie. Suddenly, I found myself standing in the living room, in front of the clashing abstract art paintings held together by that metal frame above the couch.

And this? I thought. *It is also here to confuse me.* I leaned over the couch and pulled on a loose metal rod protruding from the frame. *Over a million?* I questioned in my mind as I thought back to when Julie introduced me to the piece. I lost track of how long I stood there pulling and twisting then standing there holding it in my left hand once it broke free, ten or so inches in length.

What am I doing? I thought. "Defense or offense?" I asked aloud in a trembling whisper. My feet had already begun to take me away from the living room. "Defense or offense?" I asked myself again, scared, terrified at the loss of control that was occurring.

My right side bumped into the wall in the dark hallway, shoulder and then head as I fell to the ground, and, in that moment, I shook myself back. It was dark still, but I saw more clearly, not the clear that overtook my mind moments before, but a clear that helped explain what I was doing, what I was going through.

My back found the small wooden chair again, then it found the wooden floor. *Fixed. Almost like new,* I thought after inspecting it from beneath without the aid of light. Julie must have been playing some kind of joke on me. Or she was being sarcastic when she told me I fixed it. She was not trying to confuse me or harm me; she was just trying to be funny. She must have been. There was no other explanation.

After a calming internal conversation on the chair, under the chair, then on it again, I began to make my way back to the bed. I was hungry, tired, and my body and mind needed rest. I labeled my short mild episode a result of the above. The culminating stresses and those factors were the culprit. It had happened to me before, but only when I was a child, very few times beyond middle school age, maybe a few in college and graduate school. My mind would begin to race, putting together events and ideas and behaviors and filling in the blanks which frequently culminated in increasing paranoia. Panicked, I would grasp on to something that could protect me, a weapon of some sort, improvised or otherwise, run to the bathroom, and lock myself inside. Always defense, never offense, yet still I questioned my intentions whenever it occurred.

Julie was still under the covers and she said nothing upon my entry into the bedroom. I quietly closed the door and slipped in on my side. A handful of minutes went by before I thought I heard her say, "I miss *you*, Nick. Where did *you* go?" If she did say it, it was directed toward the other side of the room, not loud enough to push through its ambiguity of presence which made me question whether I should attempt a response. The question lingered in the silence for a few minutes during which I stared into the darkness and thought about what I needed to do to right my wrongs, but nothing meaningful came. I even felt my consciousness slip away for a duration, maybe I slept.

After those few minutes, I was jolted alert again. I looked over at Julie only to find that there was nothing coming from her side of the bed; no movement, no breathing sounds, nothing. Then a cold sliver of a slab grazed my warm body as I attempted to shift under the covers for comfort. Why did I still have the sharp rod in my left hand?

Quietly, I left the bed, the bedroom, and made my way through the dark hall to the kitchen. I shook my head and tried to forget about the episode as I dropped the rod into the garbage; I told myself to forget it ever happened just like when I was a child.

When I quietly made it back under the covers, there was still nothing from Julie, no movement, sounds, nothing, so I knew there was nothing for me to contemplate, no further conversation for which to plan or prepare, no reason to remain mentally aware. Whatever had just occurred, whatever the aftermath, I would deal with it in the morning or maybe I would never deal with it.

For a full week, I had been suffering from sleep deprivation yet the built up fatigue was powerless as I struggled to find sleep. I was starving for food, but had no appetite to eat. I decided to try to let my mind move about undirected in an attempt to drift away from reality and into a dream. My mind was going in different directions, to different topics and ideas, and then it settled on the basement.

Each tenant had a small storage space down there. Julie mostly used it for out of season clothes, but there was one box she refused to throw away that held everything from our relationship; from movie stubs to restaurant receipts to party favors to our wedding invitation, Julie kept everything. It was all there, down there in the basement, in the dark, in storage, probably never to been seen again. The life we once had, when we had direction, aspirations together, when we knew we could love one another forever, all hidden away, underground, out of sight, out of consciousness. Still present, it was as good as gone.

My mind moved from the moldy much forgotten basement to nowhere in particular; a scattering of ideas and words, images and sounds floated around, randomly colliding into one another to create undeveloped thoughts that were illogical and contradictory. I slid unknowingly into sleep, not consciously attempting to think or make thoughts; just allowing my mind to wander and slowly drift away.

Chapter 34

Bill's Tardy Status

[Two weeks later]

Echoes. Echoes of my groaning and huffing and puffing. I sneezed and it too echoed loudly, back and forth in every direction as it bounced around the room from wall to wall, ceiling to floor, all concrete and not separated by more than eight feet.

Five hundred and twelve, I thought two or three times before saying it aloud. It too bounced around the cube.

"Always late," I said to no one. "Always waiting for him." Bill was allegedly on his way. The guard, not one to share more information than absolutely necessary with the inmates, said, as he escorted me from my cell, that a visitor wanted to meet with me at three. The hands of the analog clock ticked behind little bars which protected it from the regulars of the room; it stoically indicated 3:23

p.m., and I had been sitting shackled on a metal chair in the tiny visitation room since 2:52 p.m. My back was becoming increasingly well acquainted with the discomfort the chair imposed upon it, but that was, in my mind, no reason to remain seated. It was the shackles around both wrists and both ankles attached to the chair attached to the concrete floor that determined I would not rise, not move. Apparently I posed more of a danger than I had during our previous meeting because I wore many more restraints this time around.

"Bill doesn't deserve it anyway," I said aloud, thinking about the courtesy of standing when one enters the room. At first thought, half an hour before, when I had been indelicately inserted into the cube, I wanted to show him respect when he walked in. I wanted to thank him for helping, for doing his best, taking the time to fight for me, attempting to free me from this prison, but I wanted to thank him without thanking him.

It would be strange, out of place between us, change the dynamic outside my comfort level if I said it aloud. It would result in him feeling far too superior and we would end up getting no good work done for the trial. So I would stand when he entered, maybe shake his hand and smile politely as well. That was the decision I had made what felt like an eternity ago. It was not until I attempted a practice courtesy stand after five minutes of sitting that I found it to be an impossibility. But, as I sat there after more than half an hour of waiting, I resolved that I would not even attempt the feat when he arrived. I would remain seated and maybe even let him know that my inaction was not solely due to the shackles, but by concerted choice.

Undoubtedly he had read what I had written so far; the record of our first meeting, Monday's events, Tuesday's events. Undoubtedly he would have questions, comments, maybe jokes at my expense in an attempt to cheer me up. I decided, as I sat there for the thirty-fourth minute of waiting that I would *not* smile, would *not* laugh, and *would* be insulted at the slightest humorous word or smirk. This was a serious situation and I deserved for him to treat it as such.

"I wonder what he'll ask about," I muttered. "Clearly he'll bring up the sharp rod I pulled from the frame of the abstract paintings," I said, answering my own question aloud. No one could hear me as I sat alone in there and I had not uttered more than a handful of words over the past few days, since Bill and I had had our first meeting in the other visitation room. It was not a bad idea to exercise my voice a bit before he arrived so I would not sound so strange, so different, so beaten down to nothing.

"What of the rod?" I said, mimicking Bill's inevitable question in Bill's inevitable mocking tone. "You were angry with your wife for something you could only *speculate* that she did, you were in an argument, and then you ran off and grabbed a *sharp piece of metal*. How is a jury not going to hate you, not going to think you did something wrong, not going to want to convict you?"

Still sitting in the same position because I had no other choice, I responded as myself to Bill's imaginary cruel jibes. "You know I did nothing wrong. I'm just being honest about everything, writing down everything that happened, everything that I felt. There was no intention in running to get a sharp piece of metal. It was reflexive. I was scared, growing paranoid, not necessarily of Julie, but in general. That happens to people, it can't be controlled."

Again I was channeling Bill as I said, "But that does not change the fact that you left your wife in the bedroom, went to get a small sharp metal rod, then went back to the room."

"Yes," I responded as myself. "But, I did not go back to the bedroom at first. I was going to the bathroom to lock myself inside like I did as a child when I was feeling vulnerable. It was to protect myself by hiding, no self-defense or anything, just hiding."

I paused for a minute, then two, and then three as I waited for Bill to arrive, to walk into the room. At that point, I was ready to shout at him upon his entry, but still he was absent.

I bent down and put my head into my hands as best I could before continuing as Bill, "Maybe there was no intent and maybe you were on your way to the bathroom to hide, but that does not change the fact that you eventually reentered your shared bedroom with an instrument that you self-defined as a potential weapon."

Conducting a mock debate with an imaginary Bill was beginning to feel silly despite the fact that I was the only individual present or, I supposed, because I was the only individual present. But still I continued on.

"Maybe the facts are incriminating," I said as myself, "but nothing happened that night. The rod found its way to the garbage and I went back to sleep. The next morning we went about our lives and Julie was never the wiser about my little episode, an episode that would have ended with me hiding in a bathroom, alone and scared, but I stopped myself and realized my paranoia was getting the best of me again."

Knowing Bill's stance on the matter, I knew his next hypothetical question would force an issue he had previously broached during or shortly after my few small episodes in the distant past of college and graduate school. "Why don't you take medication for your sporadic anxiety and paranoia? I think it would help you." I said it with an exaggerated Bill voice, more than the rest of the lines that I was forcing from his absent throat.

"You know how I feel about medication," I reminded him, despite his absence. I then refocused as I realized I was getting off topic or that *we* were getting off topic. "The rod, the wine tasting, the dinner, the rest of it, it's all ancillary. It merely builds, leads up to the incidents that ended it all, that left me in here. In fact, I am not even sure how useful *this meeting* is."

I paused for a moment, then a minute, then two, then three. I shook my head and began to laugh. "What am I doing?" I said aloud to nobody at all. "I'm alone in here." I had been not just talking to myself, but pretending to be someone else so I would have someone with whom to converse. It was becoming incredibly clear that I had been in there for far too long.

I became less enthusiastic about the next hour or so because the impending meeting between Bill and me, and the recent meeting between myself, would be and was just completely useless. The events from Monday and Tuesday merely set the scene for the rest of the week. They were relevant to the trial, but there was more, so much more.

At that moment of realization, the door finally creaked ajar. First the guard entered. I looked behind him, expecting to see Bill smiling like an idiot. Maybe he would apologize, maybe he would make some stupid joke. But the doorway was filled by an unexpected visitor, someone who had been there all along: no one. After a handful of seconds spent waiting, wondering, pondering, the guard said, "Your visitor's not coming."

"What?" I shouted. "You've got to be kidding me! I've been in here for forty-six minutes!"

The guard said nothing more as he unhooked my shackles, ankles before wrists. I wondered if this was standard practice, ankles before wrists, but I did not have the patience to think back to every prison scene I had watched in movies and on TV to compare the frequency of occurrences of one before the other; those were the only reference points I had, having never been incarcerated before this situation.

As he led me out of the room, I could only smile at the time wasted. Given my present location, and situation, forty-something minutes was an insignificant duration when compared to the forty-something years I had wasted. All my hard work, all the blood, the sweat, the tears, the risks taken, the peril endured, the uncertainty attacked head-on, the effort invested to move a step closer to a better life; they all just led me to where I was, this bland institution. But there was still so much more to tell and my salvation lay in the sliver of a chance that the outcome of the trial would ultimately be my release from this prison. I needed to work harder, continue to write the details, parse the story so it could speed the justice process, aid the lawyers, and get me out of here.

I will not lose. I will fight until the end and then beyond.

— The One Behind the Psychologist —
The Two Behind the Psychologist
The Three Behind the Psychologist

Made in the USA
Monee, IL
14 June 2020